Armageddon
Part Four of the Ayton Cy

By

James Lynch

Best Wishes

James

2023

ISBN 978-1-3999-7585-8

Contents

Foreword

This novel is a portrayal of a possible dystopian future for the small Midlands town of Ayton on the Wold and its surrounding region. It is not a portrayal of what will happen over a decade or so, but rather what could happen if the appropriate and adequate funding is not made available and the right policies and apposite actions are not taken by all the forces of Law and Order in the town. The town faces the need to respond in a multi-agency way to the gradual creeping spread of drug consumption, people trafficking, forced prostitution and other illegal activities by an increasing number of criminal gangs, embedded amongst the population. It must also react to the accompanying widespread acceptance of criminality as a fact of life by many sections of the community.

Little by little in the last decade the people of the town of Ayton on the Wold have become numbed to the criminal drugs market and other accompanying illicit businesses of the organised crime groups (OCGs) in the town and in its wider region. The relentlessly expanding drugs trade has been persistently but differentially buoyed, not least by demand from two major sources, the moneyed middle classes and poorer youth of the conurbation in and surrounding Ayton. The use of hard rugs and particularly ketamine, the consumption of which had become rife, especially but not exclusively, among the steadily growing student population in the region, had been reinforced over and over again by a feeling of immunity to all drugs. This feeling of false confidence continued with the more powerful drugs such as heroin and onwards to heroin substitutes such as nitazenes and xylazine as well as fentanyl and even off-prescription pregabalin.

Access to such drugs has become easier and easier and is now widely, easily and relatively cheaply accessible on the internet and from a variety of other sources. They are frequently procured through social media platforms, the dark web, a secret app or sometimes casually in a local park, side-street or alleyway and even in a local shopping centre, colleges and universities. Access to drugs has also seeped into schools and educational institutions more boldly and at an ever mounting rate. Some of these drugs, like xylazine, are currently being sold on the hidden market as normal on-the-market painkillers, and they have also been found secreted in some commercial normal pain killers and in some vaping liquids.

With a soaring death-rate from drugs in the region and especially in the town of Ayton, the budget-restrained and over-worked forces of Law and Order are now substantially outspent by the opulence and monetary manoeuvring of the affluent mafia gangs, large and small, regional and international. The accompanying financially-strengthened criminal structures are infiltrating more and more into legitimate life and business in the town, including the arms of the criminal justice system, and little by little they are corrupting them. In turn, directly and knowingly or indirectly and unknowingly, many of those businesses are lucratively supporting the activities of the criminal gangs.

Some of the arms of the criminal justice system in the city and the back-up legal and business apparatus have now been progressively but not yet terminally penetrated by associates and sympathisers of the various organised criminal groups. A layered multiplicity of criminal syndicates has emerged involving co-operative working amongst local or regional criminal gangs and the larger and more powerful transnational mafia cartels. The co-operative efforts of the various criminal organisations include the establishment of small cells of representatives from several mafias, formed from trained individuals seconded from their home syndicates to work together on a particular project. Those projects might include, for example, the production, transportation, supply or sale of illicit drugs or transportation of women for what amounts to slave labour in gang brothels or men to work in conditions of modern slavery in the indoor drug farms. The small cell-like groups involved disperse once the particular task has been accomplished and they return to their own organisation.

This highly complex system is ordered and controlled by upper layers formed by the international criminal syndicates providing the drug-wherewithall in a Cosa Nostra style coalition and overseeing the whole process. Not by a long shot is the structure entirely successful and the town is still frequently engulfed by progressively more and more violent gung-ho knife and gun warfare amongst the different feuding mafia gangs, both regional and international.

Not long ago such violence was restricted to knife and fist warfare among criminal gangs for control of the drugs trade. Now, however, with the growth of the use of guns in the feuds, members of local community are being ever more affected, resulting often in inadvertent injury and in some cases death. Members of the local Ayton Constabulary and security personnel in shopping centres and local retail outlets are more and more subjected to belligerent threats, bribery and sometimes life-threatening violence merely for doing their jobs properly and conscientiously.

To put it briefly, Ayton and the surrounding area are in the grip of a wide-ranging crime wave of epidemic proportions, with rampant tit-for-tat intergang violence in the town and a regular occurrence of such crimes as gangland assassinations and abductions, accompanied by sex-trafficking, car-jacking and widespread use of guns by criminal gangs, more often than not in petty patch and other trade disputes. Added to that is a growing plethora of street crimes, such as mugging, criminal damage, car and bike thefts, shoplifting, and various forms of antisocial behaviour, now also at endemic proportions. The crime of shoplifting is currently widespread and brazen, often to support addiction, in some cases from extreme deprivation, to buy food. Sometimes some of the criminal gangs recruit youngsters from the College to shoplift to order for them and then pay them with drugs. The crime sadly goes largely unpunished with the shop-owners suffering hostility, aggression, blackmail and physical violence as well as huge and recurring financial losses.

The demand for shop security guards has soared due to the incidence of these crimes. In some districts, law-abiding citizens have even been advised not to go out in the evening and at all costs to keep their children away from any potential contact with drugs and drug pushers in night clubs and other recreational outlets. As well the ubiquitous criminal gangs are now marketing their wares far and wide in such sites as educational institutions, shopping centres and indoor and outdoor recreational areas.

In spite of exhortations to the contrary from multiple sources, there has been a growth of family multi-generational drug-taking. County lines activity in the Ayton region, which is officially defined as a term to describe "gangs and organised criminal networks involved in exporting illegal drugs into one or more importing areas, located on the outside of a major conurbation, such as a town or city within the UK", continues to surge dramatically on the backs of the Ayton region's young people, many of whom have been enticed with gifts of drugs, food, foot-ware or clothing into being runners.

For one reason or another, the exclusion of vulnerable children from educational institutions in 'drug areas' of the Ayton region is ballooning. It is adding its own contribution to generating criminality and other drug-associated crimes such as shoplifting and physical violence. In fact such exclusions from schools and colleges tend to lead to an almost automatic pathway to county lining and addiction. Sometimes those children, who have been sent to referral centres, find themselves at an institution, which is far away from their home. They become major target for the gang-recruitment of children to be used for the sale of drugs and the recruitment of some youngsters for other criminal activities such as shoplifting. The incidence of drug addiction and overdose fatalities amongst young people has thus spiralled in the region to the extent that remedial, remediation and most rehabilitation facilities are totally overwhelmed.

The emergence of several societal factors has also made the task of the local Police more difficult and that of the criminal syndicates easier. Foremost among these is the constantly growing wealth and spending power of the middle classes in Ayton and its region. Young people as well as adults, by their hunger for so-called recreational drugs are supporting a sharp upturn in the demand. This also applies to the point where the United Kingdom is now the biggest consumer-nation of cocaine in the whole of Europe.

A second factor often at the opposite pole of the socio-economic ladder is the emergence of what is called a 'ghost army' of youngsters of school age, who consequent on the Covid pandemic to some extent or another are rarely or never attending school. Added to this is the almost costless crime of the trafficking of young-people, from which massive profits are made by the organised criminal groups (OCGs) every year. This aspect of people trafficking provides an important pool of recruitment for the criminal gangs as well. It brings with it a concomitant proliferation in petty street and shop crime as a source of initial pocket money to introduce many of these children to be able to buy drugs and participate in other drug-related activities. Sadly, in addition, the consumption of such drugs as cocaine has been reliably linked with the shocking rise in domestic violence in the town and the growing number of broken families, often throwing some young people literally on to the streets.

Thirdly there is the ever-growing influence of major drug cartels in the local market for the purchase and sale of newer hard drugs, often with direct representation of gang syndicate placemen in the production countries, such as Columbia, Costa Rica and to a lesser extent in other South and Central American countries. This co-ordinated approach generates a uniform chain for the economic production, transportation and sale of illegal drugs and especially cannabis, as well as for the return transfer of the illegal proceeds, their washing and investment in legitimate assets on the commercial markets.

These co-operative and co-ordinated approaches are perhaps especially surprising against a background, where one major transnational cartel already possesses a near monopoly on the production, distribution and in one case the sale of cocaine in the UK. The same syndicate also has a dominant position amongst the other syndicates, in some cases in the acquisition and sale of newer more powerful synthetic opioid drugs with extreme potency, such as fentanyl, ketamine and off-prescription pregabalin.

Fourthly, there is the growth of cooperative but not illegal local businesses often on-line, which provide assistance to the criminal gangs with services such as sale of drugs, above board legal support, safe and reliable money laundering and cash transfers especially overseas, as well as other legal and advisory services.

Finally in a long list of change factors in Ayton, there has been a period of rapid growth of new arrivals from a wide variety of backgrounds settling in Ayton or occupying officially provided residence in two of the central hotels in town. Many of these new settlers are genuine asylum seekers and are likely to become new citizens eventually. In this connection, the proposed establishment of a third local hotel as a Home Office residence for new arrivals in the town offers the opportunity for new pools of recruitment for all criminal gangs and especially for some nationalities already represented in the populations of Ayton and its surrounding region. This source of recruitment is now supplementing or replacing home-country recruitment of an ever-growing workforce for criminal activities.

Ardajan Nikolaj, mysteriously known to his accomplices as 'Nico the Greek', has over a number of years been the supremo of a mafia super cartel, the Mafia Shqiptare cartel, in the United Kingdom, which groups together all the Albanian organised crime groups, most of the transnational OCGs and a few of the larger regional groups here in the UK. His moods and his temper are legendary and greatly feared in his own and other clans in the town. He is clever and sophisticated and he prides himself on always delivering what he promises. He is based on an estate in the East End of London but is responsible to his masters for the efficient functioning of all the branches of the clan throughout the UK. In this role he is a frequent visitor to the Ayton region, which is seen by the syndicate as a major and expanding market for profit from the sale of the Cartel's worldwide produce.

This same syndicate had already several years previously achieved a near monopoly on the cocaine market in the UK and a firm grip on one or two of the newer and harder drugs, such as ketamine and fentanyl. Nico was also the lead member of the Mega-Mafia grouping, something like an executive committee formed by and from the membership of the leaders of a number of the more powerful crime gangs in the town, transnational and regional. He was the capo di tutti i capi, the supreme boss of all UK bosses.

This dominant assembly indirectly controls all the other criminal gangs in the country, large and small, local, regional, national and international and holds the prize of a the near-monopoly of much of the marketing of some harder and newer drugs. All other crime syndicates large and small are theoretically obliged to bow to its directives and the decisions of the committee of the Capos of the criminal syndicates in the nation, national and international. The annual turn-over of the drugs business in the UK is estimated at the present to be somewhere over an estimated ten billion pounds per annum, with over three million consumers, some three hundred thousand consumers of the most harmful drugs and scores of hospitalisations and deaths annually.

Nico's main adversaries in the town and region are the newly elected Police, Fire and Crime Commissioner, Maureen Wilson-Hayes, the Chief Constable of Ayton, Patricia Nowak, who had been recently appointed from the London Met, and the long-serving Deputy Chief Constable, Rajiv Gundara. This latter had recently been promoted to the post of Deputy Chief Constable with a central responsibility for cleaning up the drug and people-trafficking businesses in Ayton and the region. Supporting this small group is a team of dedicated and recently reinforced multiracial Assistant Chief Constables and a specialised Criminal Investigation Department, led by a Chief Inspector, under the leadership of Detective Chief Inspector Rajan Appasamy.

As was the case with her forerunner, the retired Chief Constable Heather Compton-Jones, the new Chief Constable, Patricia Nowak, was recruited from the prestigious Met Police Force in London and is now responsible for overseeing all Police services, including the CID, in the town. She also carries direct responsibility for relations with other regional bodies and for direct liaison with the regional and national crime agencies and, as appropriate, with ministerial departments, Interpol and Europol.

Like her predecessor in the role, she has a strong commitment to tackling the scourge of drugs in the town and the surrounding area, their purveyors, the criminal syndicates in the region and the local cooperating businesses, who help to facilitate the laundering and transmission of huge sums of money. She was aware of the increasing infiltration of mafia hoodlums in the town into the normal business, legal, economic and political life of the town. She was also aware of the corruption in certain quarters of the town and to some small extent in her own Force, all serving the financial interests of the criminal mafia gangs.

She was thus strongly in favour of a more focussed approach to the disbursement of the available limited public funding for the Force, planning actions within a budget. She is moreover fully willing and able to show value for money in the disbursement of funds to counter the delinquent activities of the drug and trafficking criminal barons and their co-workers. She requires that all funding be focussed on where those funds would make most impact in demolishing the criminal gangs.

She is also keen on the use of a range of new technologies, such as facial recognition technology, decryption strategies, CCTV etc. to find and apprehend criminals as well as the need for the continual professional training and retraining of the existing workforce to support such developments. She is strongly committed to working and sharing intelligence with other relevant groups particularly security agencies and the local and national mass media as appropriate. She rightly appreciates the weighty importance of multi-agency co-operation in achieving her objectives.

It is often through the experiences of the small Burnley Crowder family that we see the events recorded in this book. In the last decades, the family has changed its composition and, as with many of the families in the town, the torch of civic responsibility and charitable commitment has been passed to new generations. Emily, the grandmother has passed away and Isabel her daughter is on the threshold of retirement. Isabel's daughter, Andrea, is on the point of taking over Isabel's successful construction consultancy business in the town. After studies at Imperial College in London, she had joined her mother's business some years ago and had proved herself equally competent in business matters as her mother and much more computer literate.

Like her mother and grandmother before her, Andrea is committed to public service and particularly where drugs and young people are concerned. Similar to both of her family predecessors, she is also an active and enthusiastic governor at the local secondary education college. In that role she has acted as a major spur to the College's anti-drugs, anti-knives and anti-media-caused suicides among young people, both policies and practice.

She married her sweetheart Adrian McAllister, whom she had met at Imperial College, as soon as she had graduated with First Class Honours in Engineering. They now have two children, a girl and a boy, Melissa and Jeremy, currently studying in the local secondary college.

Adrian has his own successful financial services business in the town centre and was recently elected a town councillor. In addition to running his own successful financial services business, Adrian was well connected with other business colleagues in the area through his club and golf activities and other voluntary and charitable activities.

With demand for all kinds of drugs still burgeoning the scene is set for an even greater expansion of the drugs market in the Ayton region, with the involvement of a larger number of ruthless criminal organisations ranging from several transnational ones with scores of members to solo initiatives in a park or alleyway. In these latter smaller organisations, the individuals themselves sometimes importing new and highly potent drugs from new sources in China and to a lesser extent India. The continuing growth in the market of clients and the steady price of most of the drugs, as well as the support and sustenance of co-operants in some local business companies are also providing dubiously legal or downright illegal assistance to the criminal gangs.

The exponential curve of growth in the drugs market in the town will no doubt need to be met by a substantial increase in the counter-measures of the forces of Law and Order to bring into the criminal justice system those involved in the production, distribution and sale of illicit drugs as well as those, who facilitate and support such criminal activities. This initiative is likely to occur across the full spectrum of drug specimen strength, including the most recently arrived, hardest and most dangerous ones, as well as the growth of new hits such as nitrous oxide. The outcome of this uneven struggle between the forces of Law and Order and the life destroying criminal gangs is at this time far from certain.

Chapter One: Ayton: Remembrance Sunday

In spite of the fact that it had rained heavily during the night and the sky was still a heavy grey in parts, the morning had progressively opened up intermittently to an unusually bright Autumn day. The sunshine was now illuminating the site and the partly moss-covered Cenotaph structure and there was a growing warmth slowly pervading the site. A crowd of would-be attenders at what was sometimes called the Armistice ceremony was streaming through the town centre of Ayton to attend the commemoration of what was more generally known as Remembrance Sunday.

Bit by bit the mud on the unpaved part of the site was also beginning to dry out and the slippery cobbles and flagstones on the rest of the site were beginning to become slightly less slimy, although unpredictably, they were still very slippery in places. As usual there was a small and ever growing assembly already around the Cenotaph, (meaning empty tomb) that day, from about ten thirty. They were anticipating the commencement at eleven o'clock of the sounding of the last post and the traditional service of remembrance for fallen members of families and friends, known and unknown, British and Commonwealth, who died in the First or Second World War or later.

The design of the memorial in local stone on the only unbuilt land in the town at the time of construction meant that it was situated between two main roads. At that time trams trundled and clanked their way to the then fairly near suburbs of the town. From the start, the memorial had been controversial for a number of reasons. For example on final construction, because the members of the military portrayed on two of the sides of the monument had been represented with bayonets, some influential citizens had described the structure as a belligerent structure. This happened at a time when quite a number of the citizens were still mourning loved ones, who had died in the Great War and many were more and more citing the Great War as "the war to end all wars."

That problem had, however, been solved many years ago with a typical Ayton compromise, namely the extraction from the sculptures of the bayonets, but with the retention of the weapons. A position had been chosen for the construction of a town Cenotaph in Ayton situated on a raised site on the level main square in the town centre opposite the medieval corn mill and completion had been swiftly achieved by mid-July 1920.

In the immediately succeeding years the square had normally been packed by members of a fairly culturally cohesive citizenry in the town, some with shared loss to remember and similarly the participation rate was boosted for a while from the end of the Second World War. Those days were now passed, however, as that generation was succeeded with a young population less involved with such matters. Instead the square with its multiple cafés and shops round the sides and two busy night clubs was a major retail site. It was as well a night-time meeting place for the town's young people of all backgrounds, who let off steam at the weekend there, but of whom only very few were present at the Cenotaph on this Remembrance Day.

Today participants had been arriving for some half an hour to await the striking of the town-hall clock at eleven o'clock precisely, followed by the sounding of the last post by a sole bugler. The ranks of the local military regiments were well represented and the great and the good of the town were also very well present, sporting their formal regalia in some cases. There were very few young participants. The Public was slightly less well represented than in previous years, an overall trend that was occurring now ever more rapidly as the two world wars became more and more distant with the passing of the years.

Not surprisingly, the ranks of the senior members of the local Police, the local authority, members of the Council's Police Committee and auxiliary services and all the great and good of the town were replete as were all representatives of members of the religious and lay groups in the town such as the LGBTQ groups. National, regional and local politicians were all present, smartly dressed and attentive to the presence of a source of voters for the next election.

The ceremony was to be conducted as usual by the rather portly Bishop of Ayton, who arrived with a bevy of assistance from less senior members of the Church of England, acolytes, male and female, as well as young altar girls and boys in red or black cassock and white surplus. The lay readers were from a selection of the town's ethnic communities. Also in line with more recent precedent, representatives of all faith groups and none had been invited to participate, some wearing the traditional clothing of their country or ethnic origin, providing a colourful dimension to the otherwise sombre spectacle.

On the whole the atmosphere was calm and controlled with a high standard of dress and behaviour and heightened expectancy on the part of all repeat attenders, as the

County's regimental band commenced with the playing of "Rule Britannia", followed by a selection of solemn, traditional music and accompanying singing by the audience and choir. At the playing of Purcell's "Dido's Lament", the clergy and choir began to process to take up their places at the opposite side of the monument from the quite large gathering of formal civic and other dignitaries, including senior Police officers.

All senior members of the Ayton Police force were present in full-dress uniform, including Superintendent Charles, head of the Ayton Armed Police Unit showing a chestful of medals, white shirt and black tie, coat flashes and rank epaulettes. The Chief Constable was wearing a black and white checked cravat, marked epaulettes with rank designations and she also was wearing her medals. The actual senior ranks were small in number, but Police officers were also present, who were on duty and in work-a-day uniforms. These latter officers, all wearing stab-proof vests and in full uniform were entrusted with keeping the meeting orderly and safe and with re-directing and advising local redirected traffic. For these officers it was a normal workday.

Several town-beat officers were not unfamiliar with a recently arrived Eastract parking clearance robot, parked in an open space of the Town Square, slightly back up a gentle slope. Indeed some officers had even observed its efficient and speedy clearance of illegally parked vehicles in the city centre in the preceding few weeks since its arrival in the town. But today, in that spot and during a solemn Remembrance Day ceremony its parking location seemed somewhat incongruous. The traffic officers had already raised with Deputy Chief Constable, Rajiv

Gundara, the senior officer in charge of the displacement of all officers at the ceremony, the question of the presence of this monster and its location at this time. It was for example not situated in a recognised parking slot at the top of the short slope running down to the Cenotaph. Nor had it ever been seen parked on the Town Square before.

Although the Deputy Chief Constable had agreed that it was unsightly and irregularly parked, his judgement was that it was perfectly safe and currently of no danger to the Public. It was a paltry distraction from the ceremony and its efficient delivery. He hazarded a guess that although it was after all an ugly tank-like, tracked and remote controllable traffic clearance robot, it had presumably been parked there for the weekend by local council workmen in order to escape work as quickly as possible. In any case, the Force had no means of moving it, as they did not possess the remote control code. Neither did the Police possess the authority to do so.

The Memorial Ceremony began at just turned ten thirty with a collection of traditional national airs and some solemn music played by the band of the regional regiment. At the first note of Purcell's Dido's "Lament" the religious procession, led by a cross-bearer, approached and mounted the few steps to the Cenotaph. They were followed by the entry of the major dignitaries. At the first stroke of eleven, according to the normal order of service, silence would fall and military members and Police would stand to silent attention. The assembled audience would also fall into a hushed silence, after which a single soldier would play the 'Last Post' on the bugle. This would be followed by the sound of traditional solemn music, during which wreaths would be laid by dignitaries followed by members of the Public.

On this occasion, as the town hall clock struck the first of its eleven digits, Police Constable Margaret Pettigrew was attracted towards the vehicle by the unmistakable, laboured sound of a petrol engine starting up, which raised her suspicions. She was at some distance from the Eastract vehicle and the noise could have come from some other nearby vehicle. She was stationed at some distance behind the main body of the crowd and she turned towards the vehicle and approach the park-vehicle. When the noise was instantly followed by a gentle rumble as if from tracks moving sluggishly over the partly muddy gravel surface on the extremity of the site at the rear of the peripheral crowd, she decided to investigate more closely.

She walked up the slight slope away from the Cenotaph to apprehend the driver and persuade him or her to desist from moving the vehicle during the ceremony. But the distinctive noises failed at first to gain much attention as there were similar noises from the diverted traffic on the main road through the other side of the town square and the sound of loud music from the ceremony.

Then one of the other Police officers at the periphery of the assembly, Police constable Manjit Singh turned round to see what the noise was and to his surprise he observed the Eastract parking vehicle ponderously beginning to move forward like some threatening monster towards the assembled crowd. He quickly approached the machine to alert the driver to the fact that the vehicle, still at much less than its maximum speed of four point five miles an hour, was a danger to the crowd below assembled at the

Cenotaph. He intended to order the person controlling the vehicle either to stop it on the spot or more sensibly to drive it to a safer parking place available on the other side of the town square today. Finding neither on the vehicle nor in the vicinity anyone apparently in control, he rightly concluded that the vehicle might correctly be assumed to be remotely controlled, although once again, surveying the near distance, he failed to locate an operator. So who was operating the vehicle and why? His suspicions rose.

After conferring with Police Constable Margaret Pettigrew for an agreed estimate of the potential danger to the Public. Without further delay they agreed that he should contact the senior officer responsible for the Police organisation at the site and the roads leading to it, Deputy Chief Constable, Rajiv Gundara, indicating the current speed and directionality of the vehicle. The two Officers estimated the machine to be moving towards senior officers of the Police Force on the podium together with other noteworthy citizens at the side of the Cenotaph. As a precaution they also advised relocating members of the crowd at the front of the podium to an alternative location on the other side of the Cenotaph site where the members of the religious procession were located. They also suggested an advisory announcement be made over the tannoy advising members of the Public to move to the area of the square judged as safe.

Assessing the potential danger from the vehicle to the Public as high, the Deputy Chief Constable at once ordered attendant Police Officers to begin the redisposition of members of the crowd away from the presently intended pathway of the vehicle. As that particular manoeuvre was proceeding painfully slowly, he then ordered one of the

Police cars in the vicinity and nearest to the Eastract vehicle to move straight away to block the offending vehicle just before it had reached the part of the site where some members of the Public were standing. He instructed the officers to leave the brakes of their car hard on and then to quit their car quickly and move to a safe distance.

Both redeployments, of the crowd and of the Police car, were executed with slow but with commendable efficiency. To the surprise of the Police officers now observing, the resulting manoeuvre by the parking vehicle was to slightly switch direction, clip the rear of the Police car, sliding it out of the way to the left of the moving parking vehicle. Thus rather than hitting the main body of the Police car as the officers had planned the machine made a slight detour knocking the parked Police car out of its path, then reorienting once again towards its now clearly intended target, the podium and the gathered dignitaries, including senior Police officers.

This apparently spooky tactic by the parking vehicle indicated to Assistant Chief Constable Adarsh Khanna that the matter was not one merely of a runaway vehicle accidentally moving. Rather it was a case of someone within sight of the vehicle being in close charge and having malign designs on the crowd. She ordered officers to clear the podium right away and to move all members of the Public away from the vehicle's apparently intended target. The regimental band was also invited to move to a safer location on the site and the music ceased.

There was just sufficient time for the crowd to be cleared and the podium emptied, when the vehicle accelerated probably up to its maximum. But the small size of the mud-laden tracks meant that the vehicle snagged on the steeper set of first-stage steps up to the monument and, although whoever was remotely controlling it revved the engine ferociously, eventually the engine was switched off and the vehicle moved no further.

As a consequence of the interruption and intervention of the car removal vehicle further interruption to the ceremony was required until appropriate safety precautions had been implemented. The removal of the offending Eastract from the site also required obtaining a vehicle removal crane, which also caused further delay in the recommencement of the ceremony. In fact so much damage had been done to the ceremony that it was impossible to smooth out the passage of what remained of it, although it was resumed and completed but more than one hour later and with a much reduced number of spectators. An extensive search was also commenced by the Police around the site until the ceremony restarted with the participation of the much smaller crowd.

But no sooner had the ceremony recommenced than a single shot was heard from the area behind the Cenotaph. The wreath-laying was halted again and the playing and singing of traditional airs came to a stuttering, ever-fading halt. The Head of the Ayton Armed Police Unit, Superintendent Julian Charles, was a member of the group of senior Police officers ceremonially present. It was a simple matter for the Chief Constable to order him, together with a couple of authorised firearms officers on precautionary active duty for the event that day to investigate the provenance and intention of the gunshot and to apprehend the person or persons responsible.

Sadly, and bearing in mind the previous episode with the parking vehicle and its consequent disruption of the ceremony, many members of the crowd were clearly very frightened and some, particularly those with children, began to rapidly drift away, thinning the ranks of the crowd even further.

After a careful but thorough investigation by officers from the Armed Unit, however, no one was found and the source of and reason for the displacement of the vehicle and the single shot were only discovered much later. Initial questioning of the members of the Public, who had been present in the location behind the monument at the time of the gunshot, revealed that a sole hooded-anorak clad figure of a man had fired a gun into the air and quickly departed, but no one could recall in which direction he had left nor give any useful description details of the offending gunman other than his size and clothes.

Superintendent Charles reported to the Chief Constable the actions that he and his small squad of armed officers had undertaken and the negative results obtained. As a consequence he suggested that Senior Officers meet again that very afternoon. The aim would be to plan an outline of a full-scale inquiry to be later mounted by the Police in order to try to discover those responsible for the unhappy interruptions to the solemn ceremonies that day and their real intentions and to bring them to justice at the very least for breaches of the peace.

Ever conscious of the possible public relations disaster of what had happened, the Chief Constable added that the Police and Crime Commissioner, Lynda Barwick, would no doubt be raising some queries about the incident and its handling by the Force and there was also likely to be a storm of criticism from local media and concerned organisations, councillors and political representatives, and most noticeably the ex-service members, who had been present that day.

Thus the proposal for a meeting soonest was readily agreed by the Chief Constable and a meeting of all senior officers, including Detective Chief Inspector, Rajan Appasamy Senior Officer of the Ayton CID, was posted for the afternoon of the following day in the Chief Constable's room.t

Chapter Two: Kidnapped

The Chief Constable of Ayton, Patricia Nowak, was absorbed in reading a detailed paper, prepared for her by Detective Chief Inspector (DCI) Frank Wozny about the spreading availability of heroin substitutes such as nitazenes and xylazine in the town and region and the consequent dozens of deaths and increased sickness from those sources in the town over the last three months. Three deaths had occurred just over the last weekend The paper analysed what the DCI considered to be the main reason for the increase in drug consumption, health harm and deaths from those recently arrived drugs, the sources of their availability and the means of their sale. It also explored what was known of the loopholes, through which these toxic drugs were entering and finding eager circulation among certain sections of the local population.

The paper suggested that those drugs, said to be approximately one hundred times more potent than heroin, were being sold to unsuspecting users, mainly addicts, as heroin, which was in short supply at the time due to external factors such as measures by the Afghan Taliban to curtail the supply. The paper from the DCI proposed some specific and robust measures that could be taken for tackling the increase before it grew out of hand and, as required by the Chief Constable, the various components of the strategy had been carefully costed.

As she was still only about halfway through the reading of the proposal, there was a knock on the door and DCI Wozny had entered.

"Sorry to disturb your work, Ma'am, but I wanted to bring you up to date on the arrest of a middle aged woman and a young man on the motorway slip road for Ayton yesterday. They were arrested on suspicion of transporting with intent to sell a large quantity of controlled substances. The initial toxicologists' report indicates that the consignment being offloaded from her car to the gentleman's was a new designer drug that contained a high dose of fentanyl. They have been charged and are due to be formally questioned in the presence of the duty lawyer today. I have just spoken to colleagues in the Incident Room and I have to report that we have made no further progress on the gunshot killing in the main square at the weekend, nor on the stabbing at the local college on Friday, but I shall keep you up-to-date. But mainly I wanted to update you without delay on the results of the successful demolition of the drugs bazaar in the town park and its potential link with the apparent disappearance of one of our constables, Police Sergeant EmilyWooton."

"DCI Wozny. Thank you very much, but could you first just update me on your investigations into the fiasco at the Memorial Ceremony on Sunday at the Cenotaph? I am getting a lot of flak on this from a variety of sources including the local councillors and representatives of the local and national political parties. What is the situation with your inquiries?"

"Ma'am, regrettably I am not able to report any success in finding the culprits but a team is at this very moment scouring the local area for clues and interviewing members of the public in nearby establishments including any shops that were open at the time. Sorry, Ma'am."

“That’s alright, Frank, please do keep us absolutely up-to-date. Anyway, please take a seat. I was just reading your excellent report and proposals for tackling the arrival of those new and very powerful synthetic opioid drugs into the town and the composition and effects of a new one called tranq. But I have not completed it yet. Anyway, do go ahead and brief me on the park episode. I shall reply to your paper when I complete reading it and have considered it with the Finance Department considering your budgetary suggestions.”

“Well the upshot is that we have arrested two young men of Albanian origin and charged them with the sale of Class A drugs. Colleagues have already started interviewing them in the presence of their immediately available ‘made to measure’ lawyer. One immediate issue is their age and whether they are still minors or adults. As they have no papers or other documents it is a job for the experts to define their age physically, on which a determination may be made how to deal with them.”

The DCI smiled at his description of the lawyer but the Chief Constable remained hard faced and bade him continue. She stated authoritatively.

Well we know that the age at which a young person reaches the age of majority in the UK is 18. It is at that point that a child becomes an adult in the eyes of the law.”

Yes, Ma’am, of course we know that to be the case. Their lawyer is also aware of that legal fact. He is claiming, however, that the youngsters are sixteen and seventeen respectively. Significantly that claim also links in with something else they are claiming in order to evade responsibility for their actions; namely their work status."

The DCI hesitated briefly as if unsure how to present the next part of his report. After a few seconds he continued with his report.

"Just to continue for a moment, however, and I shall return to that subject presently. Their story is that they are just a couple of Albanian teenagers. They maintain that they were enticed to the UK from their picturesque home town in Albania near an Ottoman hilltop castle by the social media. The incentive was a promise of limitless opportunity, secure employment and wealth in the rich country of Great Britain. They were just two of the almost seven thousand Albanian asylum seekers, who travelled across the channel in small boats to the UK this year. The big difference is that their cut-price transport costs were paid for the two young men by the Albanian mafia, the Mafia Shqiptare cartel. The arrangement was made through the good offices of one of the Iraqi Kurdish gangs on the French side of the channel, who at that time dominated the cross-channel small boat transportation of immigrants to the UK. A 'fare fee' of several thousand pounds for the service was paid to the latter gang by the Albanian mafia syndicate. Their lawyer argued that this marked them out as slave labourers under the terms of the Modern Slavery Act because they were exploited in being bonded to repay a never ending loan."

The Chief Constable interrupted the flow of the DCI's delivery with a query.

"The question arises, Frank, why the local mafia gang would fund the transportation of these young men? What is in it for them?"

"The response to your very relevant question is that the two young men were committed by agreement with the mafia to repaying their ever accumulating travel costs after arrival from the proceeds of their work in the indoor cannabis farms for the mafia in the UK and more specifically in the Ayton region. On arrival in England the two did not register like the other fifty or so occupants of the boat, in which they travelled across the Channel. They were picked up from the harbour by one of the local gang 'shepherds' and driven directly to one of the indoor drug farms near the town to begin work forthwith. In a sense this arrangement has enabled them later to claim that they were prevented from registering and compelled to work and were thus victims of modern slavery."

"Is that where the lawyer came from? Paid for by the local Albanian mafia?

"That is correct, Ma'am. This is a common strategy used by the gangs to escape prosecution at all or to ensure reduced sentences. Invariably they are paying for private lawyers to defend so-called impecunious 'slaves', using the legal provisions designed to safeguard genuine victims of modern slavery. One judge has already expressed concern about the source of the funds to pay the lawyers for such cases. Suspicions have also been widely circulating about alleged corruption by some professional white-collar enablers such as solicitors, accountants and translators. But to return to this particular case, evidence has also emerged that directly on arrival and as part of their first phase training as 'gardeners' or later as county lines runners, the two teenagers, Daniel Prifti and Mehmed Hoxha, **were** engaged on twenty-four hour, seven-day a week, work in one of the largest indoor cannabis farms in Ayton."

The Chief Constable interrupted the flow to ask a question.

"So how did they move from relative slavery to a job in the park? Seems unbelievable!"

Subsequently someone in the Mafia hierarchy, impressed by their work, proposed that they be employed to try out a new small business endeavour for the sale of some surplus cocaine in the local town park. That is how they now found themselves selling mainly cocaine but also some few more potent and expensive drugs in one of Ayton's municipal parks. As an aside and coincidentally the park was the one opposite the semi-detached house of the Burnley Crowder family and it was they, or more specifically Andrea Burnley Crowder, who first drew our attention to the 'drug business in the park'. Anyway, the two teenagers successfully set up a regular market place behind a thick group of bushes in the park and on discovery had imported an old settee and some mobile stools for greater comfort. The settee and other paraphernalia remained in a thicket of bushes on those days when the youngsters did not set up shop or sold out early."

"So how long had this 'business' being going on before we managed to dismantle it?"

They had been going already for about two months and the local 'shepherd' had recruited several cyclists for the business as couriers for the delivery of goods purchased from an app on their mobile phones. Advertising took place predominantly through the dark web. Purchase of a wrap on the spot with four ten pound notes or two twenties for a gram of their product was also available and increasingly recognised as a good deal amongst the young population of the district with sometimes a queue of youngsters waiting to avail themselves of the service, many of them vaping and throwing their used containers on the ground. The two teenagers were apparently commended by the mob boss for Ayton for their successful launch and were told, according to their lawyer, that this endeavour had paid off a part … only a tiny part though … of the debt that they owed for the journey to the UK."

"Hm, very interesting, but hardly unique and, insofar as we have the information, looking at the accounts for the project, putting the two young men out of business has hardly made a major contribution to our overall aim of dismantling the local drug business, putting the drug gangsters in the lock-up and thereby reducing overall the consumption of drugs. How was the 'business' eventually suppressed?"

"Well, Ma'am, it was the very success of their business initiative that led to their undoing either through the jealousy of their competitors, who reported on them, or the voice of the street about the easy availability and competitive price of the drugs on sale. In any case the goings on right under their noses, so to speak, soon became obvious to the neighbours on the other side of the road or casual visitors to the park. They remarked that a mass of youngsters visiting the park so fleetingly indicated that something, probably something nefarious, was happening there now that had never happened before in that rather boring park, which had of late attracted such a crowd of youngsters. That judgement was also confirmed by the clouds of smoke from the assembly of vaping youngsters waiting to be served near the sale point, which could be seen from the houses on the other side of the road and the swelling accumulation of a discarded litter of coloured, plastic cases used as covers for vaping devices."

So, according to what you are saying, it was inevitable that sooner or later they would be apprehended and charged with drug offences including holding some hundreds of wraps of Class A drugs as well as other controlled substances."

"Yes, Ma'am, and this is the interesting thing. On arrest and transmission to the Police station, as I just said, they claimed in their limited English that they were slave labourers, forced by the gang to undertake the work of selling the mob's produce and obliged to pay off endlessly the costs of their travel to the UK or their family back home would suffer. A private lawyer, Mary Freeman, from the local firm of solicitors, Pitts, Short and Freeman, appeared all of a sudden shortly after their arrest. She stated that her firm had been engaged by the two young men to represent their interests and to ensure that they were fairly treated as youngsters and slave labourers. How they could do this when they had no personal money and were in debt is one of the imponderables in this case. Anyway she straightway requested a private interview with her clients and in that private interview they were clearly advised to re-join 'no comment' to any questions by the Police and not to answer any queries addressed directly or privately to them by Police officers. It is our understanding that they were assured that, where necessary, their lawyer would speak for them." The DCI paused and then said clearly and deliberately.

"But there would appear to have been further consequences perhaps from the detention of the two young men."

The Chief Constable interrupted briefly to give guidance about their treatment while at the station.

"Just a prior caveat. Please make certain that all these cases are conducted with a laser-sharp attention to the legal book. But please continue"

2Yesterday, the day following the arrest of the two young Albanians in the local Park, Police Sergeant Emily Wooton and her colleague Constable Abel Jenkins were patrolling their usual beat in the town centre and engaged in discussions with a shop owner about a young lady, who had been detained by the store detective apparently having shoplifted goods from the store. At that point they were interrupted by a clearly distressed young man of foreign extraction and limited English. He called them to what he said was a serious accident with someone injured. Due to his restricted language competence, they were unable to elicit further details and so the y decided to investigate this serious accident together."

"And how is that event connected with the case, we have been discussing?"

"Well because the two officers were deeply engaged in the dispute about an alleged shoplifting case; and theft from shops being a priority and zero tolerance crime for the

Force in the town, due to the exponential and rapid increase in the crime and the growing tendency for shoplifters to engage in violence towards shop keepers and staff, they made a decision that one of them only would accompany the young man.. As the middle-aged lady being talked to about the alleged episode of shoplifting seemed benign, Sergeant Wooten asked Constable Abel Jenkins to continue with the discussions of that case with the shop keeper and the lady concerned and she volunteered that she would go with the young man to attend what sounded like a serious incident of violence.

"Sensing an urgency in his request, she rushed with the young man round the corner and down a back alley, and, Ma'am, that was the last time she has been seen. She has disappeared completely! When Constable Jenkins had completed his work with the shoplifting problem, which incidentally was completed with an amicable settlement with both parties agreeing that there had been a misunderstanding, he found it strange that the Sergeant had neither returned nor called in. He went round the corner and down the alley but found no trace of her, nor of any of her equipment, nor of the young man who had approached them."

"Without further delay Constable Matt Jenkins reported to HQ the suspicions he held about her absence and quickly returned there to participate in the production of an identikit of the young man, who had approached them. Carrying copies of the identikit, a squad of officers was sent to the area and undertook a wide-ranging search of the area, asking members of the public about the disappearance and showing them copies of the identikit. Their search included any shop holders where the premises had been open at the time of the disappearance. But sadly they returned with little or no results thus far."

The Chief Constable was under the weather. She was consumed by a mountain of work, a budgetary crisis and a reduction in the human and material resources available for fighting crime in the Ayton region. There was the ongoing sex scandal in the Force marring her efforts to convince the Public that the Ayton Police was a clean Force. She was also facing mounting criticism from the local politicians and some members of the Public about the happenings during the solemn Remembrance Day ceremonies and how it was dealt with by the Police.

To top it all she was also beginning to have to cope with growing domestic pressure as well. Her devoted husband of some thirty-five years was complaining, in that nice way that he had of registering a complaint, that they were never together and they were both seeing less and less of each other and their three children, who were now grown up and were married with their own children. Moreover, she was rapidly losing the relaxation of the meetings and occasional meals with her friends as well because she never had time to meet them. She was not getting any exercise and was snatching unsuitable snacks rather than eating more healthily and consequently her health was deteriorating slowly but surely.

Nevertheless on that cold and dreary late Autumn morning, she had called together a fairly large assembly of her middle and higher level colleagues so that they could share with each other the details of the cases, for which they held the leadership role. Her design was to achieve some deepening of cross-fertilization of each officer's work to help improve the performance of all officers. Yet even as she entered the conference room, the Chief Constable knew in her heart of hearts that there would be few resolutions and probably many more questions than answers. She knew that her teams were weary, covering for absent colleagues and short of resources and at the same time facing mounting numbers of crimes and Public alienation.

Some of the officers were having to work unusual shifts to keep on top of the ever-increasing demands. The number of officers, who had succumbed to physical or mental illness and were on sick leave was growing every week causing staff shortages at the same time as increased demands were triggering the late circulation of urgent reports. Sometimes attempts at skimping procedural requirements caused consequent knock-on effects on the efficiency of required legal procedures and hazarded the legal integrity of the work. It pained her that sometimes criminals could escape punishment due to what she saw as these unforgiveable lapses in administrative procedures and legal requirements.

As she took her place standing at the front of the room, the hubbub of chatter in the room began to subside and an air of expectation began to pervade the audience. As silence dawned, she held up her hands to speak.

"Before we get started with the business today, I want to express my thanks and appreciation to you all for what you are doing at this tough time for the Force and for our community. I know that the situation is challenging and you are all under very great pressure, but I want you all to know that I am really proud of you all for the extra effort that you are making to keep on top of the mountain of work and produce such satisfactory results."

She then turned to Detective Chief Inspector (DCI) Frank Wozny and invited him to give an update on progress of the investigation into the apparent abduction of Police Sergeant Emily Wooton.

"Perhaps Frank you could update us on the progress of the case concerning the abduction of one of our very own officers, Sergeant Wooton."

"Thank you, Ma'am, I believe that we have some progress in understanding what has happened and why. Our officers have undertaken a widespread questioning of members of the public, and I have attempted a back-channel scan for information about the reason behind this action. The results at first were sketchy, but from these actions we have now been able to put together a pretty accurate picture of the two men involved and what they were wearing, what happened when they met the Sergeant and how the abduction took place. We have thus now achieved what we believe to be a fairly accurate description of the two men. If fellow officers regard the crime board they will see reproductions of the two men's faces and clothing, which we believe are pretty accurate, and which have already been circulated as identikits to officers including those on the beat. From reports by members of the public we now also know how it happened. The first man enticed the Sergeant into a traffic cul de sac, with few passers-by. When the two met the other young man, this latter seemed to be putting his arm round her. We now assume that he was actually threatening her with a gun in her back. She was escorted through an alleyway and pushed into a waiting car, with the engine running, which makes us assume that a third person was also involved. We also have CCTV footage of the car, because it was parked rather carelessly on a main road."

"What about the reason for the abduction, Frank. Do we know anything about that?" A voice from the audience called out.

"Using our back channels, we have been able to establish that the abduction of Sergeant Wooton has been linked by the mafia gang with the arrest of the two young men in the park the day before yesterday. Via the grapevine we know that the big boss, Ardajan Nikolaj, is in town and he is annoyed about the raids and arrests of his staff, which apparently are substantially reducing the earnings remitted to the centre, for which he is entirely responsible. Under his direction, therefore, the biggest transnational mafia mob in the country is saying, if you abduct our staff, we shall reciprocate by abducting yours. So somewhere in one of the gang's safe houses our officer is being held and we believe that she will be safe from harm for the moment, as they are looking for an exchange. If such an exchange should not occur, then she would be in immediate danger. In response we have intensified our raids of the indoor drug farms, brothels and safe houses of that syndicate, but so far without major success by which I mean the capture of senior members of the gangster cartel. We have traced the ownership of the car and it is only a matter of time before we trace the car and its users and are able to release our officer and arrest these evil gangsters, who have kidnapped our colleague."

"Thank you very much for that report, Frank, and please let me know straight away if you need additional support of any kind at any time whatsoever. There are so many cases waiting to be reviewed including the shooting dead of a man in the main square this weekend and the knifing, which took place in the Ayton Education College, incidents of domestic violence and antisocial behaviour including the barracking of officers engaged in their legitimate duties that resources are tight. If necessary we shall find some for the solution of this case."

The Chief Constable then turned to address Deputy Chief Constable, Rajiv Gundara, who had just entered the meeting late and a little hastily.

"Rajiv, sorry to catch you just as you arrive. But to give you time to get your breath back, can you brief us on the state of play in your case later on in this meeting?"

"Certainly Ma'am. No problem. But may I suggest that we invite my colleague and assistant on this brief, Assistant Chief Constable Maria Clarke to speak to the detail as she together with colleagues in the incident room, has carried out the bulk of the work these last few weeks while I have undertaken the implementation of the central government-funded project on reduction in anti-social behaviour in the Southway area of the town?"

"Yes of course. So Maria we shall call on you next. Good! But in the meantime, can we next take the drug bust on the slip road of the motorway, which occurred yesterday? Detective Inspector Margaret Spencer, Margaret, can you briefly fill us in on the slightly rare success please?"

"Yes, Ma'am. We received a tip-off about a drug deal in progress on the motorway. One of our motorway patrol cars swooped on a silver BMW, registered to James Cottony. The BMW was intercepted and ordered to pull in by one of our patrol cars. Straight away the man admitted to having cannabis in his car. Apparently you could smell it anyway. On a search of the car 20 kilograms of the drug were found as well as one hundred thousand pounds in cash and a handgun and a half dozen burner phones. On a search warrant inspection at his home address a small cannabis farm was found with 150 plants growing in it. Cottony was arrested and taken to Ayton Police station where he was charged with production and supplying a listed drug, possession of cannabis with intent to supply and the possession of criminally obtained property. He pleaded not guilty and asked to see his lawyer, Ms Mary Freeman, from the local firm Pitts, Short and Freeman. He is currently being cross-examined with his lawyer present. We think he was assisting in the conveyance of drugs from the East End of London to the major Albanian transnational mafia gang in Ayton and that he was a regular on this job. He freely admitted that this was not the first time he had conducted such deliveries for the mob."

"Thank you very much for that very lucid description of a successful arrest for controlled drug trafficking. Assistant Chief Constable Maria Clarke. I wonder if you could now take up the relay particularly on the domestic violence side of your brief.

"Yes, Ma'am. With domestic violence incidents mounting exponentially and becoming more violent at the same time, I am afraid that I have to commence with a plea for more taser-trained officers to be used in this field of work. We must also consider whether further use of Police dogs may be required. Domestic assaults are progressively more and more violent and often involve the use of knives or other sharp instruments against Police officers. Zombie knives are easily available via on-line marketplaces. Attacks with such weapons are too, frequently linked with drug and alcohol consumption. Of the domestic murders over the last year, consequent on domestic violence, more than ninety percent were carried out by men and well over seventy percent of those murdered were women."

The Chief Constable interrupted abruptly to respond to the request for additional resources."

"Of the total complement of officers in the Ayton Force, some ten percent are currently taser-trained. A number of those taser-trained officers are already allocated to your team, but they are also engaged in other areas as well. Your request will involve further training of some ten to fifteen officers and the provision of X26's for those officers. I take your point fully and would request you to set down the increase that you believe you need in taser-trained officers with a costed budget. The same for your hint that you may need some Police dog-officer, K9 officers' involvement. We can then discuss your proposal and agree a plan within a budget, which could be implemented soonest. I promise you this will be taken as one of my major priorities."

"Thank you very much Ma'am, I really appreciate your support. Now with your permission, can I hand you back to Javid? He has been managing the Central Government-funded project on antisocial behaviour in our town and I believe he has some good news to share with us."

"Thank you for your enthusiasm, Maria. Deputy Chief Constable, Rajiv Gundara. Javid, we are all waiting impatiently, perhaps a little enviously even, to hear how you have spent the extra resources allocated by central government and with what effect."

"Thank you Ma'am. Well the budget has been utilised either through additional officers or through overtime to achieve a doubling of the officers on patrol in the designated area, in fact an additional three thousand hours of uniformed Police patrols. This additional policing has seen a substantial increase in stop and searches, and also a considerable rise in enforcement actions in the form of community protection notices and public protection orders and the installation with the support and agreement of the local authority of more CCTV equipment. Reports indicate that there has been a substantial reduction in people openly smoking cannabis in public places, in acts of vandalism and intimidating gatherings in public places. Shoplifting has also declined by about twenty-five percent and violence against shop-keepers and assistant has also declined substantially. About fifty percent. Some reports indicate a reduction of some fifty percent in overall antisocial behaviour of different kinds and coincidentally a reduction in shoplifting has led to approbation from many of the owners of retail sites. Drug-purveyance and sale in districts where it was formerly rife has also declined. Interim reports indicate overall a reduction of some fifty per cent approximately in reports of antisocial behaviour, although caution is needed in interpreting the interim figures as the project still has a further six months of funding to run before it will be finally evaluated. But those are the interim in-house findings. Quite positive, I think you will agree."

For the first time in the meeting there seemed to be a general acclaim for an apparent success and some officers gave a short handclap. The Chief Constable stalled the applause and pointed out the passage of the time available for the meeting.

"Well time is flying. So I think we still have time to hear of the work of our education liaison officer and particularly with regards to the serious stabbing last Friday at the local Ayton College. Sergeant Lucy Wragg, Lucy, can you inform us how the work is going please?"

"Certainly Ma'am. I regret to say that drug sale and consumption is still rising at all our educational institutions, mainly from the secondary level upwards. I regret to say that it is rife amongst our university students. First reports seem to indicate that the stabbing on Friday was probably drug-related and an arrest has been made with the interim detention of the subject. I am working with teachers and lecturers in all the institutions of education in the area and with their governing boards to introduce new ways of reducing if not totally eradicating the passage of drugs into school and college life. An uncompleted job, I am sad to say. A report of the incident and the ongoing work is in preparation and will be available for circulation by the end of next week, after the interrogation of the suspect has been completed. Sorry it was not available for this meeting, but I am afraid that things are rather fraught at the moment in the education field.

"Thank you very much for that interim statement. In what will have to be our final contribution today, I am going to ask the Deputy Chief Constable to update us briefly and the murder in the main square at the weekend. Rajiv. As succinctly as you can please."

"Thanks Ma'am. Well very briefly. The murder has been designated as part of the ongoing gang warfare in the urban area of the region. Only one shot in the head from a silenced handgun was fired and so, although there were many people in the square engaged in rowdy conversation at that time of the evening, the attention of members of the Public was not really drawn to the incident. Those, who saw the single perpetrator do not have a good memory of him or her. But we have managed to construct an identikit and some officers, who have examined it have hazarded that the murderer was a well-known member of the Liverpool drugs cartel. No arrests have been made and investigations continue. We have found the discarded cartridge and will be testing any finger prints or other clues such as DNA on the national crime data base. I am sorry that I do not have more progress to report at this early stage, Ma'am."

Thank you Rajiv. Please keep us up-to-date. And with that we are out of time and must return to our current projects. Once again, thank you all for your contributions, which I am sure have provided great learning for us all. They are all very much valued and appreciated. As I said at the beginning, I am very proud of you and it is an honour to have the privilege of working with you all. Now it's back to our desks and to our work."

Chapter Four: Payback

An ashen faced and sombre Ardajan Nikolaj, mysteriously known familiarly to his accomplices as 'Nico the Greek', the supremo of the Albanian mafia super-cartel in the United Kingdom, was in a deeply vengeful and ruthless mood that Sunday morning. His main county lines organiser in Ayton, a man of many years of experience, always attentive to what Ardajan and his local boss were saying and advising, a key person in the region's multimillion pound county lines scheme, had been shot at the weekend in the Market Square; one shot to the head with a silenced gun, clearly from a practised assassin.

While the Police were still looking for the criminal, who had committed the murder, Ardajan knew for certain, but on the basis of no hard evidence, that it was the Ayton mob of the Manchester drug cartel. At least that was what his intuition was telling him. Those Manchester thugs had tried to move in on the Albanian cartel's patch and access to drugs before and this was a further attempt for them to have a go. But they were not going to get away with it. Not this time. Not with him in town! They had chosen the wrong moment.

One of the main reasons why he was so distraught, in addition to his sneaking affection for the business efficiency of the murdered man, was that Skelidano, his friends called him Skelly or Kelly, was one of the main links in the mobs regional business between the sale of the drugs and their dispatch to users. He had also been an innovator in many ways. For example he had introduced a system of delivery of orders by young boys from the town on bicycles. With his murder, they faced client ire, because payment had been made and no drugs received. Come to think of it, they did not have a complete list as Kelly had always kept the lists in his mind in case of interfering and inquisitive snooping by the local Police.

The Manchester mob must somehow have found out, probably from a snake in the Albanian gang's Ayton set-up, about his Firm's county lines organisation and Shkrelli's crucial and indispensable role in that section of the business. But they had way overstepped the mark this time. The time for payback and deterrence had arrived today. That silly old man heading the Manchester mob, Martin Pocklethwaite, known to his colleagues as the 'Pickpocket', had tried once too often now to try to pick the pockets of the Ayton Firm. This time he had made a big, big mistake!

Speaking to the head of the Cartel's regional business, Sebastiano Gjoni, he went over and over the plans for the day, repeating himself and his strident requests for information.

"Seb, who have you brought in? How many? How much? Why them? What experience do they have with this sort of attack? Who will do the driving, are the weapons the right ones for the job?"

Seb Gjoni, head of the Cartel's Ayton setup, tried to react coolly, sympathetically and reassuringly.

"Nico. Don't worry! All is ready for us to launch the punitive raid that we have planned at your say-so this very day. The two gunmen are hired from the East London mob at your recommendation and you know yourself how tough things have been there and how much experience they have had in this kind of thing. Their weapons, including a Skorpion submachine gun and Glocks, are the ones they have chosen themselves and are regularly used and updated by them. The site of the meeting has been verified as a regular get-together place for the Manchester mob at Sunday lunchtime. It has been cased by one of our own colleagues on several occasions and at different times of day and night. We even have a plan of the pub and the narrow rear access road to 'The Mouse' in the old downtown district of New Town. Believe me, short of a calamity, the plan is hard-wired for efficient action and a successful outcome."

"It had better be. For your sake. Or you could find yourself on an express flight back to our homeland." Nico almost shouted threateningly.

Fortunately for continuing good relations, it was at that point that the two gunmen entered. Mehmed Hoxha and Daniel Koloqi were both experienced assassins on behalf of the Firm. Hoxha was a tall, burly and muscled man probably in his mid-thirties. He had worked for the mob in his home town, Shkodra in Albania not far from the Montenegro border and later during the fight for independence for the Kosovo Liberation Army in Kosovo itself.

Daniel was smaller but still swarthy and fit-looking. He was in his early fifties and had previously only worked for the Mob in and around the town of Saranda, a vibrant tourist town in the South, where demand for drugs from the tourists was huge. He had trained as a gunman in the Albanian militia during the break-up of Yugoslavia. The two men had worked together for Nico in London for the last few years and their partnership and loyalty to Nico were very firm.

"Mornin Boss!" They chorused together as they entered, slightly comically carrying their submachine guns in violin cases and almost totally ignoring Seb except for a silent smile towards him on the part of Mehmed, who spoke politely to his boss.

"We're ready to move, when you are ready, Boss. Ideally we'd like to get back to London today as we have another job there tomorrow, as you know. The youngsters are getting a bit out of line down there on the estate and they need teaching a lesson or two, as you well know yourself from your experience there."

Nico was immediately wakened from his soporiphic mood and spurred to action by what he saw as the enthusiastic and supportive exhortation of his two faithful workers. They are right. Let's get it over and done with! He thought to himself. The die was cast. He immediately confirmed it.

"Right lads then. Let's get it done."

Everyone in the room rose and the two men exited towards their car parked carefully in a space in front of the building. There was a twenty mile an hour restriction in force on the crowded road approaching the Old Town and Mehmed drove very carefully, meticulously adhering to the restriction. When they arrived at 'The Mouse' they parked in one of the spaces allocated nearby for pub parking and paid the fee. Wearing their long, well-pocketed coats, filled with additional cartridges, they checked their fall-back weapons at their waists, unboxed their weapons and briskly and confidently they entered the main entrance of the pub, which led immediately to the bar area.

On entry, they instantly realised they had made a mistake. They had expected a few members of the Manchester Cartel to be in the 'Mouse' on a Sunday morning. But they were confronted by a throng of men with two at least behind the bar. But they had started, they were committed and they had no option but to carry on. They raised their guns.

But even before the two men had begun spraying the scene in front of them, some of the assembled mobsters from the Manchester Clan with guns tucked into their trousers at the back, noticed at once the weapons the two Albanians were carrying and reacted accordingly. They were armed and began taking their side-arms from the back of their trousers without delay, and without hesitation or warning, they fired at the two Albanians. Mehmed and his colleague swiftly up-ended a table and they both dived behind it returning the shots round the side or over the top of the table with a spray of shots in the direction of the opposing gunmen from the Manchester mafia clan.

Almost at once a head and a handgun appeared over the top of the bar and fired off-siding shots towards them. As he was standing to fire, one of these shots caught Mehmed full on in the chest. He fell to the ground behind the table beginning to bleed out but still trying to fire round the side of the table. He called out to Daniel to urge him to pull out.

"Daniel. I'm a gonner but I should be able to provide some covering fire for you to pull out and get away, at least for a few minutes. Get out while you can and leave me. I'm finished Danny."

"I'm not leaving you here, Danny Boy."

Without further ado he started to try to pull the table with his colleague, Daniel, behind it to the doorway. But as he stood up, one of the men from the bar came round the end of the bar wielding a shotgun and shot him twice in the back and head, while delivering a coup de grâce to his colleague writhing on the floor. Thus they had worked together, and now they died together in their moment of failure.

The encounter had lasted but a few short moments, when as the two men were being despatched a Police car with four armed officers in it screeched to a halt outside the front entrance to 'The Mouse' and two burly Police officers entered wielding ready-drawn Taser guns. The other two from the car hastened down a side alley to the back exit from the premises to arrest any would-be absconders. The Police sergeant in charge shouted loudly to the group of about twenty men.

"Armed Police! Armed Police. Right everyone! Put your guns on the floor and get down beside them with your hands outstretched and visible. That's an order. Armed Police!"

Two or three of the mobsters at the rear of the group, tried to escape through the back door but were caught by the two Police officers now stationed there. Likewise they were instructed to place any guns on the floor and get down with their arms stretched out and visible. One of the men from behind the bar, who had used the shotgun, tried to seek escape via a door at the back of the bar that led down to the cellar where the barrels were stored. One of the sharp-eyed Policemen saw him, however, and straight away tasered him. The man fell from the steps to the floor of the cellar in agony. Everyone else seemed to learn their lesson from the incident and began reluctantly to lie with their guns on the floor beside them and their arms outstretched on the floor.

At that point an old-sounding siren voice from their leader Pickpocket called out.

"Alright lads. Do as the coppers say. We have nothing to fear. We have acted only in self-defence, as the evidence on the floor demonstrates. I shall speak to the Police."

He stood up with arms in the air and his sidearm on the floor in front of him and spoke quietly and slowly to the Police."

"Officers. We will all obey your instructions to the letter and I shall vouch for all of my men as long as they are treated fairly and strictly according to the Law."

Meanwhile at the mafia clan's safe house after an hour waiting for the expected good news from their gunmen, Nico and his underling, Seb, were becoming gradually more concerned about the possible fate of their assassins. One of the lower order soldiers was sent to have a look. When he arrived, however, the street was full of Police cars with flashing lights and lots of officers moving in and out of the 'Mouse'. A single-decker bus was pulled up outside the pub and a large group of men was being loaded onto it. Some men on stretchers were being loaded onto ambulances, while other walking wounded were being gently escorted into a multi-sear ambulance stationed further forward. Right at the front were two further ambulances into which stretchered men were being loaded by the paramedics, some with attached medical paraphernalia. He informed himself with one or two of the spectators and was told that two men had been shot dead inside the pub.

He noted the position of the car, used by his colleagues, still silent and unmoving in the Pub car space and all-in-all he made a correct assumption that the two dead men were his colleagues. He turned round and drove swiftly to the safe house, reporting back what he had observed and his interpretation of the scene. He informed the Supremo and his own boss that there seemed to be a large number of Police and some medics collecting men from the pub into a large bus.

Some of the paramedics were stretchering some obviously injured men into the ambulances and some men, the walking wounded he called them, were also being escorted into a multi-seat ambulance. There was no sign of the two assassins. He could only advise that their men had either been killed or arrested by the Police. It was only on the late news that a senior Police officer announcing that six dead males had been evacuated from the 'Mouse' and ten wounded men, some with life threatening injuries had been taken to three separate hospital A&E departments.

Later that same night a messenger came from the Manchester Cartel to say that the Albanian assassins had been killed for their foul attack. It added a threat that the war that they had started, they would be unlikely to finish.

"We've found it! We've found it!" The normally quiet and non-demonstrative DCI Wozny was almost ecstatic as he entered the discreetly peaceful main office and called the news out in an excited voice to his fellow officers, some of whom were conferring with colleagues and most working away at their desks and computers.

"What have you found? Your wallet?" One witty officer called back.

"No; something much more important and valuable to us than that. We've found the car that Sergeant Wooton was kidnapped in."

At once the room was electrified and filled with a babble of excited conversation, which continued as the DCI passed through the office and to the room of the Chief Constable on the far side of the main office.

"What have you been doing to my officers, DCI Wozny?" The Chief Constable chided humorously

Nothing really, except that we have found the car in which our colleague was kidnapped. I've put a watch on it and we are currently tracing the ownership of the car. My personal view is that there is a good chance that the street, where the car is parked is where we shall find our colleague. I recommend that we set up the means for a raid right now. Ideally it will need to be spearheaded by officers from the Armed Response Unit and I suggest that yourself, myself and The Head of the Unit, Superintendent

Julian Charles, should meet here this morning to set down the parameters of the raid to free our officer."

"Well, I concede that we three need to meet urgently, I suggest this morning soonest, before we share our planning with fellow officers early this afternoon. Ideally the raid should take place after dark this evening. So we have little time for preparatory work and presentations to fellow officers. I shall get my Secretary to arrange the meeting of the three of us. But firstly tell me how the car was discovered and where it is located at the moment."

"The car was discovered by two of our beat constables on patrol earlier today. Being an out-of-the way cul de sac, they had not visited the street for a couple of days. The car is located in front of a large, old Victorian House in St Michael's Road, in the St Michael's downtown district. The street is cluttered with vehicles some of which appear to have been abandoned. On both side there are similar large houses in the street, which are mostly now partitioned into separate lettings. The street is a cul de sac with a back alley behind each side of the street. The target house is in the centre of the row of houses on the right hand side going into the street"

"DCI Wozny, you will need to set in motion the means to obtain further details of the location and ideally a diagram of the house and a plan of action. Discreet non-uniformed observation should be undertaken as soon as possible. Any details of how many and if possible which of the gang are in the house and whether they are armed or not would be useful also. You will also need to obtain a search warrant for the property. So, let's get started and please come without delay, when my secretary calls you and says that she has arranged a meeting of the three of us at a given time."

"Can do, Ma'am." The DCI said as he rose and departed from the Chief Constable's room at speed.

When the three officers met later that morning, the DCI brought additional information about the car and its owner, provided each of them with a map of the area and a diagrammatic representation of the house and details of the subdivisions, advising that at the moment there appeared to be no other occupants in the premises than the members of the gang and hopefully the Police officer. The Chief Constable thanked the DCI and turned to Inspector Julian Charles, Head of the Ayton Police Force's Tactical Firearms Response Unit.

Inspector Charles, have you had chance yet to draw up a plan of action or can you share such with us this afternoon, when we meet the other officers?"

"I have a draft plan prepared that I have drawn up with details of the physical and material resources that we shall need. But considerate of the many unknowns in the situation, I shall leave a copy with you now so that you have advance notice of what I shall be proposing to the larger group this afternoon and may give me your comments and advice. Allowing for the many unknowns we have to make allowance for a worst case scenario. In consideration of that I am suggesting we commence the raid at midnight. Eight members of the Tactical Firearms Unit and six Authorised Firearms Officers (AFOs) and two specialised firearms officers ((SFOs) all armed with their usual side firearms, Glock 17s, and six of whom will be carrying H & K carbines, led by myself, similarly armed, will constitute the assault team. Other than the members of this team no other officers of any rank will enter the property until it has been cleared by the firearms team and the clearance has been declared by myself or one of my other senior officers in the assault team. We shall, of course, need the assistance of other unarmed officers as back-up for traffic control, taping the area, arrest and temporary on-site detention and, of course, trained medical officers to cope with any eventuality. I'll leave the disposition and number of those officers to you Ma'am, if I may. Six officers will attend at the front of the house with me and two at the back of the house. The six in front of the house will be in two squads, each of three officers." We shall be travelling to the target scene in three BMW X5s. Two of those can be located at some distance from the house, but in the road, the other car will be carrying specialised equipment such as stun guns and grenades, rams, etc. and it will need to be unloaded at a close proximity to the house. We have planned to be there at eleven forty-five and the first loudspeaker call to open up the premises will be at twelve midnight exactly, made consecutively in English and Albanian, because we believe the opposing group to be from the Albanian mafia."

The larger meeting in the afternoon started with a display of pictures and diagrams on boards at the front of the room, which were used by the CID Chief to explain the location of the house and its internal divisions, the relative distributions of the duties and the timings. This was followed by a presentation by Superintendent Charles, based on his brief, which had been circulated to all before the beginning of the meeting. It included the roles of his smaller team and the timings and placement of vehicles.

After a very few sporadic and generalised questions, posed particularly about the size of the contingent of officers participating in the raid and its impact on the Force's budget, there was general approval of the plan and the Chief Constable called the meeting to a close with a salutation of good luck to all of those participating.

All officers participating in the raid were given an afternoon's exceptional leave to rest and be with their families. They all assembled again at eleven o'clock, as usual, and tension was high among the officers. At eleven fifteen the first vehicles and officers arrive. Occupants of the other houses were informed of what was going to happen and advised to remain indoors. The street and the alleyway behind the houses were taped off and access and egress were controlled. At eleven thirty, the main force of Police and their vehicles arrived and the vehicles were parked and sometimes double-parked with a space remaining at the front for the armed unit's equipment vehicle.

At eleven forty-five officers from the Tactical |Firearms Unit arrived and unloaded their equipment. After checking each other's body armour, body worn camera, weapons and equipment, two squads moved, one comprising two men to the alleyway and the other six in front of the house led by the head of the Unit. Exactly at midnight a loud speaker announcement was made in English and Albanian saying that armed Police with a warrant wished to enter the premises to search. The occupants were instructed to open the front door peacefully and discarding any weapons they were holding they should exit the building with their hands help high. After a couple of minutes with no reaction, the announcement was repeated and after a further two minutes the order was given to use the ram. The first squad of three men, one of them bearing a ram advanced to the door and began to demolish the front door.

Almost instantly there was sporadic firing of small arms from the house, from the downstairs windows and particularly accurately from the upstairs bay windows. Superintended Charles ordered the discharge of stun grenades into the downstairs and upstairs windows and into the house through now open doorway. At that point the first squad of three men under the leadership of Superintended Charles entered the building and split two to one side of the doorway and one to the other. They then began to return the fire coming from behind tables and chairs, formed into a small barricade. Superintendent Charles ordered the second squad waiting outside to enter the house and to take up the positions occupied by the first squad. At that point, the first squad moved forwards on each side and off-sided the two men behind the tables and chairs.

The neutralisation of the two men was instantly followed by a barrage of side-arms fire from another man halfway up the stairs. But he was too exposed and was easily felled. The first squad began to climb the stairs one man at a time with two colleagues some few steps behind covering their colleague and keeping watch in particular for further appearances of further mafia gangsters above. Meanwhile the second squad began the process of clearing the downstairs rooms. Two men had also been apprehended by the two officers stationed at the back of the house. They were trying to flee out of the back door of the house into the alleyway.

Meanwhile, as the two squads reached the top of the staircase they were greeted by a barrage of gunfire from the doorways of rooms on both side of the corridor and one of the team went down with a gunshot wound to his leg. Superintended Charles immediately pulled the officer to safety and took his place off-side at the front of the squad, using his shield to advance against a hail of gunfire. He eliminated the man in the first doorway on the right and shot the man in the opposite doorway. He called one of his colleagues to come forward to that doorway and another to take his place where he was standing.

At that juncture he received a call from the squad downstairs that the rooms had been cleared, two men had been shot and two had escaped through the back door. No further personnel had been encountered.

He ordered the second squad to leave one officer at the front door and for the other two to proceed to the upper floor proceeding with extreme caution as the upstairs was still not clear. He then invited one of the two remaining officers from the first squad to accompany him up the rather narrow ladder stairs to the attic area, where there were two rooms on each side of a narrow corridor, both with their doors closed. He approached the first on the left-hand side and as the door appeared to be locked he kicked it open and scrutinised the inside. No one was there and the sparsely furnished room appeared to be a dumping ground for rubbish and discarded items from the history of the house.

He then turned and bidding his colleague to take up his position in the first doorway, he approached the door on the right-hand side. The door was unlocked and he pushed it open. He found himself face to face with a young man, probably a teenager, holding a gun pointed at him. The young man was dithering with fear and the gun in his hand was oscillating. The Superintendent could have shot him and floored him there and then. But instead he said quietly looking straight into the young man's face.

"Put the gun down, young man and you will not be harmed."

"Whether by intention or accident the gun went off and a bullet pierced the Superintendent's face shattering bones and entering his brain. It exited his head at the back narrowly missing the officer standing at the other side of the corridor. As the Superintendent fell to the floor, the second officer waiting at the opposite doorway had a clear view of the frightened young man. He shot and killed the young man and called out, "Officer down! Officer down. Medic needed upstairs in the attic urgently".

But it was too late and the Superintendent was already dead when the medics arrived and was certified as such.

. At the memorial service the Ayton Police Force and his family mourned a man of great decency and fairness, who had served a long and distinguished career in the Ayton Police Force and who was universally liked and respected. He had died in the line of duty adhering to the values that had guided his life.

The Forensic team that afterwards examined the premises, found evidence that Sergeant Wootton had been there until very recently. Unfortunately, it was a great disappointment to the Chief Constable and all the officers that she was no longer there. All were determined that the search would continue.

Chapter Six: Accountability Time

"Are you going to be able to attend the fourth session this year of the Police, Fire and Crime Commission Panel? You know; how you **personally** are always welcome and members of the Panel very much appreciate, nay even admire, what you and your colleagues do for the area covered by the Police Authority in the face of such a mountain of adverse challenges." The elected Police, Fire and Crime Commissioner, Maureen Wilson-Hayes, was coating an invitation to the, Chief Constable of Ayton, Patricia Nowak, with a modicum of flattery. She was hoping to encourage the Chief Constable to attend what she herself recognised was an unwanted and tiresome further duty for what she readily accepted to be the overworked and now somewhat weary Chief Constable.

"Yes, I already have it in my diary for next Monday at nine o'clock sharp. Unless some further urgent crisis arrives I shall be there. But as you know, Maureen, nothing is every certain in this job except retirement."

The quip raised a smile on both their faces and the Commissioner expressed her satisfaction.

"Good, I am pleased that you intend to come. Just to alert you that someone will surely raise the subject of the fiasco at the memorial ceremony last Sunday and the kidnapping of one of your officers will also be likely to be a popular target. But there will of course be many more goodies besides. We all know how busy and overcrowded your timetable is, Maureen, so people do appreciate your **personal** appearance." The Commissioner emphasised the '**personal**' attendance of the Chief Constable because it she had frequently sent an alternate member in the immediate past and it seemed to her that the Chief Constable had rather overdone the permitted 'alternate' representation in the recent past.

When the day arrived all ten elected representatives of the Panel were present as well as the two co-opted members, both of whom were from minority communities, one from the local Moslem community, and another from the local Sikh community. Both were members and leaders of a place of worship of their faith, the one an Imam from a Mosque and the other a Granthi from a Gurdwara. Andrea Burnley Crowder was one of the elected members and had also been unanimously elected Chairperson at the first meeting. She opened the meeting with a warm word of welcome to all attendants. There were no apologies for absence.

"It is good to see a full house today at an important even critical time in the life of our community. I want to express my personal appreciation for your attendance. I know what busy lives we all pursue. You have all received a copy of the reports from the Police, Fire and Crime Commissioner. Maureen Wilson-Hayes, and one from Chief Constable, Patricia Nowak, and I want to pick out the issue of the kidnap of one of our officers, which appears in both. Chief Constable, can you update us on the situation, what efforts you have made and with what results."

"Yes, of course, Chair. We made a midnight raid on one of the mafia mob's so-called safe houses two days ago on the basis of the tracing of the details of the car used in the kidnapping and its ownership and latterly a tip-off. There was a lot of evidence in the remaining personal belongings that Police Sergeant Emily Wooton had been there very recently. Unfortunately the mob appeared to have obtained advance knowledge of our raid from somewhere or someone unknown and at the very last moment she had been hastily moved elsewhere. Two of the members of the gang had been tardy in moving out and they were arrested and taken to the Station for questioning. The results of that interrogation are still ongoing and we shall keep you informed. We shall also be pursuing the person or persons, who leaked the information about the raid and we shall bring them to a full accountability."

"Thank you Chief Constable and the Panel wish you every success in you endeavours. Could we next turn to the matter of the disruption, some might say, chaos at the Remembrance Day Ceremony. What progress has there been on identifying and arresting the persons, who initiated the successive interruptions?

"We are using our behind the scenes contacts to follow up the investigations."

"So, no results so far then, indeed on either issue?"

"Correct!" The Chief Constable's retort was rather edgy if not petulant.

The Chair sought to move on away from matters of such contention.

Mr Bilal Damyal, you have given notice about a problem of stop and search and what you think is ethnic profiling. Would you like to put your question now please?"

"Yes, well more members of the Pakistani community in Ayton, both men and women, seem to be stopped and searched than those of a white complexion. I have received quite a postbag full of complaints about this and the allegation is rife in local mosques that we are being discriminated against. Is it correct? Are there any exact statistics publicly available on this matter, broken down by ethnicity?"

"I can say categorically that there is no ethnic profiling allowed in the Ayton Force. I cannot give you the exact details of numbers, but I assure you that ethnic profiling is not permitted, would never be permitted and it would be a disciplinary offence for any officer to attempt to adopt such an approach."

Mr Lashley you have a follow-up question to that. Please go ahead."

Dr Horace Lashley was of West Indian ancestry. He was an academic from the local university, whose area of expertise was race relations. He was also a long-standing member of the Institute of Race Relations.

"Thank you, Chair. I have to say that members of the Ayton Black community have also raised the same topic. I believe as a fact that proportionately more members of the Black community are being stopped, searched and arrested, than other groups, sometimes with excessive force."

The Chief Constable swiftly and vigorously refuted the allegation.

"Such a racist approach would not only be outlawed by the Ayton Police Force, but it would be illegal in the Law of the land. If Mr Lashley has instances of such an approach being adopted, there is a well-used complaints procedure and I or one of my officers would be happy to facilitate such as approach. In the first instance, if preferred, I am always happy to receive details of such complaints, which I would pass to the independent Police complaints authority."

"Mrs Adarsh Khanna you had an enquiry about the co-opted members of the Panel. Please put your question."

"Thank you Chair. I and my quite large Hindu community in the Ayton region are very happy that we already have members of two of our communities co-opted onto the Panel. We feel that the Indian Hindu community should also be represented with a co-opted member of the panel. What can be done to facilitate this happening?"

In response the Chief Constable spoke supportively of the idea.

"This is a matter for the Commissioner. But I have to say that personally I am very sympathetic to your request. Commissioner would you like to add anything to that?"

"Yes Chair. Just to say that I would be happy to put forward such a proposal for a further co-opted member of the Panel, if requested in writing by the appropriate community. If Mrs Khanna would like to meet with me after the end of the meeting I should be happy to acquaint her with the procedure and assist her and/or her colleagues in assembling an appropriate community case. This Panel would have to agree such a proposal. I am open to correction but I believe such a proposal would in addition have to be approved by the Home Office."

Mrs Emily Haigh, you had a question concerning misogynistic behaviour in the Ayton Police Force. Would you like to elucidate, please?

"Yes, of course, Chair. There is some evidence of male officers ganging together to make misogynistic comments about women and particularly and specifically about women officers. They do this among themselves in a group or via postings on the internet. Officers also sometimes treat women suspects in a denigratory way, almost as though they were second class citizens. The same applies to members of the LGBTQ+ community. Is the Force in need of a retraining programme for some of its officers? Some members of the Public have also raised a concern about alleged improper relationships between some officers and women, and perhaps particularly with innocent young girls."

Realising that some of these accusations were true, the Chief Constable was somewhat incensed by the conglomeration of these 'touchy' concerns, but tried to acknowledge them accurately and coolly.

"I'd like with your permission, Chair, to take these three matters together. Racist, sexist and homophobic behaviour, including communications through whatever channels and illicit sexual relationships will not be tolerated in this Force. Such behaviour, if proven, will lead to an automatic dismissal, where discovered. If Mrs Haigh has specific details of any such cases, I would be happy to receive and review them and if they infringe our Force policy of equality before the Law, immediately on proof, the officers concerned will be dismissed."

"Thank you Mrs Haigh for raising this subject and Chief Constable for enabling us to consider these matters rationally and according to the Law of the Land."

The Chair now attempted to steer the meeting to a major issue, which was central to their agenda today and had been raised in advance by several members of the Panel.

"Now we really must consider the matter of drugs and the Cartels and individuals, who peddle them here in Ayton. Drugs are encroaching more and more into the daily life of the town and they are having a corruptive and detrimental, and sometimes totally destructive, effect on people's lives, especially our youngsters. Mr Rupert Chambers-Jones, I believe you have a proposal to make and you wanted to raise some issues with regard to this problem?"

Rupert Chambers-Jones was a highly respected member of the local community. He had his own very successful firm of twenty or so solicitors in the town centre, where pro bono opportunities for advice to any member of the Public were frequent. He was a local philanthropist, a mason and an ardent Anglican.

"Yes, Chair. Thank you. For some time now I have observed with mounting concern the penetration of drugs into the everyday social and business life of our town and perhaps particularly the lives of our youngsters, sometimes with fatal consequences. With the increasing arrival of ever more powerful drugs, which can and do kill, and the growing penetration of drug Cartels into what was once our normal social and business lives, I am concerned about the Police reactive strategy to the problem and the failure to marshal Public opinion against what I am going to call the drug life, which is taking over our town. If I may, I want to ask what further measures the Chief Constable is proposing to halt the absorption of ever more powerful drugs into our town and to eradicate this venom and its perpetrators from our town's life? Let me say also that we need more remedial and rehabilitation facilities, especially for youngsters in this area, although I accept that such is not the arena or brief of this Panel."

Dr Charles Beatty interrupted the delivery of the expected and indeed imminent reply of the Chair to endorse what Mr Chambers-Jones had been saying. He was a well-known local GP, who also worked in the local hospital with particular reference to the rehabilitation of young drug addicts.

"Madam Chair, please forgive my interruption. I just wanted very briefly to endorse what has just been said with a few specific facts about our locality. The drugs problem in Ayton is getting worse by the day. There have been dozens of fatal drug overdoses during the last year. Across the Summer alone we have had some forty cases, some of which we believe are due to synthetic opioids of extreme potency. We are now faced with a situation where we believe that, due to the shortage of heroin, such synthetic opioids as nitazenes and xylazine with extreme potencies are being substituted without the consumer knowing and they can prove fatal. They are just appearing surreptitiously in this area disguised as vaping liquids and in alleged pain killers. Alarmingly, they are twenty times more powerful than fentanyl and one hundred times more potent than heroin. Even a small amount can kill. These drugs are being cut and sold as heroin without the user being aware of what they are and conscious that their potency is some one hundred times greater than heroin. The Ayton Coroner has already considered several of the cases of death from drug overdoses and he has concluded that nitazenes were the primary cause of death. We are now seeing more than twice as many deaths from drug overdoses as usual at this time of year. What is the local Police force doing to seize, arrest and make the case for the prosecution and imprisonment of the monsters, who are beginning to bring these drugs so damagingly to our area and to our young people in particular. I realise that any effective action will need to include the Police, public health officials, drug charities and the Police in a multi-agency effort. But we can begin to make a difference here in this Panel. Thank you Chair and once again, my apologies".

The Chair replied soothingly.

"No need to apologise, Dr Beatty. What you have shared with us may be unwelcome news, but it is nonetheless essential to our own efficient functioning and overcoming the crucial problems that you identify. Chief Constable, you now have the floor."

"Thank you for that question, Mr Beecham-Jones. Let me assure Dr Beatty that we are hot in pursuit of the monsters, who are causing such mayhem in our community. We have launched a crackdown particularly to staunch the flow of such substances into our community and a section of the staff in the incident room is dedicated specifically to tackling this concern. A mounting number of seizures of drugs, closures of properties and arrests have been made and prosecution of the offenders is advancing satisfactorily. The drugs have been destroyed in environmentally friendly incinerators, except where they are needed as evidence in court. The situation is, however, very complex. But I can mention, for example, the Central Government-funded scheme in the Old Town area to put more officers on the ground. Interim results for this experiment are encouraging in keeping drugs and drug sellers off the street but also in information and intelligence gathering especially about the location of the gangs' drug cultivation premises. We also have an ongoing programme within a very tight budget, for closing down all the indoor drug farms and brothels in the town, intercepting the delivery of drugs, especially the new more powerful one, which you mentioned, to the locality and putting the purveyors of such noxious drugs in prison. Last year we closed some fifty indoor drug farms and arrested those providing and tending them, most of whom were successfully prosecuted and are now in prison. Of the twenty or so drug cartels in the town, ten have been closed this year and their members have been successfully prosecuted. I very much welcome Mr Beecham-Jones and Dr Beatty's contributions and the suggestion about a mass publicity campaign would be helpful in addition to the other measures we are taking. Unfortunately the Ayton Police Force does not have either human or financial resources for such an effort at this time. I would be happy, however, to meet with the two gentlemen to discuss how to engage charitable organisations in the area and individual community members to seek the funding and commence the campaign as soon as possible. This evil business is driven by Public demand for drugs first and foremost. No demand. No cartels! No indoor drug farms! No drugs!"

Dr Beatty expressed his thanks and Mr Beecham-Jones also responded appreciatively.

"Thank you, Chief Constable. I shall get my Secretary to contact you and my friend, Dr Beatty today to arrange an initial meeting just as soon as our respective diaries permit. I would also suggest, if I may, that if she has the time, the elected Police, Fire and Crime Commissioner, Maureen Wilson-Hayes, could also join us, and I shall include her in my round robin."

....The Chair expressed her personal support for the idea and willingness to participate in any discussions or activities that would facilitate its materialisation. There also seemed to be a general and in some cases enthusiastic welcome and support from the members of the Panel for the idea now being advanced. Several members even volunteered assistance there and then and some even offered to make modest donations to get the thing started. As the Chair was just about to close the proceeding of the Panel, Mr Stanley Bewley, a retired research chemist at the local university and a long standing member of the Board, interrupted and added another item to the agenda.

"Madam, Chair, with your permission, I should like to raise the issue of the cruel and inhuman practice of people trafficking, which is rife in the country and for many women it ends in this town. Not long ago a new route from Pakistan was opened up to complement the two major existing routes from Romania and Africa. Members are probably aware, several other routes already exist and some of the women trafficked also end up here from as far away as Africa, serving as unpaid prostitutes. Each woman has a small hen-hutch size room with a dishevelled bed and a camera high up on the wall directed towards the bed in each room. Such brothels are a gold mine for the criminal trafficking gangs. For example if a sex worker had ten clients a day, not unusual, each paying £80, that would produce more than a quarter of a million pounds a year to an organised crime gang. With four similar-sized brothels, they could easily pull in a million pounds a year. That is the main reason why new bordellos are being established ever more rapidly, in some cases more quickly than the authorities can close the existing ones down, with all the resources then needed to care for the liberated sex workers and interrogate and bring the keepers to justice. If required they need to give the women protection, legal advice and other assistance, which could be done under an existing scheme overseen by a well-known and respected national charity. There is another charity, which provides what are called victim navigators, who would also be available free to support the traumatised women twenty-four seven for as long as they need one. This would be one way to save life, enable the building of new lives or to facilitate repatriation according to the women's own wishes. Sorry about the length of my statement but please could we have a major item on our next agenda concerned with people trafficking and its impact on this town and its facilities, as well as the lives of those sorely tortured and abused women. The item could include a statement, circulated in advance, from the Commissioner and the Chief Constable about the role of the Ayton Police force in such an effort."

"Yes, of course, Mr Bewley and thank you for raising the matter. I shall ensure that your suggestion is the first major item on our agenda for the next meeting of this body."

Dr Charles Beatty rushed to interrupt again much to the consternation of the Chair.

Madam Chair! I really am so sorry to interrupt the termination of this meeting. I have just recalled that I would like the problem of media-induced child suicides to be put on the agenda for the next meeting. I understand that there have been one or two in this College. Please forgive me. I thought it was so important."

The Chair answered with immense graciousness.

"Please, Dr Beatty, your contributions to this Panel are always welcome. There is no need for forgiveness."

As the meeting of the Panel was now out of time, it was on those unusual and rather happy notes that the Chair closed the meeting. The Chief Constable gave a sigh of relief and returned quickly to her desk and a further mountain of work before arriving home to her family late again that evening totally exhausted.

An urgent meeting had been called by the secretary of the Ayton College on behalf of the Board of Governors of the College to consider the pressing problem of what were called 'ghost students'. Andrea Burnley Crowder, Chair of the Board was presiding over the meeting of the Board, to which the Principal of the College, Dr Andrew Ziegler, senior members of staff, the Police liaison officer for the College, Police Sergeant Mary Rigby. Mrs Marjory Robinson and other staff members from the local hospital and Mrs Gillian Reagan some others from the local authority Social Services Department were invited as non-voting observers but would not be refused permission to speak.

Calling the meeting to order the Chair welcomed all members and the guests and gave an interim definition of what was meant by 'ghost students'.

"Welcome to this important meeting of the Board of Governors of Ayton College and especially to our guests from the hospital and social services today. By ghost students, we mean the significant number of students who are enrolled at the College but regularly do not attend, attend intermittently or having attended for a period of time and then never attend again. We are trying to discover the reason for these different kinds of absences and how they can be tackled more effectively so as to enable the students to return to full-time education. Dr Ziegler would you like to start the ball rolling, please?"

"Yes, thank you Chair. Excluding those who are absent through legitimate reasons such as illness, the outline of the problem is as follows. Something like twenty-five percent of the enrolled students are caught within the net of absenteeism. Some attend and then leave without any notice and in spite of several calls by staff and secretaries to them and the attention of our colleagues in social services never reply. The other group is those, who enrol, attend sometimes for an extended period and then leave for varying periods before turning up again without reasonable explanation. We need to know the reason for both kinds of absenteeism and how they can be tackled so that students at the beginning of their lifespan can benefit from what the College has to offer. There is also another small group of ghost students who attend sometimes for a protracted period and then stop attending and never return to the College. Later we shall consider how they can be attracted back. Any ideas please."

The head of Social Services, Mrs Gillian Reagan, indicated that she would have a go.

"I would emphasise that I am speaking off the record and not on behalf of the local authority. I would also say that my explanation may not cover the whole of the group of students that you indicated. There seem to me to be two main reasons. Firstly and especially for those who are intermittently absent I would suggest county lining work and secondly and particularly for foreign students recently enrolled, there is the offer of work by the mafia drug gangs based in the town as what I am going to call slave labour in the indoor cannabis farms."

"Thank you very much for those outline definitions. Very helpful. Would anyone like to address and enhance the first group of students, the intermittent attendees? Yes, Dr James Sproat from the hospital side of social services."

"Well, thank you Chair. This is not my prime area of expertise of course, but I do see the consequential results of some of this in the hospital. I would suggest that the group of irregular absentees is made up mainly of young people, who are engaged by one or other of the mafia gangs in Ayton, to illegally transport controlled substances across boundaries and return with cash or the reverse process. For short it is referred to as county lining. They are often engaged by payment of free drugs, food, fashion foot-ware, drugs and other incentives, but sometimes instead or in addition with a pittance of cash. In either case they eventually, sometimes quite rapidly, become dependent on and later addicted to the gifted drugs they are being fed with and in many cases they end up with us in the hospital for remedial attention or rehabilitation. The great danger here is that synthetic opioids drugs they are given are sometimes cut with a powerful drugs such as heroin and onwards to heroin substitutes such as nitazenes and xylazine as well as fentanyl and off-prescription pregabalin. Indeed this year such drugs have led already to a spike in addiction, health harm and hospitalisation and drug deaths. Sadly such deaths have occurred amongst the young as well as older addicts. Young people must be told that the consequences of drug abuse can be very serious or even result in death. Just to round up and specify what I have said in numbers we have had thirty deaths from such overdoses in the last few weeks, the majority youngsters and the toll is rising exponentially with consumption of noxious substances by youngsters now including, nitrous oxide and vaping. On the second group, the long-term absentees, I cannot pronounce. I have little or no specific experience. I would advise that such absences are a matter of the Police, hopefully liberating what have in the meantime become modern slaves."

"Thank you Dr Sproat. I think you have expressed the problem exactly and helpfully. Anyone else like to add anything?

"Yes, as Principal of the College I should like to add that some of this absenteeism regrettably begins here in the College with the precursor illicit seepage of drugs into the life of the College. This is something, which we have never been able to completely halt, and it still occurs in spite of College rules stating explicitly that the import of drugs into the college buildings or grounds is strictly prohibited and that such activities will be subject to sanctions, wherc uncovered, or in some more serious cases, referral on to the Police. But regrettably it does still occur and where students get a taste for what they call recreational drugs, they sometimes progress further to their own detriment and in some cases an early death."

"Thank you Dr Ziegler for that additional comment."

The College Police liaison officer, Police Sergeant Mary Rigby raised her hand.

"I should like to add that, in my humble view, the College may have need to refresh and expand it procedures for dealing with the different problems, which are not all the same and, therefore, not all susceptible to the same action and solution. I do not wish to appear to be telling the College what to do. But Ii I may say so, there is clearly a need to reinforce professional development programmes in this rapidly changing field and especially in recognising the dire effects of drug-taking. Tragically, the College has suffered three deaths from drugs and a half dozen stabbings so far this term. I am sure that some such incidents are avoidable with the right policies and further action on the part of the college. If I or the Force can be of assistance in that process of evaluation and revision of the staff development programmes, we are happy to help. Can I also say that the local Force is expanding and intensifying its actions against the criminal gangs, who get rich by the misery of others, especially the youngsters? One additional comment. New synthetic opiates are already pushing drug consumption, health harm and deaths from drug abuse of one kind or another to record levels. But experience shows that one factor in the 'death from drug overdoses' enigma is the fluctuation according to the availability of drugs internationally. According to experience in the UK Midlands, however, one way of tackling this scourge has shown that multi-agency approaches are most effective in stemming the rapidly climbing number of health harms and deaths."

"I wonder if we could move to the second group of long-term absentees. Would anyone like to hazard a few words on the causes and effects of the much smaller incidence of long-term absence?"

Police Sergeant Mary Rigby indicated a wish to speak again.

"Chair I think what I have to say, can be encapsulated in a few words. Those who quit their education long-term, usually do so for a job or what they are convinced is one. Most of these are foreign students, recently and sometimes illegally arrived in this country and unknowingly enticed by one of the mafia drug gangs' 'shepherds' to work in slave labour conditions in the indoor drug farms, of which there are still far too many in this town."

Thank you for that contribution, which amplifies the earlier statement on modern slavery.

"Well, I believe that we have circumscribed roughly the composition of the two groups of absconders from the College. As time is passing rapidly and we are all busy people, could we now turn to what the College community can do to discourage young people from making a disastrous decision and consequent mess of their lives? How can we in the first place prevent the importation of drugs into the learning environment, which is so critically important for the future lives of our students?"

"Firstly, Chair, if I may, as Police Liaison Officer, do we have any idea of how many drug trafficking students we have in the College at present and whether the number is steady, declining or, worst case scenario, constantly growing?

The College Principal offered to make a start on the subject raised by the Police Liaison Officer.

"Chair forgive me for breaking in again. In terms of hard data responsive to the Police Liaison Officer's question, I have to admit that there is a relative penury of hard evidence. What I can say is that we know how many such students this year have been caught in the act, namely ten, only one of whom was so serious as to be referred to the Police for further action. But with regard to the Chair's invitation I would suggest that we turn over our discussions and conclusions to the College Academic Board for advice and, where appropriate, action. Secondly we need to install some kind of checks at all entrances to the College; perhaps a table at each entrance to the College with an invitation to anyone carrying drugs to place them on the table and go on their way. Perhaps there could be a big warning notice above the table that taking drugs into the College is subject to severe sanctions and in some instances reporting to the Police for further action. We could also brighten up the health education section of our curriculum with advice against taking drugs not prescribed by a doctor by dint of illness. As well, we could ask the Academic Board to request those responsible for each component of the curriculum to closely examine how it can contribute to the College's struggle against drugs and the safety of our students."

The Chair reacted enthusiastically and alerted the Governing Body to the fact that all the papers and minutes of the College Governors meetings were freely available to the Academic Board and indeed to all members of staff. She invited further contributions.

Mrs Marjory Robinson, long-term Governor and a leading member of the local authority Social Services Department, indicated her wish to make a contribution to the debate.

"Thank you Madam Chair. A statement and a question! Firstly a statement. Unless we can tame this monster of new more potent drugs, which is even now beginning to seep into our very own community, we shall have to face the kind of soaring death rate from synthetic opioid poisoning that has been experienced in the United States, where there have been hundreds of deaths, principally from fentanyl. Next a question. Of the students, who have been discovered selling controlled substances in the College, what was the male/female distribution?"

The Principal answered clearly and unambiguously.

"The vast majority of sellers of drugs on College premises are male. Only one female purveyor may occur very exceptionally each academic year. Female sellers of drugs on the College premises are almost totally absent; very rare indeed."

Andy Bowers, a longstanding member of the Governing Body and a very successful local business man, who owned a large furniture shop in the main square, held up his hand in a gesture to speak.

"Yes, Mr Bowers. Please go ahead.

"Well!" Firstly, we have heard today of drugs, drugs and more powerful drugs arriving in our country and in our town and in our College with desperate and sometimes fatal consequences, especially for our young people. We have heard of knife fights and fatalities as a consequence of such fights amongst students in the town and in this College. I just do not understand how they are getting into our country, our town and our College. My second point is that this illegal trade is powered by demand. If there was no demand, there would be no drugs. Has everyone gone mad or just blind? I ask myself. When I was a lad, we didn't have much money or anything else for that matter. But neither did we have illegal, controlled substances at all, let alone in the quantities currently available. Third point! In that context, this College has got to get its act together and make sure that no drugs or knifes, not just some or a small amount of illicit substances, enter this College, and senior staff and governors had better get on with delivering that objective sooner, or we shall all end up smothered in chaos under a huge heap of drugs and with many of us needing a doctor to heal our knife wounds."

"Thank you Mr Bowers for that very honest and forthright, apocalyptic statement. I am not sure about the ominous picture that you paint, but I strongly agree with your overall message that both drugs and knives must be banned from the College and its grounds and that anyone who breaches that ban should be subject to severe sanctions. Implicit in your words is the advice that it is insufficient to ban these things and then sit back and relax. We need to urgently consider and implement the ban and follow up by continually monitoring, evaluating, revising and improving ways and means of enforcing the bans. I would suggest that this meeting request the establishment of a small working party jointly of staff and governors to draw up a plan of campaign to cover the two issues and prepare a rapid interim report, if you like, back to this body at its next meeting in two weeks' time. Would members and guests be agreeable to such action, please indicate your view."

The whole meeting indicated their support and there was no need for the Chair to ask for an indication of dissenting voices. And that was how the meeting terminated with members better informed and strongly supportive of the need urgently for further action by the College itself.

Chapter Eight: Retaliation

It was a normal Sunday relaxation for the dozen or so senior members of the Ayton Albanian drug cartel to meet with the men of their syndicate in one of their own restaurants to socialise, mostly over a cup of Balkan coffee or a glass of Raki and cheese or honey Petulla. It was in fact part of their regular relaxation from the arduous business of serving the demands of the Clan in its Ayton business. It was also conveniently situated in the Ivegate in the old town centre, although not very accessible for motor vehicles. But as it was their own, or at least the Clan's restaurant, they felt themselves safe and secure there.

They appreciated the chance that the restaurant offered them to unwind. But they also valued the genuine Balkan home cooking served free of charge as well. In those rare moments of relaxation, there were opportunities to escape business and to gossip instead about football, local, national and international, families, politics and their home far away. It was a haven of peace and recreation for them all to enjoy.

Some way, however, by dint of a deliberate action for the receipt of money or by accident in an incautious conversation, the regularity and location of the get-together became known to their enemies, not least the main enemy that they competed with for the drug business and prostitution in Ayton, the Manchester mob. They had themselves attacked members of the other syndicate a short while ago for trying to impinge on their drug, people trafficking and brothel businesses. But that was a while ago now and more or less forgotten as nothing had happened since then.

The Manchester cartel was premier amongst the most embittered enemies of their clan, one of a large number of the criminal gangs based in the Manchester Metropolitan area, but for the moment the only one with an out-posted extension based in Ayton. The Head of the Manchester cartel was Martin Pocklethwaite, known to his colleagues as the 'Pickpocket'. He had strong roots in Ayton and was fixated on revenge against the Albanian mafia, due to a recent attack on his group's county liners, which had killed six of his own members and wounded several others. In addition, due no doubt to a tip off of details to the local Police by his Albanian opponents, he had had the local Police Force crawling all over the place for several days after the attack, asking questions and probing the premises and his business. Moreover, two of his men had also been charged with unauthorised possession of a firearm. He was burning for revenge.

He had called in two of his thugs, experienced gunmen from the Manchester mob, to help him plan and deliver that revenge. Sam Beardsell and Joe E Landsman were very experienced in the kind of work that Martin was wanting done and indeed together they had carried out similar attacks for him in the Manchester Metropolitan Area to the one, which he was envisaging in Ayton. They were not strangers to working with Martin.

They had just arrived on that Monday morning and were being briefed about the job by their boss the 'Pickpocket', in one of the mob's safe houses on the outskirts of Ayton near a large multi-business industrial estate. Martin spoke first to give them their instruction and commenced by telling them what he did not want.

"I don't want a massacre, which brings the local Police down about my business. The aim of the job is to hit the top men in the Albanian gang: the boss of the Albanian mob's regional business here in Ayton, Sebastiano Gjoni and his direct superior, Ardajan Nikolaj, known familiarly to his accomplices in crime as 'Nico the Greek'. He is the supremo of the Albanian mafia super-cartel in the United Kingdom: a real prize if we can get him. One of the best opportunities to get them both is their weekly Sunday morning get-together at the mob's restaurant in town called 'The Balkan Kitchen'. The problem is that the restaurant is visited by just ordinary members of the Public as well and prized for its Balkan cuisine throughout the whole region. Sometimes the Manchester mob are accommodated separately on a table curtained from the main area occupied by the general Public. Sometimes not! I am not interested in civilian casualties or even common or garden mobsters. That would cause me too much hassle from the local cops for little or no gain. What I want is the two foreign yobs at the top of the tree in this organisation cancelled out, which should decapitate and debilitate the group at least for some little while. Now tell me. I realise that you have not done a recce yet, but what do you think you will need for the job and what do you think about its feasibility as described to you today?"

Joe answered in a fairly middle-class and sophisticated accent, as befitted his family's background and his education. A tall and well-muscled man, he spoke in a confident and self-assured manner.

“Well boss, firstly we want good photo shots of the two men that you are alluding to. We shall also need a map of the area and we want a briefing paper on what they do, both business wise and recreationally. Clearly we shall have to case the restaurant one day, inside and outside, to prepare for next Sunday and also scan the surrounding area. We shall want one of your most reliable and experienced drivers and a very fast car, a fast top of the range BMW or Audi, if possible.”

He halted briefly as if thinking of further additions to his list.

“As well, Sam and I will need to get started today to discreetly reconnoitre the rest of the area frequented by this mob to see if there is any scope for a distance attack. We have brought our night and day telescopic attachments for our rifles with us as that could be one possible swift, safe and efficient approach to solving this little problem, for just such an eventuality as we face. We can get started this very morning on reconnoitring of the area around the restaurant and possibly one of us can get a look into the restaurant for a coffee and a visit to the toilet. We might be able to use our car for today’s work.”

“No problem! You will be accommodated upstairs here. You will have free access at any time of day or night and security for your equipment and your weapons. Jack Jacobson is waiting outside to meet you and he will take care of any food or comfort needs that you may have or indeed anything else, including one or more of the ladies from one of our brothels to accompany you if you do aim to visit the restaurant on Sunday. Needless to say we will cover any costs, as usual in our joint enterprises and, if you need any cash at this moment, I have a limited amount here in the desk. Would you like a cup of coffee or other refreshment before you go upstairs to your quarters and start on your day's work?"

Martin offered encouragingly.

"No thanks. We shall get started without delay. We have other jobs lined up at home. So we need to complete here swiftly but of course also successfully."

With that the two men rose and prepared to depart. At the same time, the door opened and Jack Jacobson, their 'butler' for their stay, entered the room and introduced himself. They walked together out into the corridor conversing about their immediate needs and turned to go up to the first floor to view their accommodation. After only a brief talk, they asked Jack if he could drop them off at the top of the street where the restaurant was situated and park somewhere nearby.

For the beginning of the reconnoitres, they changed their minds and decided to ask Jack to drive them in to the road where the restaurant was situated and drop them off outside the premises. En route it would be helpful if he could alert them to any matters of interest that occurred to him, which he thought might be of interest to them and useful to their task. He pointed out that the restaurant was at some distance from their accommodation, but he was always available to them for lifts, wherever and whenever they wanted to go. They asked to be dropped off at the top of the street or road where the restaurant was situated and they would call him when they needed him.

The road, called Ivegate, was a very narrow fairly steep road, probably of medieval origin, lined on both sides with retail food and clothing premises and the one restaurant more or less in the middle on the right-hand side descending and with the road ending in the very middle of the very busy town centre. There was a large sign at the top indicating that there was no entry except for delivery vehicles. The road was very busy with pedestrian shoppers on the roadway as well as the sidewalk and as the two men mingled with them, they made a mental note of any anomalies that might be of future use to them. They also agreed that Joe would enter the restaurant and case it for access and egress. He would buy a cup of coffee to hide any suspicion and at the end go to the toilet to explore the place for other entries and exits; perhaps at the back of the restaurant. Sam would also seek out any alleyways that might give back access to the rear of the restaurant.

Instantly on entering Joe noted the long hard-wood drinks bar on his right with the whole of the dining area adjacent except to one long table not at that time in service on the right with a heavy, drawn back curtain. On his left almost the whole wall was taken up with windows onto the road. He ordered a coffee and a piece of cake. After completing his refreshments he paid the waiter including a generous tip. Afterwards he went to the toilet situated at the side of and behind the bar and significantly with a half glassed door leading out to a narrow alleyway at the back, which Sam was investigating. On exiting the restaurant, he looked to his right and saw his colleague at the bottom of the road beckoning to him.

In the meantime, Sebastiano Gjoni and his boss Ardajan Nikolaj, were busy discussing just such an eventuality as was being prepared for in the Manchester mob's safe house. They were planning the prevention measures that they would need to adopt in case of a repeated attempt to impinge on their empire. Ardajan Nikolaj was speaking first as was his arrogant wont.

"I sincerely hope that the members of that small-town outfit that tried to move onto our patch has learnt their lesson. Unfortunately we did not get their top man and that may mean that he may want to have another go. You must be on your guard against that and build up you defences. Those criminals, the local coppers, are also attempting to close more of our houses and that also needs to be dealt with. As a branch office, we need to step up our county lines sales and that means recruiting more youngsters as runners. Delivery by bicycle locally is worth increasing for small amounts of wraps at competitive prices. Deliveries of stocks of the new drugs are also being interrupted by those hammer heads, the local cops, and we need to rethink the routes, times and vehicles that we use. I've set this all down in this little sheet here, which I shall leave with you to study after my departure."

He halted and waved a brief for a second or two and looked at his underlings as he regarded him severely then explained the reason for the homily of desired actions and precautions.

Sebastiano just nodded in silent assent.

"I need to return to London this week and soon, as I have obligations to fulfil towards customers and my bosses there, and many other routine items demanding my attention as well. When I return I shall bring two replacement gunmen back with me. I want to emphasise that during their stay here they will be a cost to your budget here in Ayton not to mine in London. Their time here will be limited and their job will be first and foremost to propose measures to defend against and prevent an attack against us by anybody at any time anywhere. And secondly to train some small number of your staff to take over from them when they return to London. I cannot just keep providing you with your sharpshooters. I shall be away as short a time as I can make it. Surely not more than a few days to a week. You can contact me if you need to on my usual smartphone number. Any questions?"

Sebastiano did not like the non-participatory pontification of his boss, Nico. He found it very trying but he did not dare to speak up about what was really troubling him, namely where he was going to get the financial and human resources for what was being demanded of him. He acquiesced with a faint smile and a silent nod of his head.

It was with a demonstrative flourish that his boss rose throwing the written brief on the table in front of Sebastiano. He left the room and hastily departed for his fiefdom in London.

Chapter Nine: A Birthday Celebration

It was Sunday, the day of her husband, Martin's, fortieth birthday and Andrea Burnley Crowder had planned a special surprise for him and for that very evening. She had advance-booked a table for the evening at the Balkan Kitchen restaurant in town for seven o'clock that evening, a restaurant of local renown, but one where they had never dined before in all the time they had lived in Ayton. They normally dined at home in the evening during the week and on Sunday, partly due the exhaustion of their many other commitments in the busy life they led, as well as their voluntary and charitable ones, some of which were evening ones. But today was a different and very special occasion to them both.

Andrea had arranged for Isabel, her mother, to attend to her children in their parent's absence. Isabel was on the threshold of full retirement and, having given up much of her Public work, she was becoming ever more dissatisfied with her rather boring routine life. So she was only too happy to babysit her two grandchildren for as long as was required and even to see them to bed if necessary. As she no longer went into work every day, she would stay with them until Andrea and Martin returned home, however late that was.

After all there was a small box-room bedroom for her, set aside for this very purpose upstairs next to the two children's bedrooms. Just in case, the bed had already been prepared for her, if needed. Everything had been pre-prepared by Andrea as a surprise for Martin. For example, a taxi to take them both to the restaurant had been pre-booked and they would dress for the evening in their best clothes. They intent on arriving in style there for their birthday dinner

When Andrea told Martin of the arrangement she had made for the restaurant and taxi, he was absolutely delighted. He thanked her profusely for her imaginative proposal and continuing love and gave her a big kiss and a prolonged hug before departing bright-eyed and bushy tailed for an extra day's work at the office. When the children had been dropped at College nearby for Sunday recreational activities, Andrea also drove into the office to deal with a pile of post and written information left by her secretary of the appointments on Monday.

So the commencement of another very crowded success. She thought to herself that success brings with it its own problems. Certainly, the business had improved its performance as her mother, Isabel, had decided to retire from the business and hand over the reins of the company completely to her daughter. Isabel only attended the office intermittently now and more and more rarely as time went by. As word spread about the new ownership of the business and the accession of her ambitious and well-qualified daughter, her pleasant, client-oriented way of working attracted lots of new customers to the business with a very substantial increase of revenue … and work!

On that particular day, both Andrea and Martin found that the day dragged as they both looked forward eagerly to the evening's celebration. Given that consideration, it was no surprise to either of them that they arrived home early from their extra day's work more or less at the same time. So early in fact that it was not yet time for her mother, Isabel, to arrive for her evenings baby-siting duties nor for the children to be collected from their recreational activities at the College. Over an afternoon cup of coffee on the settee in the front room, they reminisced about their time at Imperial College in London and the different foreign placements they had experienced. Andrea had spent time in France and Martin had attended university in Frankfurt in West Germany as it was called then, as an integral part of their studies.

They thought back with appreciation to the way that those experiences had broadened their minds and their circle of friendships and the visits they made afterwards to their new-found friends in Bad Ischl in Austria and to Rennes, Capital of Brittany, and France. They also visited North America to meet up with Martin's cousins in Vancouver and new friends also in nearby Seattle and Washington DC in the United States.

When the time came for the children to be picked up, Martin said he would go for them, while Andrea began to prepare herself for the evening. When he returned Isabel, grandmother to the two children, had already arrived and she took charge of the children's snack and got them down to their homework, acting as substitute adviser to their many questions. So Martin also had time and freedom to get himself ready for the evening's dinner.

At six thirty the taxi arrived slightly early and, as planned, they were at the restaurant for quarter to seven. They had to wait for no more than a few minutes, until they were taken to their table by their waiter for the evening, who rather doubtfully said his name was Sandy. They noted straight away that they had a table in front of a long, drawn curtain at the side of the main restaurant, from which a gentle noise of conversation was emanating. But that fact did not trouble them at the time. The waiter asked them if they would like to order a preprandial drink and they ordered a bottle of the house rather expensive, young Albanian sparkling wine, Shëndeverë! The waiter then presented each one of them with a rather large and ornate menu and left them in order to bring the sparkling wine glasses and a few snacks, as ordered. When she returned they ordered a dish of grilled vegetables, fergese, fasule and byrek but with a soft drink, dhallë, as they had not yet finished the wine.

Two coincidences contributed to the situation that the two of them, Andrea and Martin, unknowingly found themselves in. Firstly the Albanian drug gang had decided to move their already arranged Tuesday get-together for that week to a Sunday to celebrate the anniversary of Albanian independence in 1912, which was always a Public holiday. Thus the closed curtain, behind which senior members of the Albanian mafia mob were meeting that evening. And secondly Sam Beardsell and Joe E Landsman the two gunmen, who had been hired by the Head of the Manchester criminal cartel and head of its interests in Ayton as well, were intent on neutralising Martin Pocklethwaite, to exact revenge and punishment on the Albanian gang for a previous very damaging and costly attack by that gang on the branch of the Manchester mob in Ayton.

The two experienced gunmen commissioned by the Manchester mafia gang in Ayton had completed their reconnoitres and decided that further delay would not be merited nor would there be a better place for the execution of their allotted task than the restaurant. That evening,

Sunday National Independence Day, would be the best time to quickly complete their work, pick up their loot from headman, Martin, and speed off to their next job in the Manchester Metropolitan area the following day.

In preparation for the hits, they pulled on their masks, collected their Glock side-arms, which they placed in a holster at the back of their body, and ample ammunition, synchronised their watches and went downstairs to meet Jack Jacobson, their driver for the night. They aimed to arrive at the restaurant about eight o'clock when the evenings celebrations were well under way and perhaps some of the group would be at least a little drunk. In any case, they were confident the top brass of the rival mob would be there. It would be a snub to their colleague mobsters if they were not. The two gunmen had not heard that one of their intended victims, the supremo of his mob in the UK, had already departed unexpectedly for London the day before.

When they arrived at Ivegate, Jack ignored the restriction on entry only for deliveries, and drove straight down to the bottom of the road, and parked directly round the corner, where the two men dismounted and he agreed to wait for them there. They checked their watches again and agreed that they would both enter the curtained area of the restaurant at the same time, in ten minutes time. This would allow Sam to go round the bottom of the road and up the narrow alleyway to enter the back of the restaurant behind the curtain, while Joe would have time to walk the few meters up the road to the restaurant's main entrance and directly into the restaurant.

After the passage of the ten minutes, they both intended to enter the restaurant, one from the front, walking the few yards across the main part of the restaurant and one from the back so that they had their victims in a pincer. When Sam arrived at the back door, however, he found it locked and bolted. He had to break the windows on the upper half of the door, affix his silencer, shoot out the lock and reach through to withdraw the bolts.

The noise attracted the attention of some of the men at the table and two went with their handguns withdrawn, to investigate what was happening. Sam shot them both dead and proceeded to the back of the table. This unplanned manoeuvre had the advantage for Joe that it directed the attention of the remaining diners to the back of the table and away from the direction, from which he was advancing at some pace. Joe pulled the curtain back. He spied at least one of his intended targets in the middle of the long table and put several bullets in Sebastiano Gjoni's head.

But of Ardajan Nikolaj there was no sign. So for good measure he shot the two people on either side of Gjoni at the table, just as with their attention fixed behind them, they began pulling out their handguns and rising to join in the fray at the back. Joe then fled back through the customers in the main restaurant, violently pushing aside and threatening with his gun the few diners, who tried to impede his flight. He exited the restaurant safely re-holstering his handgun as he went and walked swiftly down the steep road to where Jack was waiting for them both in the car.

In the meantime Sam was fighting a rear-guard action shooting almost randomly in his panic towards the men hiding behind the table and shooting at him. He exited the shattered back door of the restaurant firing into the restaurant. One of those shots pierced the curtain and hit Martin, still sitting at the table opposite Andrea, in the chest, shattering bones and dislocating limbs, injuring intrathoracic and extrathoracic structures and resulting in profuse bleeding. His head slumped forward onto the table, splashing into his plate of food.

Andrea was horrified but reacted instantaneously with a call for an ambulance on her mobile and also to the Police. She lay Martin on the floor and whispered to him that the ambulance was on its way and he should not despair. Whether he could hear her on not she could not know, but she also whispered her undying love to him.

Eventually after what seemed like a lifetime to Andrea, the ambulance did arrive and park directly outside the main entrance to the restaurant. Two medics, a man and a woman entered carrying a stretcher and medical equipment and began treatment for Martin, eliciting as much information as they could all the time from Andrea. By this time, he was still, pale and waxen and not showing any signs of life. But after initial emergency treatment by the medics and the application of breathing equipment and attachment of a drip, they put him on a stretcher and placed him in the ambulance where with Andrea watching with tears in her eyes, the man continued to treat him while the woman drove them, alarm claxon sounding loudly, at some speed to the A&E department at the main hospital.

In the meantime Sam was besieged at the back of the building. He was conscious that he was probably not going to make it. But he fired a volley and began to sprint down the alleyway in the hope of escaping before his pursuers could catch up. One of the shower of bullets, which pursued him down the alleyway, however, hit his leg and slowed him down. Still hoping he staggered on more slowly now, but he was cut down with a further volley of shots in the back from several gunmen before he had gone a few meters and finally one of the men came, stood over him and gave a final shot to Sam's head although by that time he was probably already dead anyway.

Jack and Joe waited a few tense minutes for Sam, even putting at risk their own escape before they realised that it was probably up for him. They departed sadly but swiftly and safely to their safe house just as the Police began to arrive and to prohibit entrance to and exit from the road.

For several months now there had been a growing crescendo of feedback from senior Officers in the Force about ever louder rumblings in the ranks. The causes were manifest: the mounting workload; the lack of appropriate human and financial resources for all the different tasks they were asked to undertake. There was also the swelling and unprecedented absenteeism in the ranks of the officers, causing a growing the burden on the remaining officers. All of these causes of disquiet in the Force were beginning to take their toll. Added to all this were the mounting numbers of injuries to officers, especially in raids, and perhaps particularly the untimely death during a recent raid of the well-respected indeed popular Head of the Police Armed Police Response Unit, Superintendent Julian Charles, which appeared to have brought all the unrest to boiling point.

Something had to be done urgently, her senior colleagues advised the Chief Constable or there was the danger of a revolt in the ranks, but also from amongst some senior officers. Consequent on the snow-balling clamour for action, the Chief Constable of Ayton, Patricia Nowak, decided to try to diffuse the situation by calling together a meeting of senior officers and representatives of the Police Associations.

The meeting was set for nine o'clock on Monday morning, when it was assumed that most colleagues would be rested after a break and ready for a frank and positive, perhaps even a creative discussion about how to solve or at least assuage the anxiety. The place of the meeting was set for somewhere comfortable, the station conference room, and simple breakfast refreshments were available of a side table. To encourage an atmosphere of polite collegial interchange the usual serried ranks of the seating in the room had been changed and the chairs and tables had been arranged in a circular constellation with the Chief Constable at the place facing the door.

The meeting was opened with a few short and appreciative but lengthy and bombastic words by the Chief Constable.

"Colleague Police officers, welcome to this review meeting. My thanks are due to every one of you for attending in the context of what I know are very busy lives. I want to express my gratitude also to the whole Force for the extraordinary service, which they constantly give for the Public of Ayton. I am always the first to express well-merited my appreciation to politicians and the general Public about the high level and quality of your indispensable contribution to the lives and security of the people of Ayton and district. I know we all accept that there is enormous pressure on both human and physical resources in the Force and that brings with it its own burden, sometimes of overwork and illness. The overall aim of this meeting is not to correct that impression of strain, but rather to find ways of coping with it, in order to lessen the strain. I would encourage you all to speak frankly and politely of any grievances, of course, but also to indicate, if you can, any potential solutions. Who would like to speak first?

Deputy Chief Constable, Rajiv Gundara, indicated with his hand that he would like to start the ball rolling.

“Ma’am, thank you for convening this meeting. Thank you friends and colleagues for attending. We are all aware, I am sure, of the disadvantageous situation of basic human and financial resources in all Police forces across the country. Confronting us we have an ever-swelling diversity of crimes, some new, some ancient, but many of them perpetrated by criminals, who have human and physical resources far superior to ours own, now or in the foreseeable future. These criminals now use the most sophisticated means of communication, sometimes superior to our own. These days, we all face a level of threat and violence from these criminals, which is unprecedented and that brings with it, its own emotional stress. The question we all pose to ourselves is surely, will we get back to our families at the end of the day? These days we all experience the feeling that the diverse wave of criminality in the area is forever expanding in volume and sophistication so that we have to make sometimes unpleasant decisions. We all know that a raid, is not just a raid in work terms, but that it involves sometimes quite massive preparation and post-raid toil as well. We are all aware that a single raid will often involve many hundreds of hours of preparatory and follow-up activities. That is the world we live in my friends and that is the world we accept to live in when we join a Police force in this day and age. The question is how can we make it more conducive to our officers and not forgetting also their families?”

“Thank you, Rajiv, for that succinct and encouraging presentation to get our meeting going. Assistant Chief Constable Maria Clarke, I perceive that you wish to address the group.”

"Yes, thank you Ma'am. We all know that our budget is largely determined by the local authority's rates. But as our colleagues in this Force have shown, there are also other ways of growing our income, which can at the same time enable us to offer a better level of and more successful service to our Public. I refer to the central government-provided funding of a substantial increase in the number of officers to cover foot patrols in one of our central districts. So far as we can tell, this project had yielded excellent results for the Public and our officers so far. It has also led to a substantial improvement in crime figures as well. In other words it has brought about a reduction of crime in the area and provided a more relaxing and less hazardous environment for our officers and for the local community. Or let us take the conjoint multi-agency efforts to produce an anti-drug strategy for the town, in which anti-drug flyers and other publicity instruments have been paid for by our colleagues in national and local charities and other local and regional voluntary organisations. It is currently being launched. Turning to rather more animal comforts, let me just add finally that the new franchise of the cafeteria here at the station is widely accepted to have provided a better and more comfortable and relaxing environment, furniture and facilities-wise as well as a wider and better quality of food at roughly the same price."

She smiled at the audience as she made her last point and it seemed to go down well with the assembled officers, some of whom also registered smiles of understanding and one or two even exchanges of hushed words accompanied by smiling agreement. The Chief Constable thanked the Assistant Chief and turned next to the Police liaison officer for the whole education sector including the College in

Ayton, Police Sergeant Mary Rigby and invited her to address the meeting next.

"Ma'am, I just wanted to say something that we sometimes forget. I personally spend most of my time away from stations and other officers. I hear nothing but admiration and praise for the work that our officers do. I find enormous refreshment of my professional competence by listening to others from very different backgrounds. I am very happy in my job and feel that I make a positive different for many people."

"Thank you, Sergeant Rigby, for that very positive and welcome contribution. Who is next? Yes, Sergeant Birch."

"As pro tem Acting Head of the Armed Police Response Unit, after the terrible killing of Superintendent Julian Charles, I just wanted to ask for a special compassionate dealing with members of the Unit at this time. In my many years of service to the Unit, I have never known the level of emotional upset that there is currently amongst officers in the Unit. We shall of course continue in our duties as best we can but we lament our personal loss of a courageous and well-liked officer. Rest assured this Force is well regarded and desperately needed by our local community"

"Thank you Sergeant Birch and …."

At this juncture, Detective Chief Inspector (DCI) Frank Wozny burst into the conversation in his usual forthright manner but this time somewhat more impatiently even irascibly than usual.

"Look, fellow officers. The discussions so far reveal to me a yearning to deny that there are major problems. Our officers, my colleagues, are suffering attempts at blackmail, bribery, threats and actual knife and gun violence as the mobs of Ayton try to infiltrate the Ayton and region administration of business, finance and justice. The same criminal gangs are expending huge sums of money trying to try to infiltrate local business and the economy of the city in general and to corrupt the local Police Force with bribes, corruption, extortion and downright violence. Drug related violence against the forces of Law and Order is rising. Gang-on-gang violence is mounting too with the most recent being the other evening, where a mobster called Sebastiano Gjoni was shot in the head four times, whilst having his dinner in a local restaurant. Sadly, the use of violence against the Public is also escalating. Innocent members of the community are being affected with injury or fatality as Adrian McAllister, a local businessman and husband to Andrea Burney Crowder, who does so much for this community voluntarily, found to his cost this very week. Staff in the Force avoid being photographed for fear of being subject to intimidation attempts and sometimes their spouses or family are cited to force compliance with the wishes of the gang. Many officers and employees in the Station are not rich. They are poor, with debts or other vulnerabilities, which the mobsters constantly seek to exploit. The mobsters in our mist are also conspiring to work together, their business is more corporate, and more multinational, with cells from different gangs in specific areas like production, transport, supply for a particular project, money-laundering, and teams for the introduction of new more powerful drugs, etc., etc. But I think I have said enough. It does seem to me, however, important to establish firmly, clearly and frankly some of the areas of challenge to us all or we shall surely find no solutions to solving them."

Police Sergeant Lucie Brockenbank, a long-serving beat officer from the centre of town and a representative of the Association stormed in to the discussion

Ma'am. I don't wish to be contentious, but I strongly agree with what DCI Frank Wozny has just said. We have to face up to the problems in the Force or fail to remedy them. At this moment out on the beat, where I exist, it frequently seems to me that it is the criminal drug cartels who are pulling the strings and winning the game. We must take really seriously as well the fact that there is a very acute possibility that someone in our ranks, sometimes and somehow is passing drug interception intelligence and advance notice of indoor drug farm and brothel busts here in Ayton to the mobsters. As quickly as we close those establishments, the mobs with much greater resources than ourselves are replacing them. These criminals aim at approaching respectable people in business, politics and elsewhere in our society with incentivised offers to corrupt them into co-operating with the gang. There are strong rumours on the streets of officials in the town hall, legal services firms, as well as national and local civil servants and elsewhere accepting bribes. Clearly I do not know the exact details, but insofar as these leakages are occurring, our efforts will always be in vain and an expensive waste of our scarce resources." Two suggestions. A confidential welfare set-up a bit like the family liaison room we now have for officers and their families and a strengthening of the evaluation of our work and achievements by an independent unit of our own officers and employees."

Police Constable Margaret Pettigrew, another beat officer came in swiftly to endorse the idea of a dedicated independent welfare service for officers and their families.

"Ma'am I strongly support the idea of a dedicated welfare unit for officers. Unless we act now the poison of criminal gangs on our community life with their drugs and ambitions to take over civil society will infiltrate all of our social, economic and political life and the criminal justice system. We need to act quickly to address this matter or in a few years' time … well can you imagine?"

Assistant Chief Constable Maria Clarke stepped in to try to make the contributions of fellow officers more focussed. We have had numerous informative contributions about what is wrong with society and its Law enforcement systems. Some of them come within the purview of this Force. Some do not. But we have had little that has addressed the problem of the strain and overwork of officers and how to tackle it. Along the lines of the last two contributions I would like to formally suggest that this group make a recommendation to the Chief Constable today for the establishment of a dedicated and confidential welfare facility to be established in this station for officers and their families. On the issue of overwork we have had no specific suggestion on how to deal with it in a satisfactory way. The establishment of the welfare facility may well provide officers, who are feeling stressed, an opportunity to share their concern with someone in such a facility and receive advice on how to cope. Other major commercial organisations have such a facility. You know, often just talking about your trouble seems to help. One might also suggest a lightening of loads by more co-operative sharing of tasks amongst several colleagues, rather than the burden falling on one pair of shoulders. I'll leave to fellow officers to express their opinions on that."

Everyone had more or less expected that the Assistant Chief Constable's statement was the final rounding up of the debate. But at that point a young Constable Marjorie Macnamara spoke up with a rather ground-breaking suggestion. Marjorie was recently out of university, imaginative and ambitious.

"Ma'am, as I see it the major problem here is an overburden of work. If that is correct then we have to find ways of lightening the burden on officers. Onc area where we could save ourselves a lot of work is in the busts that we regularly do of brothels. They involve both substantial preparatory and follow-up work as well as time, money and resources for the actual raid. Yet, within a very short period of time, the brothel and its prostitutes have been replaced by the criminal mafia gangs with a couple of minibus-loads of women from London. Rather than spend all that time money and resource, I wonder whether we should just accept that some men … and I abhor this … require sex and are willing to pay for it. I know the situation of the women is intolerable and unjust. Could we not turn the tables and get the local authority or relevant health body, for example the Health Protection Agency, to institute a system of inspection to approve premises and the treatment of the women there as they do in several countries abroad. Would not such a move improve the lot of the prostitutes, get the mafia gangs to spend their own money on the provision of the brothels and at the same time save us a lot of money and stress for staff releasing the money and renewed energy for other activities?

The Chief Constable was a little horrified by this radical suggestion by a very young and new constable and she responded to the debate in general in a sympathetic manner, but without mentioning this final radical contribution specifically.

"Thank you all for a very interesting and frank debate. On the welfare facility, I support the idea. Of course we already have a family welfare suite in the station, and we shall have to consider the suggestion in a budgetary context when we have put together a firm proposal. On the issue of overwork and stress amongst officers, we have come to no conclusions. That does not mean that our discussion today have been useless. Sometimes just sharing your frustration about matters of stress, strain and perceived overwork can help and that is what we have done today. So I would suggest that we have regular such meetings on this matter in the future. So please, if you could, before the next meeting try to muster some of the concerns raised by your staff and other officers, who are not present with us here today and try to elicit their suggestions of how to deal with the problem."

Everyone seemed satisfied with the suggested actions and the meeting dispersed with officers still discussing with other officers, conversing in small groups about the issues and the meeting and some no doubt about the far-reaching proposal of a newcomer constable.

Chapter Eleven: A Final Raid?

The Police team was meeting to put the final touches to the planned raid on a large mafia brothel on the outskirts of the inner town centre. Some of the twenty or so officers, who were attending the meeting in the main office were unconvinced of the need for this raid, as talks were already advancing with the local authority about an alternative, more humane way of regulating them. They felt that other tasks, such as stopping of the increased influx of more powerful, lethal drugs into the area, was where the resources should be spent.

Others were still convinced of the need for raids such as the one being planned to release the 'entombed' women from their cruel bondage and to keep clipping the wings of the mafia gangs, who were running the brothels and earning a fortune in doing so. Assistant Chief Constable Maria Clarke had been requested by the Chief Constable to take overall charge of the raid with the close assistance of Police Sergeant Tony Birch, Interim Head of the Armed Police Unit.

The meeting discussed the arrangements for the raid, which was timed to begin at midnight, when Police officers would approach the front door and quoting the search warrant, which they held, request that the door be opened. At the front of the room were displayed several pictures and diagrams of the surrounding area and the internal dimensions and location of the rooms inside the premises. Pictures were also displayed of the four men and two madams, who were expected to be present in the building. There was no mention of whether they were expected to be armed or not, as firearms had never been used by either side in previous raids.

Promptly at eleven o'clock the advance party departed to cordon of the access road and the back alley and to make sure there was parking space for the rest of the Police vehicles, such as the paddy wagon and first aid vans and other Police cars and vans. At a quarter to midnight, the members of the Armed Response Unit arrived in three of their own vehicles, as did the rest of the complement of Police officers and civilian assistants from the local authority health and social services departments.

The usual announcement was made twice and on receiving no reaction, three authorised firearms officers were dispatched with a ram to break down the door. The officer with the ram stood back after felling the door and the other two armed officers made to enter the building. What happened now was totally unprecedented for this kind of raid. The two officers were instantly felled by a rain of small Kalashnikov fire from the inside of the premises, most probably the quite large hallway. The injured officers were pulled away and taken to the first aid vehicle by their colleagues.

In the meantime, special body armour was donned by all authorised firearms officers, with a chest-attached bodycam, and they were also equipped with ballistic shields. Stun grenades were fired through the front door and front windows and two fully armoured quads, each of three officers, advanced towards the front door holding their ballistic shields in front of them and calling out loudly, "Armed Police, Armed Police". The rest of the Unit quickly arranged themselves, fully body armed and with ballistic shields, in squads of three and began to advance towards the building to be straightway ready to aid or replace their colleagues, when and as required.

The first squad entered the building without resistance and it was clear that those who had fired before, had retreated from the hall. As the first squad advanced deeper into the hall, the second squad entered the building and positioned themselves to cover the first squad.

The next hostile fire came from the stair way and the first criminal was killed with a single shot to the head from the long gun of one officer, using an H&K G36C carbine. The squad advanced to ascend the staircase and a second gangster fired on them. He was also neutralised by a single shot to the head. The other two men came down the stairs with their hands held high, having discarded their Kalashnikovs upstairs. They were frisked and cuffed and escorted by officers to the detention van.

The rest of the raid comprised the detention of the two madams and the freeing of all twenty of the women, who were straightway handed to social services staff, taken in a comfortable coach to a dedicated safe house and subjected to a medical examination. They were also offered a shower, given fresh second-hand clothes and presented with a nourishing meal. They were not detained but were offered safe accommodation in social services safe properties. All would be available for Police and immigration questioning later on, when they had begun to recover from their ordeal. It is at that point that they could decide to try for permission either to remain in the country or to repatriate to their home country of their own free will and at the state's expense. If the latter, their return journey would be planned and funded by the UK government according to their wishes.

Finally, cash and several wraps of different drugs, discovered by the squads in the house, were handed over to forensics and all other officers withdrew from the house to make way for the crime scene investigation officers and the cordon of the road was relaxed. Further finds by the forensics team included notebooks recording sales income and expenditure including on bribes to named persons in local employment, and data about production and import from other centres in the UK of different drugs, including some of the very potent and new ones.

As the raid had finished somewhat later than expected the evaluation meeting was postponed to a day later than usual to allow forensics to do their work and officers were given a day for recuperation, rest and recreation.

When the officers met for the evaluation meeting at two o'clock in the afternoon two days after the raid, it was Chief Constable, who chaired and she began with an announcement about the two officers, who had been shot at the beginning of the raid.

"Fellow officers, I can begin today's meeting with a piece of good news, namely that the two officers injured at the commencement of the raid yesterday were only severely bruised. Their body armour took the force of the bullets that hit them, destroying the chest attached body worn camera. Happily medical opinion is that they will be back at work with us in a few days' time. I am sure that is a great relief to all of us."

There were calls of "Here! Here!" from all the other officers.

She paused for a second or two before making her next announcement.

"I am not sure whether to be pleased or sad about this second announcement. The body of the old man, who was head of the Manchester mob, Martin Pocklethwaite, known colloquially as the 'Pickpocket, was found early this morning at the side of the canal with six bullets in his head! Forensics are still at the sight and it is unclear whether this was a murder by a competing mob or an attempt by the young Turks in his own outfit to pave the way for a new and younger leadership. We shall see. But now it's over to Assistant Chief Constable Maria Clarke to introduce the evaluation of the brothel raid during last night. Maria over to you."

"Thank you Ma'am. Well on the whole the raid went well. Two gangsters were killed and two arrested. The ones that have been arrested are currently being questioned under caution with their lawyer present. Two so-called matrons are currently helping the Police with their inquiries and they have proved to be very co-operative. Interviews of the women freed by the raid have not begun yet on the advice of medical and social services. Handguns, a further stash of money, several hundred pounds all in cash, large stashes of drugs in wrap and pill form, valuable items such as diamonds and expensive wrist-watches were also uncovered in the so-called office of the premises. Vehicles have also been impounded. The forensic examination of other items seized is continuing. Conditions for the women in the brothel were appalling and it is only good luck that they have survived so far mostly in fair health. We do not yet know, how many women did not survive their time in sexual enslavement in the brothel. I'm now going to turn the meeting over to my colleague, Acting Superintendent Anthony Birch, interim Head of the Armed Police Unit, which took the brunt of the activity during the raid."

"Thank you for that introduction, but my name to colleagues is just Tony!" He smiled a little and there was some sympathetic low-key amusement from his colleagues in the Police Armed Response Unit. He proceeded confidently.

"Colleagues I would like to claim that this was a model raid. But I do not believe that to be the case. Apart from liberation from sexual serfdom some two dozen sorely abused young women, the value of which I do not under-estimate, this raid was a lost cause. Firstly the preparation was lacking in some essential elements. Secondly, in spite of more wides-spread gun ownership by our mobsters in Ayton, we did not sufficiently prepare that such an eventuality as the armed defence of the premises would arise. Thirdly, there was too much resource available. We did not need so many officers. Fourthly, was the expenditure of such scarce human and financial resource merited, when in spite of such brothel raids things like drug availability and consumption, health harms and deaths have increased and are continuing to grow at an exponential rate? Finally, we have currently no effective mechanism for cost evaluation in this Force. Well that is my reaction about the raid. You may not like it, then you are free to advance your own assessment of what was achieved by the raid."

DCI Wozny rapidly claimed the floor trying to smooth a pathway for further positive discussion in the meeting, as he saw it.

"Tony is a colleague of long and dedicated service to this force and I always take carefully his forthright and clear way of presenting an argument. I think there is a lot in what Tony has just said, from which we can derive a new policy about raids and what kind of raids we expend our resources on. His comment about the preparation from the raid, I find, I must say, a little bit too harsh, but with a kernel of learning for us embedded within it as well. He is right in implying that the balance of our budget is inadequate to current ever-changing needs and we need to revisit where our priorities lie and prioritise our budgets. I'll leave it there for the moment for other people to speak."

Police Constable Marjorie Macnamara spoke next amplifying her previous recent comments about similar concerns.

"Ma'am. I really do believe that we have to change our priorities in this war against the new drug lord and their much more nimble, adaptable and co-operative ways of doing their business. The old organisation where a single godfather headed a criminal gang has long since been discarded. The drugs business has become much more corporate and international and much less family- or clan-based. There are even a few instances of joint ventures very similar to the model of classic commercial companies. They now cooperate and work together on particular projects such a growth, transport, sale and money laundering. I personally believe that the drug mafias are a bigger threat to our security and freedom than terrorism. We need to attack and break up the new working parties and confiscate their funds. We need to close down those apparently legitimate businesses that support and work with the mafia gangs and we need to throttle off the supply of drugs, especially the more recently arrived more powerful ones, which are killing ever more of our young people, the future of our nation. Those are the objectives, which I my view, should be priority funded."

Police Constable Margaret Pettigrew indicated her wish to speak and she was beckoned by the Chair to do so.

"Ma'am. I must say that I have found this meeting very frank and informative. I have learned a lot today and been prompted to think seriously about matters that I had previously taken for granted. To my perception, there is a consensus arising for a more rigorous realignment of the budget resources that are available to us with our strategic aims. Of course some of those are determined for us, for example in re swiftly to any and all emergencies. But that is not the case for all expenditure. Could I politely suggest that we establish a small working group to consider the fundamental reconfiguration of our budget against our major priority objectives, perhaps with the assistance of an outside financial expert of integrity? I don't know. What I do know is that if present trends continue unchallenged, well where shall we be in another few years' time? Over spent and under-achieved!"

Almost before she had finished making her presentation, another officer, Sergeant Joseph Latham rushed into the fray.

"I strongly support the presentation of my colleague, Sergeant Pettigrew. It is nice to know that the government-backed project is showing up well, but in the other districts of the town and outside in the rural area, we lack the necessary intelligence capacity to do our job efficiently. We do not know, for example, the names of our opposing criminal mobsters. Nor do we know the names of those who are wickedly importing the new more powerful drugs into our area. By and large we do not seem to have the old intelligence-gathering community-Policemen any more. I believe because of lack of resources. I also support Sergeant Pettigrew's proposal for a thorough look at this force's priorities and a matching financial pathway for the construction of our budget to those defined objectives. One proviso only, namely that the working party should be small but representative of different ranks and specialisms and that it should reach its initial conclusions and recommendation rapidly. Those should then be presented to all officers in written and oral forms, this latter at a meeting such as this one, so that any proposals can be available for comments, additions and corrections by all officers."

The Chief Constable was a little taken aback by the avalanche of support for a fundamentally different way of working, choosing and matching work objectives and budget allocations. Finally, however, she saw the loci of what was being propose and took up the relay to bring the meeting to a close. She spoke somewhat dryly.

"I should like to thank most sincerely all those officers, who prepared, launched and have taken part in the evaluation of it this raid I am also grateful to all those, who have participated in this extremely frank, dynamic and creative meeting. Let me assure fellow officers that I shall move to set up the kind of small budget group that is being envisaged soonest and that the group will be able to propose changes to our priority objectives as a Police Force not an army and to the eventual structure and use of our budget. Thank you for a very productive meeting!"

The Chief Constable felt a little out-manoeuvred and the big question now was whether the proposals made in the evaluation meeting would ever see the light of day?

Ardajan Nikolaj, mysteriously known to his accomplices as 'Nico the Greek', the supremo of the mafia super cartel in the United Kingdom, was is a good mood. All the leaders of the major criminal groups in Ayton had agreed to join his meeting with each bringing a financial assistant or underboss. The place for the meeting was a country house in the countryside outside of Ayton, which had recently been purchased by the Albanian group, quite legitimately, but with laundered money. A large table of different dishes was available with a soft drink of different kinds, but no alcohol.

The main participants were the transnational syndicates and the progressively more powerful regional ones, some of these latter having recently grown from individual or small-group beginnings and including those from Manchester, under the leadership of its new head Gary Buxton and his underboss and financial assistant Giles Campbell, London, Liverpool, Birmingham and as far away as Newcastle and Middlesbrough. Even the rebellious Hellbanianz, a gang of brash young Albanians based in Barking, East London, had been invited and had sent a member of their group, who turned out to be a rather diffident participant: more like a spy, some participants actually felt.

There were none of the old-fashioned single big name led-groups of days gone-by. Those present were representatives of company-like syndicates run largely like other commercial big businesses with chiefs like any other company. The whole constellation of their businesses and its staffing had fundamentally changed. The internationalisation of new criminal syndicates now earned their illegal income not just from one crime area or one regional area, however large. Rather they locked internationally into several markets, from drugs to firearms, people trafficking, prostitution and beyond to money laundering, cryptocurrency, information technology and the internet, as well as more and more to penetrating normal economic life with legitimate investments in areas like real estate, property development schemes, car washes, hotels and fast-food restaurants purchased with laundered funds

Somewhat surprisingly they were now also in the healthcare business, in children's care homes and those homes for older people, usually through off-shore companies. London, the Capital of European money-laundering and hub by dint of the new crime common language, English, was now the centre of European organised crime and its financial heart. Ardajan Nikolaj was proud to be part, an influential part indeed, of the new crime empire.

When all had sated their appetites and informal getting-to-know you had been completed, Ardajan Nikolaj, stood up smiling and politely tapped one of the spoons on to a china cup to call his audience to order.

"Fellow business friends, welcome. I have been requested to bid you all welcome not only on my own behalf but also at the behest of our Firm's senior colleagues in London and abroad. We are here today to discuss the collective interference in our trade by local, regional and national agencies of so-called Law and Order, but also international organisations such as Interpol, currently boasting as having dealt with over sixty thousand cases last year, Europol, Frontex, etc. I am here to facilitate our new mode of functioning and conglomerate syndicates to increase turn-over and to ward off the depredations of these vultures. Multi-agency groups, where in particular cases, for example, document fashioning, we set up a group together to undertake the task, which represents all those who wish to be involved, in the delivery of the service and in the combined income from that endeavour. The days of our conflicts over market share and revenue are over and done with. Today we are looking for ever greater corporate, multiagency working with the one major aim only of accumulating additional income for each individual organisation that participates. The other rapidly changing area where we can benefit by deepening our co-operation is in the internet and social media, but that requires the availability of tech-savvy technicians with the necessary knowhow from each participating Firm. Believe me the internet offers a brighter future for us all and for our profits. The dark web is not my speciality but reports from colleagues on the basis of a rating system confirm that we are marketing almost four hundred thousand different items, the bulk of which are drugs, through that channel but the quantum of which is rapidly expanding in areas such as guns and new, more potent drugs. Anyway, that is the agenda for today. There is no compulsion on anyone to participate, but I believe that we all share a commonality in wishing to improve our balance sheet … substantially. And here is the opportunity."

Strangely, the first to speak, in a rather brazen and combative, manner was the representative from the London estate-based Hellbanianz, an Albanian street gang of retail drug dealers, known for their extreme violence but also for their strong alliance with the Italian mafias such as the powerful NDrangheta.

"Nico. Thank you for the introduction and the free victuals. I'm proud to tell you that we can manage very well by ourselves, thank you very much. To be frank, one item in what you had to say seems to me a little two-faced. On the one hand, you speak about co-operation, co-working and sharing of income, but my friends and I find that we are largely excluded from the very profitable market of new more potent drugs like most synthetic opioids such as fentanyl and heroin substitutes such as nitazenes and xylazine in the UK and European markets. What kind of co-operation and income do you offer to us in that area of the market?"

Nico took the abrasive question very coolly and tried to give a correct but not very helpful rejoinder.

"Well, thank you for your question. I am not in the market today to offer anything. My job today is to facilitate contacts that can result in co-operative business endeavours in a particular area of the market in a way which will increase profits for all participants. One prerequisite for that is what the group seeking participation can bring to the table. For my own organisation, I can share with you that we have forged a multinational group from several different cartels that import new and more powerful drugs, mostly synthetic opioids like fentanyl and heroin substitutes such as nitazenes and xylazine, and distributes them in a particular market to organisations, small groups and individuals at a very competitive and constant price. We have had to forge the market ourselves with substantial initial investment costs and that has involved working closely with our cousins in the US and the Americas and others, who obtain their products from several countries in South and Central America. But some freelancers have already tried importing drugs like fentanyl directly from China and India with a modicum of success."

The representative of the Liverpool mafia clans, Joe Buchanan, barged his way in to the discussion at this point.

"Chair thanks for inviting us and for the excellent food. I not sure that there is any point in my remaining here any further. Our Cartel is the only one in England, which does not normally sell Albanian-sourced cocaine. As I say, Chair, thanks for inviting us and for the excellent food. I not sure that there is any point in my staying for the rest of your meeting. We are an independent group, with its own source for obtaining cocaine usually on the continent and selling it to us directly into our international port. We have also negotiated our own source for whatever else we need directly with our own friends in South America and we are self-sufficient. But just to deliver a word of warning to our friends here today and any others with malign intentions towards our patch, our trade is jealously guarded by our own gangs. So as you can see we do not need the kind of macro-organisation that you are presumably, or at least seem to me to be, offering. Farewell and thanks again for the invitation and good food."

At this point in the proceedings the Chair had the strong impression that his meeting was going off the rails.

The next person to speak was the new young chief of the expanded Manchester cartel, Gary Buxton.

"Chairman, I should like to say that the former supremo, the old man heading the Manchester Firm, Martin Pocklethwaite, has had an unfortunate accident and I Gary Buxton, have been requested to stand in his place. I am here with our financial assistant, Giles Campbell. I very much welcome this meeting and agree with its purpose of helping to put us in a cooperative mode of work across common areas involving several organisations, so as to maximise our earnings. We have already tried this with our Albanian colleagues in the field of the acquisition and sale of cocaine. They are providing us with the cheapest and purest cocaine on the market and we are hoping and planning for further developments in that field in the future. One area in which we would like to engage in further co-operative development is information technology and the dark web, where many thousands of business items are now processed. Anyway that is our pathway for financial progress in the future. Thanks for organising this meeting."

The representative from Birmingham, Raymond Abaddi, indicated his wish to speak and addressed the meeting.

"I fear that we are a little in front of the aspirations of this meeting. We already participate in corporate endeavours covering investment in real estate, hospitality, car washes, hotels, restaurants and leisure, and we are also working corporately with other cartels in the field of the purchase, transportation, marketing and sale of the main drugs. We are, though, still a little behind on the more recent and more powerful drugs and like our colleagues in Manchester the use of the dark web. But thanks for arranging the meeting anyway."

The next person to address the whole group was the chief of the Middlesbrough cartel.

"To begin with, we are not the Middlesbrough set-up. We are the Teesside group. That is our main patch. Despite our geographical location, we are also working co-operatively and corporately with cells made up from different nationalities for specific market purposes, which usually disband when their goal has been achieved. One example is cocaine that is shipped clandestinely in containers or more recently by air from various countries in South America to Antwerp but also through LeHavre in France and Hamburg in Germany. Immediately on arrival it is transported to the Netherlands for cutting and packaging before export to the different countries in Europe. Incidentally, as well as the largest ports in the UK, it is also imported through smaller ones such as Harwich and Hull. From Antwerp, the main seaport, and after its transfer and market preparation in the Netherlands it is exported without delay to other destinations and of course including Middlesbrough for marketing throughout the North East of England. This whole complex process before the drugs get to the consumer is governed by a multinational cell of bespoke experts from several sources in order for it to be successful. It does work and it has enhanced our profits. Just one example!"

Nico was reassured by the previous two presentations and was feeling a little more comfortable about having organised the get-together.

The next person to address the meeting was the chief of the Newcastle contingent, Mark Elderson, to whom the new business system being advocated appeared not to appeal at all. Nonetheless he had a friendly smile on his face as he addressed the other participants

"Chairman and friends. I have listened quietly and respectfully to all that has been said in the fundamentally different presentations of my friends here today. There is an obvious division between those who would like to embrace the new, more big business oriented system, and those like ourselves, who are content with a system that has grown up over the years and fits the area well at the same time as yielding a good level of profit on total income. We, and by the way we are Tyneside not just Newcastle, we receive our products from trusted friends in the Netherlands, known and tested over many years, and receive from them the drugs that we then market fully independently here in the North East. The drugs that they send us are already cut and packaged as wraps, tablets or other means and are fully ready to hit the accumulating demand of the market for our products. As a consequence of our region being not just Newcastle but North East we have a very wide and well developed county lines system, which yields a good fifty percent of our income. We are a business that concentrates almost exclusively on drugs and we are content to satisfy that market, without engaging in other major markets like our colleagues here today do. So thank you for inviting us, my colleague, Jimmy McGee, and myself, but no thanks we would not wish either to adopt the business model that you are advocating and the complexity a new relationships with a dubious association with increased yield. We already have a system that works smoothly and is hard-wired to deliver good profits. Oh, by the way thanks also for the excellent refreshments. My compliments to those, who prepared and delivered them and of course to those who paid for them! Good taste!"

He smirked at the Chairman and then scanned the table with a friendly smile.

The final speaker was the representative of the London syndicate, Mike Lawrence, who had come to the meeting alone, stood up and raised the tone of his voice in great seriousness, to ensure that he engaged the full attention of all participants.

"Friends the system that our host has described and which has been variously endorsed by some friends and declined by others, has proved a protective barrier for us in London against the ardent but unsuccessful attempts of the local metropolitan Police to close our business down and also as a stimulant to greater efficiency and profit. I would urge everyone here to cast their suspicions aside and pursue this model and I look forward to working with some of you later perhaps. If I can help in any way, please do not hesitate to approach me at the end of the formal part of this meeting for a chat."

Given that highly positive endorsement by his close friend from London, whom incidentally he knew very well before the meeting, and the cordial and supportive tenor of most participants in the meeting, Ardajan Nikolaj stood up once again. He suggested to participants that as they had had a good meeting and there were still lots of refreshments available, they could now adjourn and leave time for the consumption of some more of the snacks and for informal contacts and chinwags before departure. Some of them had quite long journeys in front of them, and that is how the meeting completed with individuals and groups leaving in dribs and drabs.

As he was driving back to his base in London, Nico felt a certain unease about the meeting, dissatisfaction even. It had certainly not been as universally successful an event as he had hoped and planned for. Perhaps he should have intervened and guided it more closely? Perhaps the composition and organisation had not been quite right? That sense of unease was compounded when he received two messages from Ayton.

The first message informed him that the Police Sergeant taken hostage had been liberated uninjured by a night action of the local Police, during which three of his men guarding her had been killed. The second was a message from the same source saying that another of their brothels in Ayton had been raided by the local Police and two of his men had been shot dead with another two arrested, who were currently being interrogated at an unknown site. All the women in the brothel had been freed and were currently under armed Police guard in safe houses with the local social services department looking after them. His car nearly came off the road as he exploded and vowed that someone would pay for this outrage. He would have his revenge!

Chapter Thirteen: Some Police Gains

For a very long time, there had been rumours and widespread suspicions in the Ayton Police Force that there were officers and other employees, who were leaking crucial information on planned action by the Force to the criminal gangs in return for cash payments. Senior officers were concerned at the number of occasions where the mobsters seemed to anticipate the actions of the Force, for example the number of occasions where a raid was planned and executed only to find the property deserted, with all the consequent loss of financial assets and the incalculable time of officers.

Linked with this suspicion were the multiple stories that some officers, not many, it is true, were using classified Police databases and confidential personal information about other officers to feed information to the mobs about those officers, who might be vulnerable and, therefore, susceptible to some form of coercion to serve the interests of the mobs. These officers were said to be disclosing information, via the web, email and mobile data storage devices such as USB keys and laptops, which would be useful to criminals in their search for officers to pass on critical information to them. The acquisition of such an officer would provide the gateway for the leakage of information concerning for example plans for Police raids of criminal gang properties.

It had been known for a long time that criminal gangs were preying on officers in the ranks of the Law enforcement agencies as well and trying to infiltrate their ranks too. It was also known that a set of characteristics such as poverty, over-spending, financial difficulty such as defaulting or other form of financial debt, what they considered sexual deviation or promiscuity or other vulnerabilities had been assembled by the criminals to make up a profile of officers likely to be amenable to corrupt practice. The criminals then used the profile to pinpoint an officer to assist in the identification of suitable further officers for bribery.

The criminals, it was alleged, used the consequent profile to get the bribed officer to scan national and institutional financial databases against the list of characteristics to profile potential prey. When elements of the profile were found, the information was leaked to the gangs and consequently an approach was made, sometimes over a friendly invitation for a drink, to firstly engage and then to corrupt the person so identified for information about officers, covert Police activities and plans. From time to time the profile would fit a minority of officers, who are judged to match one or more of them, and therefore reveal themselves as potential victims for bribery and exploitation.

To try to tackle this problem and cut off the flow of crucial information to the mafia gangs, a small confidential working group was set up to investigate the issue, led jointly by Deputy Chief Constable, Rajiv Gundara and Detective Chief Inspector (DCI) Frank Wozny with the able assistance of Assistant Chief Constable Maria Clarke and two trustworthy and experienced officers, who had skills in information technology, encryption and decryption and wire-tapping. In fact one of the early successes of these two officers was the cracking of an encrypted phone service, which revealed the level of collusion and bribery between drug gangs and a senior Police detective, corrupt lawyers, civil servants and customs officers locally.

It was stipulated in the terms of reference of the working group that it would report directly and exclusively to the Chief Constable. They began by scanning the records to look at officers' lifestyles and insofar as was possible their income and expenditure in order to identify potential bribery targets amongst the Force's ranks. On the basis of the examination of those sources by the investigating group and of further personal information gathered about them, the Deputy Chief Constable the DCI and their working group identified such a potentially delinquent officer as a fairly new recruit, Police Constable Robert E Miller.

DCI Wozny, on behalf of the group, requested the permission of the Chief Constable to see the man's confidential record, to examine his telephone records, etc. and then to interview the man. These requests were granted on certain conditions, including finding out more about his family background and what persuaded him to do this, when he had such a good, secure career ahead of him. In the meantime, he was placed under surveillance and his phone records were examined and indicated frequent calls to a known member of a criminal gang.

When his family background was investigated, as instructed, the Deputy Chief Constable, a most empathic man, was deeply moved by what he found, as he explained to the Chief Constable.

"Ma'am, I must say I was deeply saddened by what we, the Assistant Chief Constable Adarsh Khanna and I, discovered about the man's family background."

"Is it relevant to our investigation?" The Chief Constable asked.

It is highly relevant to your query about why a man with such good career prospects would risk everything for a few pounds extra, Ma'am. Let me explain."

"Go ahead!"

"When the Assistant Chief and I visited his home with the family liaison officer Bob Marlowe and met his wife and his three children, one of whom is about eight month and is suffering from a hernia, which needs repairing. The house, a three bedroomed back-to-back in Leyburn Street, one of the very few such houses remaining in the town near but not in the centre, it seemed at once clear that they were struggling. They had a house round the back opposite a midden and no garden. The property was meagrely furnished, hardly furnished in fact at all with only old tab rugs covering the stone floors downstairs and bare boards upstairs. The bedrooms upstairs were reached by a cold stone floor with no covering, nor was there any covering in any of the bedrooms. The only furniture in any of the bedrooms was beds. The only water in the whole house was a cold tap in the cellar-head kitchen. The range was not working properly and the only source for hot water was provided by heating a kettle on the coal fire. When we attended the house, only a meagre flameless fire was hardly surviving in the grate of the range fireplace. The house felt cold and damp. When we spoke to the officer's wife, she revealed, and I believe her absolutely, that they were under pressure. The landlady had recently raised the rent and it consumed one quarter of her husband's pay as a starting

Police constable, even though he is at the beginning of his second year. Her clothing and that of the two children was ragged and darned or patched. The one relief was a new cradle for the baby with clean and warm bedclothes and baby clothes. She said her husband had come into some money recently … she did not honestly know where from …and they had spent it all on the children, particularly the new one. She admitted that they were in deep and accumulating debt and her husband needed to go once a week to the nearby foodbank so that the family could eat and the baby's bottle could be filled. She herself was pale and emaciated, but courageous for her family, including her kind and gentle husband, as she described him. Ma'am, no one should have to live like that in this day and age. Destitution on this scale should be against the Law. I felt ashamed and gave her all thc money I had with me, about thirty pounds. I was almost persuaded that we should bin the prosecution."

"Deputy Chief, I am pained and disturbed by your description. I agree it is disgraceful that any family should have to live under such conditions. But we cannot just suspend the prosecution. That would be illegal and we could ourselves be prosecuted. What we can do is twofold. We can quickly refer this case to the Benevolent Fund and our colleagues in the Station family room and ask for urgent action to assist and relieve the distress of the wife and children, to which you have alluded. Secondly, if he agrees to co-operate, we can place the man's circumstances before the court, and we could ask the Court to consider a lighter more compassionate sentence. Given his co-operation with the Police inquiries, perhaps some of which might be suspended."

“Yes, of course Ma’am. Anyway I shall be meeting him and his lawyer tomorrow to continue the interview and I will put it to him that in his own best interests and those of his family he should admit what he has done and plead guilty.”

“I wish you every success, Deputy Chief.”

The next day, the man was informed that he would be interviewed under caution with a member of the Association to accompany him or a lawyer if he so wished. An early time was set aside and in the meantime the duty solicitor, Mrs Simpson, came along to assist and advise him. In the presence of his solicitor he was warned that he faced a serious charge of Misconduct in Public Office, for which the sentence could be life imprisonment. He was advised that if he co-operated with the Police investigation that would be conveyed to the court and would be likely to result in a lighter sentence. He was given time to consult further with his solicitor.

When the interview was reconvened the next day, the man indicated that after consultation with his lawyer, he wished to admit his guilt and co-operate with the Police investigation. He would plead guilty when the case came to court. He said it had all started with a pint of beer in a Pub and subsequent friendly meetings in the pub, which had led to the new friend offering an amount of money to help him feed and clothe his family in exchange for information about indebted, alcoholic or addicted officers. When questioned further he said that the sum for each delivery of information was about five hundred pounds in cash.

Several months later the officer was convicted of misconduct in public office, perverting the course of justice and unauthorised access to Police computer material. He was sentenced at the Crown Court to three years and four months in jail, two years of which was suspended in consideration of his assistance to the Police. He was dismissed the service.

Further cases came up shortly after this one and were turned over to the same Working Group to investigate. One case concerned collusion between Police officers, immigration personnel and officials in the regional office of the Crown prosecution service and the leakage of information about covert Police tactical and strategic targets. But this was deemed more appropriate for regional or national prosecution services to undertake and passed on in the first instance to the regional offices of The Crown Prosecution Service.

Some further referrals were more parochial. One related to a fairly senior Ayton Police officer, who was alleged to be passing intelligence on drug plans for drug interceptions to mobsters in return for a series of payments of substantial sums of money. This was followed in quick succession by a whole sequence of further cases delegated to the group to investigate or to pass on to outside agencies, such as the regional and national prosecution services. Those cases included credible allegations of sexist, racist and homophobic misconduct by a small group of male officers and plausible claims that a senior officer had procured information from Police systems to demolish an accusation of bullying against himself.

As agreed at the installation of the working group, a review meeting was called by the Chief Constable at the end of the three months period of probation. She also chaired the meeting, at which all members of the working party attended. As she was once again overwhelmed with her workload, she wanted to get the meeting over as soon as possible. She, therefore, addressed her colleagues at a rapid pace.

"Welcome and warm thanks for the work you have all done over the past three months. You have had several cases referred to you and some you have quite correctly turned over to the relevant regional or national agencies to deal with. So the sum total of completed cases for the past three months has been one. I just wonder if any one of you might like to speak to the record?"

"Well Ma'am. Thank you for your support during the first period of our work and as you have said we have had a largish number of cases that were referred to us and we have opened up exploratory investigations on most of them. Some of these reflect on the reputation of this Force and we shall be pursuing them with great vigour and alacrity over the next phase of our work. Moreover the work of this group is not the sum total of the tasks that we are undertaking, as we all have other jobs, responsibilities and work obligations, some of which demand urgent attention. I think you will agree that the case of homophobia and sexual behaviours is one of those urgent cases with convincing evidence that something in the Force is not quite right."

"Yes I agree with your choice of first priority. I would have all my officers feel that they belong and they are comfortable and valued with us. I shall have no sexual discrimination, no matter what the sexual orientation within the Law of any member of staff and that includes of course the LGBT+ community. It is just unacceptable. I should like you to treat that matter as part of your top priority and try to identify any transgressors as soon as possible. I want no reprobates in this Force. We do not need them. So once again thank you very much for your efforts and your dedication and integrity. Please proceed as agreed today in terms of priorities."

Ardajan Nikolaj was fuming as he drove his car at some speed intending to return to London after the meeting. But he was so incensed at the messages he had received during the journey that he curtailed his return and decided instead to return to Ayton, announcing his arrival in advance. Since the assassination of Sebastiano Gjoni, Head of the Ayton office of the Mafia clan, the succession had been uncertain and Nico had had other things to occupy him so he was not sure who would meet him when he arrived. There was a Police check point on the slip road to Ayton from the motorway but Nico managed to pass through unhindered.

On arrival at one of the Firm's safe houses in Ayton, however, he was received and greeted by Tristen Plackici with two henchmen, Luan Berisha and Vishnak Asllani who clearly had decided that together they were the leaders of the Ayton office and that the three of them had voted Tristen as their overall leader. Tristen, dressed slickly in designer clothes and looking very smart, greeted Ardajan Nikolaj warmly and addressed him cheerily by his nickname.

"Nico, my dear friend. To what do we expect this unexpected pleasure? Welcome!"

"I heard of the cowardly killing of your leader, Gjoni, and the death of our men at the hands of the upstart Manchester mafia gang, who thought themselves to be bigtime. That debt of honour has already been repaid with the killing of the head of that amateur set of local bums together with four of his men. But even more seriously, I was informed as well about the raid on another one of our brothels and the accompanying deaths of our workers there at the hands of the despicable local armed Police Squad. Not least, there have also been a swelling number of interceptions of the delivery of cocaine from our London office to Ayton, amounting so far this year to some ten percent of our stock overall or thereabouts so far, again by the devious local coppers. These deaths and robberies cannot be allowed to pass unpunished. There is now a blood death that falls on the rest of us to pursue and settle."

"Nico, before we speak of the expiation for the death of our workers at the hands of the local coppers, I am afraid that we have another blow to record. The local fuzz raided one of our main offices yesterday and they have arrested six of our workers and taken away precious mass of our belongings. All of our computer and telephone equipment there have been confiscated, as well as all the files, our cryptocurrency stash and valuables in the office, including cocaine and other drugs, cash, weapons, luxury items including diamonds, and three of our vehicles, which were parked outside. These attacks are an additional very big blow and, considered cumulatively, they represent a huge depletion of our assets over quite a short period and an enormous reduction in the revenue available for remittance abroad. What worries me as well is also the fact that these successful depredations are also regarded by our competitors as a weakness to be exploited. I agree with you, Nico, we have to react to this kind of thing or the local Police might begin to think they can have a free hand in stealing our goods and workers and getting away with it. And the same with our competitors! By the way, at the weekend we also had another interception of a drugs cargo in transport on the motorway nearby and the arrest of another two of our men, one driving and the other with a gun escorting it."

Tristen sat back with an almost satisfied look on his face; happy that he had got this sorry tale off his chest at this early point in the encounter and, as he thought, being accepted as the new Ayton boss.. But he was in for a shock. He froze before the vicious gaze of the boss and there was more to come.

"It seems to me that the events and the information needed to commit these leaks, cannot be attributed to the swine having extra-sensory perception or some other capacity to anticipate correctly what we intend to do. They suggest to me that you have a leak, or perhaps several in this branch. I want the reprehensible traitor or traitors, who are betraying their fellow workers found and punished. I want it done in such a way that it will show to all members of the syndicate in Ayton that they cannot get away with such behaviour and also what will happen if they do try it on. It has to be an example to everyone else in the Ayton Firm. I want that as your first major priority and soonest."

Tristen tried unsuccessfully to deflect Nico from his attack by rebutting Nico's expressed impression that they had not done anything to respond to the alleged traitorous behaviour of some of the men at the branch.

Yes, Nico, we have already started the search, haven't we guys?"

His men nodded in silent assent, unconvinced about the accuracy of the assertion, but fully convinced of the healthiest rejoinder for their futures.

"I want to be kept informed of the progress of that at every stage and I expect to see results within the week. In the meantime, I have interrupted my crowded programme to assist you in reacting in such a way as to deter the local Police from further depredations. My time here today is very limited. On the other hand we have to teach them that they cannot get away with plundering our assets and slamming our men in prison with impunity."

At that point, the two replacement gunmen that Nico had ordered before his departure from London for the meeting with other syndicate heads and their finance underbosses entered the room confidently. They were a substitution for the previous ill-fated gunmen, borrowed from London, who had perished in an ill-fated attack on the Manchester mob. Klodjan Shkreli and Roan Kelmendi were both burly six-footers, clearly physically very capable of taking care of themselves and with mouths to match as it turned out. They had both had a menacing look about them, which was enhanced by the fact that they both had handguns tucked into the back of their trousers. They had worked for Nico in London over several years since their illegal boat crossing to the UK. Before that they had served the same syndicate in the same roles in Albania, after fighting for the Kosovo Liberation Army during the liberation war.

With their entry the six men became the cell for the design and execution of the revenge envisaged by Nico against the forces that had stolen the Firm's human, material and financial assets, and that is the way he shaped the conversation. On arrival the gunmen had already met their three Ayton colleagues as the leadership clique and needed no introduction. As typical Nico started the ball rolling.

"We should now turn to the urgent problem of how to show the local coppers that they cannot get away with thieving from us and locking up our mates. Have you had any chance to think of the ways and means whereby we can make our repugnancy at their actions against us felt by the local Police?" Klodjan, you and Roan have had a chance to think about this issue and the most effective means of executing the task. What interim conclusion have you come to?"

"Yes boss. We narrowed the range of targets for one aspect of the plan to the most senior members of the Force and also felt that a random selection of targets, unexpected and unpredictable by the enemy, would be the best way of putting the fear of god in our adversaries."

"Can you be a bit more specific?" Nico requested and Klodjan spoke this time.

"Yes boss, but these are outline plans subject to your approval in principle. In the first case we would case the two top officers, the Chief Constable and the Deputy Chief Constable and their usual locations including their home terrain for taking them down. We do not know yet where that can best be done. We have not had time to case the prospective sites. We have not yet had time since our arrival to do so. The second category is rather easier. Any bobby on duty anywhere would become a potential target and we would select the most simple and accessible ones with the easiest escape route. We would be alert to whether any of them are armed, although I suspect that they are all now trained and equipped with a taser at the very least."

Nico acknowledged the information appreciatively and suggested the future staffing arrangements. He liked being in charge of things even though he would be in London not in Ayton when the plans were carried out. He also endorsed the proposals.

"Well that sounds a very satisfactory start to my mind. I would suggest that each one of our guests from London team up with each one of your colleagues Tristen, so that Luan would work with Klodjan and Vishnak with Roan. That staffing arrangement would guarantee that each team has the expert knowledge and experience and also someone, who knows the terrain. What do you think, Tristen?"

"Well, it sound like not only a good arrangement but a functional one too."

Nico turned to the others.

"Ok, lads?"

They all nodded their approval, asking themselves what else they could have done.

"Tristan, what are you going to do about the transport and who do you think should drive. Do you have cars that will be swift enough but with unrecognisable number plates so that we're not pestered too soon after the events by the coppers?"

“Yes we have a couple of BMW X5s and it seems to me to be clear that in each case the Ayton lads are the most suited to driving in Ayton. They know the terrain like the back of their hands with all of its quirky traffic regulations.”

“OK, lads?” Nico asked and received once again the silently nodded approval of all four.

“Boss, we shall need pretty reliable photos of the two top targets.” The two Londoners requested.

“Yes, good point and Tristen, can you please provide them?

“Yes boss, certainly. Tomorrow morning.”

Nico spoke again to emphasise the importance of the job being done and being done cleanly and not bungled like the previous one.

“Well, I have to continue my intended journey back to London now. There are some other pressing jobs that need my attention today. But I shall be back towards the end of this week to see how you are getting on. Perhaps both teams will have completed their work when I return. Remember! These two jobs will be an important deterrent to the local Bobbies not to mess with our syndicate. It is important that they are undertaken rapidly and successfully. Not botched like the previous job! I wish you all good luck.”

With that, Nico stood up and departed to his transport with some haste, but feeling pleased with himself that he had managed to complete his intended task successfully and rapidly.

Over a good strong cup of Balkan coffee, Tristen allocated the jobs that each pair would do.

"Luan and Klodjan, your task will be to take out the two top people in the Police and Vishnak and Roan you two have the task of finding footslogger Police out on the streets and killing one or two of those."

Vishnak and Roan left the other two still drinking their coffee and Vishnak drove them to the main shopping mall near th square in the centre of town, where they parked the car and sought out any Police who happened to be patrolling in that area. There were very few Police, all in twos, and both seemed to be equipped with a Taser. Klodjan expressed his concern at the amount of pedestrians in the shopping centre and the distance they might have to weave through crowds to collect their car after the event.

So Vishnak drove them to a more expansive shopping centre on the outskirts of town, where there was a very large mall with dozens of shops and several coffee shops on two storeys. Unfortunately when they arrived there, the place was teaming with shoppers but devoid of Police. They walked slowly down the centre of the out-of-town shopping mall appearing all the time to be looking in the large shop windows in the shops mostly filled, some to overflow with customers but saw only an occasional pair of Police, hovering in a protective corner, one of whom actually seemed to be armed.

They drove back through a further two local shopping centres on their way back to the safe house but encountered no Police patrolling the pavements. They returned to their home base, facing a dilemma about where to mount their attack and invited Tristen to say where he thought might be the best place to mount the attack. "The huge out-of-town shopping mall", he replied unequivocally.

For their part, Luan and Klodjan drove to the nearest multi-storey car park closest to the main Police station and did an exploration of the station itself from the outside, its location and the surrounding area all the time seeking to avoid looking obtrusive. They then sought out and visited a number of the sky-scrapers in the neighbourhood where rooms were being offered for sale or rent and actually entered one or two, none of which met their criteria of clear and direct, unhindered visibility to the Police headquarters.

They also returned to the safe house somewhat down-hearted and exchanged experiences with the other team and Tristen. They all agreed that these were early days and that they should continue their searches the next day before making a decision, but without rushing it. Tristen brought in a Chinese take-away meal for them all and they all turned in early, hoping to improve their luck tomorrow.

"Can you come to an urgent meeting in my office straight away please?"

This was the message from the Chief Constable of Ayton Police to her senior officers first thing on that cold and drizzly Autumn morning.

DCI Wozny, the Deputy Chief Constable and the two Assistant Chief Constables, Maria Clarke and Adarsh Khanna, and Acting Superintendent Anthony Birch, interim Head of the Armed Police Unit, all knew an urgent message from the Chief Constable when they saw one, and in the whole time of her tenure, this had never happened before. They all dropped what they were doing and hastened to her office, bristling with questions. When they arrived the Chief Constable addressed them with an unusually 'unsteady' voice.

"Please sit down. DCI Wozny has a very important message for us all and later for all our officers. DCI Wozny, over to you!"

"Thank you Ma'am. We have received important intelligence from two reliable sources that the head of the Albanian mafia, the Mafia Shqiptare, cartel here in Ayton has ordered hits on senior officers of the Police Force and randomised attacks as well of officers, such as for example officers on the beat."

There was an avalanche of questions addressed to the DCI, mostly about the source and reliability of the intelligence to begin with, about which DCI Frank Wozny gave clear and unambiguous details.

"There were two corroborating sources for this intelligence, both of which are highly confidential and must not go beyond this room."

He looked round as if seeking the agreement of all his colleagues and, seemingly concluding that he had received their full concurrence and having reassured himself, he proceeded with his statement.

"The first of these sources arises from the interception of encrypted messages in a system called Encrochat, an encrypted communications platform and a popular means, used with great frequency. The system is confidently assumed to be fully impregnable in terms of security, the organised crime groups seem to assume. These criminals have full confidence of the secrecy of the covert transmission for their information, instructions or orders or indeed many other things, such as purchasing information of drugs or sadly the sale of young women as sex slaves. It is in our interest that this assumed invulnerability remains. I do not need to emphasise how important it is that these groups do not find out that our officers have cracked their app and their language system. Anyway, in brief, our investigators tracked and traced the extent of the transmission through Encrochat, some messages corroborating the others from different sources in different positions of the syndicate and in other organised crime syndicates. The second source is from our sources within the organised crimes groups. This is equally confidential too. The third source is the street chat communications system, which comes from a number of sources such as unguarded conversations, data lines, walkie-talkie transmissions, etc., of which our officers are appraised. Again what I am telling you is one hundred percent confidential."

Fellow officers were so convinced of the validity and reliability of the intelligence, shared with them by the DCI, that there were no further questions about that and the attention was focussed rather on how to share this information with colleagues and what measures should be considered to protect all officers. At this point the Chief Constable took over the steering of the subject by the group.

"I would suggest that we separate out the two concerns, namely the safety of all officers, especially those on the beat and the measures to be undertaken to give protection to senior staff. Let's take the overall issues first."

Assistant Chief Constable Maria Clarke put a question about general measures affecting all officers.

I would suggest that we look to measures that will assist in protecting what I am going to call public-facing officers, such as beat officers or those interviewing members of the Public after an accident or such like."

The normally taciturn Assistant Chief Constable, Adarsh Khanna, endorsed the idea and proposed a concrete way of implementing it.

"Ma'am, for a start and with regards to those on the beat or attending an accident, etc. etc. I would suggest a pairing system whereby two officers work together closely together and insofar as possible always stay together. One of those officers should be a firearms trained officer and the other officer should be taser-trained and armed with a taser. But at all costs, they should try to stick in each other's company at all times."

The Acting Superintendent Anthony Birch, interim Head of the Armed Police Unit, found the idea certainly doable, but pointed out the additional training needs and the current shortage of staff in the Force who were already trained to make it feasible. There was also the backwash from the awful killing of the former Head of the Armed Response Unit, Superintendent Julian Charles. In addition, a recent decision to charge a firearms officer involved in that event as a consequence of his use of the weapon in an emergency situation would also have a dampening effect on further recruitment in the Force.

"I would strongly support Adarsh and Maria's idea. It does, however, imply a massive commitment to training and retraining and might have the effect of denuding our Armed Response Unit, of officers, who are already arms-trained, and required for raids on for example indoor drug farms, criminals' safe houses, brothels etc. This measure will require very careful planning and it will need to be introduced over a minimum period of weeks, prioritising one group of officer specialisms over another in the time and rate of implementation. This whole process will be adverse affected by the murder of Superintendent Julian Charles and the decision to charge an authorised firearms officer for his use of his weapon in what was seen as an emergency situation."

The Deputy Chief Constable, Rajiv Gundara spoke next refining a possible approach to the training needs.

"We shall need a detailed and carefully articulated programme of training to begin straightway with several different pathways, lasting different lengths of time. So let us concentrate, not on what we do not have. But rather what we shall need as priorities. For example all officers are not taser-trained at the moment, but many are, perhaps more than half. How long is a taser-training to meet the need identified, namely that all officers are taser-trained and that in the meantime the pairs that we spoke about include at least one taser trained officer?"

The Chief Constable was able to offer some positive information in her rejoinder to one of her Deputy's questions.

"We are fortunate that we have already placed greater emphasis on taser-training than many other forces. So to calm at least some of the concerns, let me say that we have approximately fifty percent of officers in the Ayton Force, who are Taser-trained, and, by the way, the training usually lasts for three days. Perhaps more senior mainly desk-bound officers do not need training with the same urgency as for example beat and some CID officers. There is a government scheme at the moment to train an additional ten thousand authorised armed Police officers and, if we are swift, we could apply for some of the places on that scheme."

The Acting Superintendent Anthony Birch, interim Head of the Armed Police Unit gave a detailed answer to the question about the timeframe for training an armed Police officer.

"For an initial training at basic level as an armed Police officer, the period is five weeks full-time. Of course for more complex and sophisticated roles, further training is required and the period of training can vary according to the role required."

"What about the sex balance? The Deputy Chief Constable enquired.

Like a flash the Chief Constable fired a swift reply.

"Neither sex nor gender orientation is a criterion of selection for any training in this Force. Or anything else for that matter! Officers are, however, in a sense self-selected, insofar as they have to make the application themselves. So application for training is first and foremost an expression of will, or ambition if you wish, on their own part. That does not of course rule out that senior officers may offer encouragement to a fellow officer to participate if we find that there in an unequal sex balance for example in applications."

Acting Superintendent Anthony Birch anxiously posed a question about senior officer protection.

"Could I just for one moment address the issue of a planned attack on a senior Police officer? Is this scheme that we are discussing going to imply their preferential firearms training or the constant accompaniment of an armed officer with each senior officer? We will all be aware that such schemes would impose a further strain on our already stretched force of authorised firearms officers! More constructively perhaps, what do colleagues think can be done feasibly to protect the senior officers? And how can new demands on the Armed Response Unit be made compatible with our agreed priority objective of targeting the criminal mobs and their properties in the region, where authorised firearms officers are essential, as we now know to our cost."

The statement by the Chief Constable was forthright and unequivocal.

"I hope I speak for all senior officers, when I say that there shall be no special treatment or protection for the senior officers in this Force. We shall of course all take action to make ourselves less vulnerable. But armed protection or preferential training for senior officers is out of the question. On the other hand, we do need to discuss what precautionary action is desirable, such as for example, not using the front entrance of the station and stationing armed officers visibly at the rear entrance where in future we shall mount or dismount from our vehicles or enter the building from our carpark. We should also undertake a scanning of local high buildings with a clear view of one of our exits or another. We should as well all double check our security at home and the safety and security of our loved ones."

There was a subdued but not unenthusiastic endorsement of the Chief Constable's statement. "Here! Here!" Came from the other members of the group. The Chief Constable added further suggestion for action.

"But let us return swiftly and briefly to the issue, sharing the information about the attacks planned against our officers by members of the Albanian mafia. How do we do that so as to inform and encourage officers to take additional precautions for themselves and their families right away? How do we do that without encouraging panic or a run on resignation applications? We also need to draw up pretty rapidly a programme of taser and firearms training for officers that does not weaken our efforts to fight criminal drug gangs in our area and close them down. That programme needs to be produced pretty rapidly. Even today!

A swift call action came from the Deputy Chief Constable, Rajiv Gundara.

"Ma'am. I think that deferring the announcement of the wicked intention of this criminal gang to fellow officers could be considered negligent. You yourself, if I may make so bold Ma'am, should call a meeting of all staff today, probably this afternoon and all of us should make every effort to be present and support you. I also believe that we should in this meeting divide up the tasks and agree to different people or groups preparing the documentation you require to get this juggernaut moving. This group could have a further meeting late this afternoon to consider each other's plans."

"A good idea!" Cried out Sergeant Tony Birch, currently Acting Head of the Police Armed Response Unit." "I'll be happy to assist with a plan for firearm training, bearing in mind the comparatively extended duration of that procedure."

"Then let us commence now. Any offers?" The chief Constable asked.

Without further ado, the Deputy Chief proposed that the little group that was established just over three weeks ago to address priority objectives should undertake the preparation of a plan of Taser and handgun training, and that was swiftly agreed to by all.

Assistant Chief Officer Adarsh Khanna, normally a somewhat reticent officer, raised the concern about the raids on existing premises and the need to be true to their objective of abolishing the criminal gangs from Ayton.

"Ma'am. If the criminal gangs in Ayton knew that we had spent the whole morning without discussing their demise, they would sure be delighted. I know that we are all under extreme strain. But our stated objective is the destruction of these criminal gangs and their extinction here in Ayton. We owe that to the local population and our discussion of our own welfare and safety must not exclude us from what is in effect a sacred duty. By the way, any protective measures must include our civilian staff as well as officers. We owe them our protection as well, not least because of the excellent expert contribution they make in our incident room and elsewhere of course."

The Chief Constable picked up the relay and supported the Assistant Chief Constable.

"If I may, Adarsh, I strongly support your comments. We must not lose sight of our most important objective, namely to abolish these wicked gangs from the streets of Ayton for ever. What action would colleagues propose to show them that we are not deterred by their threats, but rather we are twice as determined? Shall we increase the number of raids perhaps? Or should we be arresting that strange man, who keeps on visiting our fair city from London and creates all kinds of alleged mischief, unhindered when he is here. He should be stopped in his car on the motorway and asked to dismount while his car is searched. If both he and his car are clear, he should then be released to proceed with profuse apologies, but asked to assist the Police with their inquiries at the station at a given time with his lawyer if he wishes. I shall draw up a covert list of how we can interrupt these wicked men from their activities in our town during the period, when they are still with us and before their complete extinction from our lives. Always of course within the Law and our regulations!"

And that was how it remained as they all dashed off to prepare their part of the defensive measures to try to protect all the Police officers in the Ayton force. But given the complexity and time-boundness of many of the measures proposed and accepted, was it remotely possible that they could succeed in protecting all officers and staff of the Ayton Police Force?

Vishnak Asllani drove himself and his new companion, Roan Kelmendi, into the centre of town early the next morning, along a familiar main road that he knew well. As normal and as a precaution, he drove carefully and slowly into the town centre that he had come to know so well since his arrival from the glittering Ottoman and Byzantine glory of Berat, his home town in central Albania, some five years ago. He had had no training as a gunman, but he now had a gun and the very passion of possession of a handgun filled him with misplaced confidence. He did not want his new companion in crime to know that he had never had any experience as a gunman before. So of course he said nothing about his inexperience.

The two men were anxious to make their first kills and were frustrated with the lack of progress they had made the previous day, as was their boss. When they arrived in the town centre, there were still a few places in the main square carpark and that is where they parked and started their search for a prey.

"What do you think? Should we stay together and jointly search further until we find a target? Or do you think we should separate and fan out to find a suitable target and then come together to execute it?" Roan Kelmendi asked Vishnak Asllani smiling at his double entendre. "After all you have been here much, much longer than I have. So you should know the best places to seek our quarry better than me."

"I think we should stay together. Otherwise, how will I know where to go? In any case if we did separate, by the time one of us had located the one and found the other, the Police officers might well have disappeared." His colleague retorted self-evidently and rather irritably.

"OK! Let's go. I should like a kill before lunch and one in the afternoon. Certainly we shall need to leave time after the first one to avoid the aftermath, before we try the next one. Now let's plan to make a break for lunch." Roan suggested eagerly.

So they set off to trawl the row of shops in the main square and encountered no Police officers. Then they tried the major Gateway shopping mall, which was slightly aside from the town centre and there they straight away spied two Police officers. It was so early that there were very few prospective customers. Moreover, the officers were walking very slowly up one side of the centre of the mall, not looking in the shops, but scrutinising the remaining area in front of themselves not behind them. The situation looked ideal for a kill … or two!

"This looks like it." Roan muttered to Vishnak keenly.

"Yes, but let's get closer. Are we taking out both of them?"

"Yes, I guess so or the unharmed one could attack us. And if he was armed, that could be curtains for us. So, I'll take out the one on our right and you do the same on our left."

Without hastening, which could have drawn attention to themselves they reduced the distance between the two of them and the two Police officers.

"Right, let's do it now!" Vishnak urged drawing his handgun and Roan did likewise.

Just at that moment, the two officers swivelled to their right and one of them seemed to be touching something on the wall. The next thing that happened was that the two officers had disappeared through what appeared to be the wall. Vishnak and Roan imprudently raced to catch up to the place where the officers had stopped and found themselves facing a firmly closed staff entrance door. There was a keyboard at the side requiring a code to open the door. Having built up their adrenaline for the kill, they found themselves totally deflated, and they sought an alternative occupation to relax for a little while. Fortunately the mall was sparsely sprinkled with shoppers and no one seemed to have noticed their drawn guns.

"Let's go for a cup of coffee and relax for a little while." Suggested Vishnak. There is a good café shop on the next floor in the mall just up the escalator on our right over there. I've been there several times and they serve an excellent coffee and some tasty cakes."

So with no mean fervour, they ascended the escalator with no thought of their mission and relaxation and coffee and cakes in mind.

Meanwhile, the other two gangsters had also driven to the centre of town, parking in a multi-storey carpark near the main Police station. They had combed the area at the front of the Police station for apartments for sale or rent, looking for a place with some height, from where they had an uninterrupted view of the Police station. Eventually they discovered a flat for sale or hire in one of the tower blocks not too far away from their target, which appeared at first sight to have a perfect view onto the front entrance of the main Police station and was situated on the top floor. It also had an emergency exit stairwell. This seemed ideal.

So they persuaded the rather gullible young man, who was working part-time from his studies, as the receptionist to let them stay there for a while to allegedly observe the amount of sun the flat received. After a while as the receptionist was becoming impatient, they also asked if they might return in the afternoon to observe the same phenomenon and explaining that this was a very important and an expensive investment for them and they wanted to be certain. The receptionist willingly agreed thinking that he had at last made his first major sale for some considerable time. The sale was in the offing!

In the interim, they returned to the ground floor of the apartment block walked down the road and sought a café for a morning break. Not too far away, they found they found the Gateway shopping mall and the upstairs café, where they arrived rather later then their two colleagues but at the same café next to the wooden barrier surrounding the café. That left them and their colleagues with a dilemma. Should they show recognition and join the two already seated? Or would it be safer to feign ignorance and sit elsewhere in the smallish café or indeed find another café? Wishing to acquaint themselves with what the others had done and whether they had already scored a hit, they decided to go and sit with their colleague, all four together, to update themselves on what their partners had done.

It just so happened that as they sat chatting away in their native Albanian, with other customers looking inquisitively at the group, two Police officers passed by the outside of the café and glanced to closely scan those inside the wooden enclosure over the top of the wooden barrier, which demarcated the cafe from the mall walkway. They seemed to look carefully at the Albanian group at whom most of the other customers in the café were also looking.

On closer sight from the inside, it turned out that one of the Police officers was male and the other female. They both wore body armour and the woman officer looked as though she was armed. Both wore bodycams. The other officer had a pouch probably with a Taser gun in it. The sight and equipment of the two officers scared the group and after the officers had passed down the corridor away from the cafe, the group got up intending to separate outside and leaving their coffee cups half full on the table.

As the men departed from the cafe, they saw the two officers talking and looking back towards them and they quickly split up and departed their separate ways.

The rest of the morning passed uneventfully indeed even tediously with neither of the two pairs finding alternative targets. That mood bred carelessness in Vishnak and Roan as they approached the afternoon have scored no hits at all that Day. They feared the scorn of their boss, Tristen, and even more the wroth of that man from London, the supremo of the clan.

“We have to hit a number of scores this afternoon, no matter what.” Vishnak volunteered. “Or we shall be in really hot water. So let’s get back quickly to the Gateway shopping mall, where we shall surely find a couple of cops, who are available."

When they arrived at the shopping centre the place was packed with shoppers busying about like bumble bees. There were also security guards much more in evidence now than they had been in the morning. They had to wait some half an hour after entering the centre before they actually spied the same two Police officers walking slowly and determinedly up one side of the shopping centre. The two mafia gunmen did not notice the security guard, who was approaching them as they drew their handguns and prepared to shoot both the Police constables. As he saw them the security guard called out to warn the Police.

"Look out! Gunmen behind you on the right with drawn weapons!"

The two Police officers turned and saw the two men approaching with handguns aimed in their direction. They sought cover behind the mall central reception desk, which was fortunately unstaffed at the time. In the same moment the woman constable, Police Sergeant Rosie McAvoy, a very experienced Police woman in the process of introducing a newly appointed officer to the work of a beat constable, recognised the two men they had seen in the café that morning. She gestured her charge to get down further behind the solid front of the reception desk. She leaned beyond the side of the desk, drew her handgun, aimed and fired to disable the gunman advancing towards her. She fired two shots at Roan, one at his leg to bring him down and one at his gun arm to prevent him from using his weapon. Screaming loudly at the top of his voice he fell to the floor shouting that he had been hit and his leg and arm were hurting him.

Vishnak dived away to his right behind the desk and out of sight of the woman Police officer. He cannily ignored the distressed calls of his companion for assistance to escape and he scarpered quickly using a crowd of cowering shoppers as cover. Quickly he picked one of them, who appeared pretty fit, as a human shield and rapidly hastened with him to the exit.

Roan was now lying on the floor but was still holding his handgun limply in his hand, incapable of aiming it or even firing it.

The officer approached him cautiously pointing her gun straight at his head and shouted. "Armed Police. Drop your gun now! Drop your gun!"

Roan now realised that he had a choice, but only for a very brief period. He could throw down his gun and live, or he could try with his limp and bleeding arm to shoot the Constable as she now neared him. He chose life and threw down his gun with a clatter on the tiled floor. Medics were summoned to give him first aid and he was then searched and restrained before being taken to the local hospital A&E department for treatment, accompanied by two authorised firearms officers from the Ayton Unit.

In the meantime, Vishnak Asllani, having reached the exit, released his hostage and ran back as quickly as he could to the car. From there he drove back at some speed, all the time, his nerves shattered and his whole body dithering with fright, to the safe house. Fearing retribution from his boss and perhaps even a one-way journey back to Albania, he did not announce his return but tiptoed without a sound straight upstairs. He did not have the courage or will to face his boss yet.

In the intervening time, the other two gunmen returned to the block of flats, which they had visited in the morning. They asked a number of question of the young receptionist to give him the impression that they were about to place a deposit on the room and concluded by asking him if he would mind if they went back upstairs and continued to observe how much sun the room had in the afternoon. Of course he gladly agreed.

The men raced up to the lift and rode up to the top floor with the receptionist accompanying them. He opened the door for them and even offered them a couple of folding chairs for their greater comfort, which they accepted with feigned gratitude. When he had delivered the chairs and departed, having asked them if they would like a cup of coffee, which they refused, the men began their task of observing through their binoculars what they confidently expected would be the hectic comings and goings at the main entrance to the Ayton central Police station.

They spent the whole afternoon observing, but all that they saw were a few cleaners and delivery men. Not one Police officer came in or left through the front entrance during the whole afternoon nor even at the usual going home time. It became obvious to them that the main entrance was not being used by any member of the force. The facile assumption that the main entrance would provide a rich choice of targets was totally false and they would have to change their approach and prepare a different plan tomorrow.

Dismayed at the failure of their plan they bade the astounded receptionist a curt farewell and said that they had found the apartment inadequate to their needs for a sunny quarter. Luan Berisha drove them back slowly and deliberately to the safe house, where they found equally long-faced, the one remaining man, Vishnak Asllani, from the other team and the Ayton boss, Tristen Plackici, decidedly upset at their report. They all knew full well that the supreme boss of their syndicate in the UK would be returning before the end of the week and they needed to be able to show him some returns. They all feared his anger and the sharpness of his tongue at what had happened so far.

There was some pride and joy, in a few cases verging on euphoria, in the ranks of the Ayton Police force that morning. Not only had no officer been killed or injured in the shooting incident at the Gateway Shopping Mall the previous day, but they had a captive, who was rumoured to be singing like a blackbird in the Spring. A programme of systematic training of more officers to be Taser-competent had already begun and as a result senior officers were projecting that all officers would be appropriately trained within the next couple of months. The Ayton Police Station was a hive of productive activity.

Training of more firearms officers was already at an advanced stage of planning and the selection of the first cohort of eight officers, four male and four female, had passed muster. The names of the officers had already been approved by the Force and the relevant government department for the new government scheme, which would, the Force was informed, commence presently. A small group of officers had also already commenced computer training for skill sets like cracking encrypted material sometimes on secret platforms. Training for legal telephone interception and covert listening devices, including bugs and wires, had also been stepped up and had proved a very popular training, sought by officers. Demand for places for that training was very brisk.

The subcommittee set up under the Deputy Chief Constable, and assigned the task of drawing up a revised plan for prioritised financial disbursement for some areas of the Force's objectives had already submitted an interim report to the Chief Constable. Its recommendations were already having an impact on the overall shape of the Ayton Police Force's plans and actions. Under the specific threat from the mafia of assassination, the senior officers of the Ayton Police Force and some of the senior civilian staff had been undergoing a series of training sessions on personal and family safety, carried out by a team of officers briefly seconded from the London Metropolitan Police Service, Specialist Firearms Command.

Links with schools, colleges and the local university, in which drug-taking was rife, had been strengthened and assistance given by education liaison officers in the training of school and college staff, including strategies for keeping drugs and weapons out of the institution and for dealing with them when they were discovered on the premises. As a consequence some schools had installed screening devices on any entrance to their premises. Follow-up measures had also commenced to trace and reduce the large number of so-called ghost students, many of whom had become county lines runners for one or the other of the criminal gangs in Ayton.

A social meeting of the Board of Governors had also been called again to review the effectiveness of the measures and the impact of people trafficking on the College, in line with the resolution proposed by Mr Beecham-Jones at the last College Board of Governors meeting. The Academic Board of the College had undertaken a thorough review of the timetabled curriculum with regards especially to the matters of drugs problems and sex equality.

Much more emphasis was now being placed by the Ayton Police on the collection of intelligence from local communities, including a variety of sources, with due appreciation of the intelligence gathered in the course of their normal duties by the now paired beat officers. A flyer had been produced listing the indications in a Public street or square, which might confirm the presence of an indoor cannabis farm, a brothel, a mob safe house or other premises used for illicit purposes. No cost fell on the Force for the preparation or delivery of the flyer, as with the permission of the charity's business managers, it was printed and circulated as a Public service, free of charge, and delivered together with the normal volunteer posting of deliveries of local magazines.

A week after the officers' evaluation meeting, the flyer had been prepared and had been circulated to all households in most of the districts of the conurbation within the week, an exercise which would be completed within the next few days. A small special unit of officers had been set up to receive intelligence from the Public and was already fully occupied, sorting what was received into categories of importance and reliability and passing the details mostly electronically on to the appropriate officers not least in the incident room. The new system for receipt of intelligence from the Public was soon yielding rewarding dividends.

Over the week succeeding the big evaluation meeting, the staffing of raids had been made more efficient. Each raid was now evaluated for its efficient use of available staff and funding. The process of preparation for raids and the interrogation of any mobsters captured had been streamlined without infringing any legal requirements. The allocation of officers from the Ayton Police Armed Response Unit had been reviewed and streamlined to provide for more raids carried out with the allocation of the same number of officers for raids on mobster premises. Other projects were also carried out within a revised overall number of staff in the Squad. Raids had been radically redesigned and the allocation of officers had been tailored to the perceived needs of the site, also resulting in a more economical use of staff.

A further bid had also been prepared and submitted to the Home Office for a second tranche of the funding for the experimental programme to increase feet on the ground in some districts through more intensive patrolling by specially trained officers. One such programme was already in action in Ayton and interim evaluation was indicating good results. All of this activity to refocus the priorities of the Ayton Force and rationalise its use of human and financial resources, while seeking to obtain outside funding through bids and requests to charities and local organisations, as in the case of the flyer, was undertaken during the completion of the normal programme of work.

Meanwhile during the course of the implementation of the detailed programme of training and evaluation, preparations for raids continued unabated, each on completion being thoroughly evaluated and the results fed back into the planning of future raids. Raids were consequently proceeding more efficiently, more rapidly reactive to information received and more frequently.

Often based on tip-offs received, interception of transport carrying illegal substances on the nearby motorway and slip roads to Ayton and being transported from London or the ports or sometimes delivered by air to the nearby airport or by rail to the local main station, had also been stepped up, with the process being more rationalised, concentrated and financially efficient and often based on information received from the Public and leaks from OCGs.

The revised system were soon yielding other successes as well. There was some jubilation in the Police Force that the new system for the receipt of local intelligence had already provided the Police with information about a derelict old people's care-home, where a cannabis farm had been established. The premises were duly swiftly raided and a number of men were arrested and some other very young men taken into care as victims of modern slavery.

The contents of the farm were valued at approximately five hundred thousand pounds in annual income to the mafia gang. The cannabis plants were confiscated for later incineration after any criminal proceeding had been completed. Those men arrested were due to face the Magistrates Court the following week. The raid had been conducted very swiftly and efficiently and without any injuries on either side. The whole enterprise from the telephone call to the raid itself and the post-raid work was considered a great success at the evaluation meeting.

A new vehicle had been purchased and a few staff retrained for the interceptions. In other words in the midst of all the innovation normal policing such as seizure of drugs continued. But the very success of the increased confiscations was becoming manifest. Special drug incineration facilities and holding space were exhausted and there was always the further danger that the criminal gangs would attempt to steal the drugs back and return them to the market.

The drugs seized in Ayton originally came mainly from two sources and seizures were escalating exponentially. Firstly they arose from the interception by the Police mobile squads of drugs being transported from a number of sources to Ayton via the motorway. Secondly a huge amount was now coming from the increased raids on indoor drug farms in the Ayton area, with a small amount accruing from independent initiatives by one, two or a small group members of a freelance initiative for the market and often subject to attempted violent attack by the 'big boys'. In the light of criminal legal proceedings against drug dealers some of the drugs had to be stored often for some considerable time in secure holding facilities such as special warehouses, whose location was usually strictly confidential.

Where the location of seized drugs had been uncovered by the OCGs, caretakers were often confronted by violent armed men intent on stealing the drugs back. On occasion, the warehouse staff were threatened, sometimes bound with ropes and assaulted. Even after their use as evidence in a criminal trial, the drugs had to be destroyed in special non-polluting furnaces. Both the storage and the burning as well as the Court proceedings involved the additional use of scarce human and financial resources. So the Police had in some ways become victims of their own success. The very accomplishments of the policy on drug seizures was threatening to cause further problems and dangers down the line in other priority policy areas for the Ayton Police Force.

But the policy of increased closure of the drug farms was illustrated by the intended action this very day. Preparation was underway for a further raid that very evening, the third that week, which according to the senior staff work rota, was to be led by Assistant Chief Constable, Adarsh Khanna. As usual the site had been surveyed again by a covert group of officers in civvies just a few hours before the commencement of intended 'bust'. The premise to be raided was a closed former old cinema,' the Little Vic', whose main entrance formerly faced onto a not very busy main road with a bus stop directly outside the premises. That entrance was clearly never used nowadays and the metal shutters had been closed some time ago.

The main entrance now was the former rear exit from the quite large cinema, which backed onto a small cinder-covered parking area, backed by a large mound of mill and factory waste covered with ash and cinders. There was a small highly polluted rivulet running through the middle, which made the car park rather soggy and messy especially at times of precipitation. The differential indentation of vehicle tracks indicated that the premises were subject to frequent use by cars, vans and lorries. At the time of the reconnoitre during the night time, however, there were only cars parked there, indicating that work was maintained during the whole twenty-four hours, seven days a week.

There were no close neighbouring houses, so there was little intelligence to be gathered from that source, but the frequently used bus stop just outside the old no longer used main entrance of the cinema and its counterpart on the other side of the main road yielded some interesting information from passengers indicating regular use at night-time with what were describes as lorries, vans and cars coming and going, lights flashing and lots of noise. This picture was confirmed by those living in houses on the other side of the main road and using that bus-stop for journeys on the one side of the road directly into town or on the other side to the shops, friends or relatives further out from the town centre.

At exactly quarter to midnight two Police cars pulled up on the main road in front of the former cinema and two officers dismounted from each. Two of the officers went and stood in front of the former main entrance of the old cinema. The other two went round the back to supervise the arrangement of the parking of further Police vehicles including a detention van, a first aid ambulance, a control station and two minibuses, as well as the vehicles containing the authorised firearms officers, with the Acting Superintendent Anthony Birch, acting as interim Head of the Armed Police Response Unit, and four officers from the squad.

At precisely midnight the usual warnings in English and Albanian were proclaimed through a megaphone and the armed officers led by Acting Superintendent Anthony Birch approached the door and banged on it announcing, "Armed Police. Open up. We have a warrant to search these premises." To their great surprise the pulling back of bolts and the sound of a key opening a lock was heard and the door was opened fully. Two armed men stood in the doorway looking as if they were asking themselves what was going on. It would emerge later that they had thought that it was their boss, a senior member of the Albanian criminal gang in Ayton. The men were disarmed and offered no resistance. A back-up squad of unarmed officers then searched them and handcuffed them and led them out to the detention van.

In the meanwhile, the first squad of officers started to move through the lines and lines of trestle tables which were loaded with cannabis plants and some other drugs. Every now and then they came across a wretched youngster, probably all teenagers, hollow-eyed, under-nourished and clothed in rags, asleep or just waking from their sleep on the cold concrete floor. None of them spoke any English and the interpreter was asked to instruct them to go to the front door and to wait there for further instructions. Members of social services, including Albanian-speaking staff, collected the young men, obviously victims of modern slavery and loaded them all into a minibus. The social services staff drove them away for a shower, replacement clothes and a decent meal.

Upstairs in what had formerly been the cinema's balcony, fertilizers, compost and plant cuttings were spread on trestle tables again and there was a small office at the side with a telephone, computer and printer. Two further men, armed, but non-resistant looked totally perplexed as if they did not understand what was going on. They were arrested then disarmed, searched and cuffed and handed on to the squad of unarmed officers at the back entrance of the former cinema, who gently invited them to take a seat in the Police detention van. A skeleton squad remained to await the men, who would collect the plants for destruction and the arrival of the forensic squad.

The next day, when news of the 'bust' spread like wildfire throughout the main Police station, with the added bonus of no Police casualties nor on the other side, there was nothing less than what can be called triumphal cheering and loud applause. The squad that had undertaken the raid was cheered and applauded for several minutes. There was now a growing feeling among officers that an important corner had been turned in the battle against the criminal drugs gangs, which were molesting their fine city and its youngsters.

Chapter Eighteen: An Ultimatum

As he drove back to Ayton at the end of a busy week in London, Ardajan Nikolaj, supremo of the Albanian super-cartel in the UK, known casually as Nico to his mates, was hoping that his colleagues in Ayton would have achieved progress in the tasks that he had left them with at the beginning of the week. It might even be said that Ardajan Nikolaj was looking forward to meeting up once more with the team of colleagues he had entrusted with the important action against the local Police Force. The action was intended as a clear demonstration to the Police and the other criminal gangs of who was in charge in Ayton, and it wasn't the Police or local authority and it certainly was not the other mobs.

After all, he thought to himself, they had carried out the disruption of the Cenotaph ceremonies to show the city's Police, who was really in charge in Ayton, very effectively. They had shown commendable efficiency some two weeks previously and they showed that they had the will, determination and skill to successfully undertake complex operations. Surely they would do whatever was required of them again to send a strong message to the local Police not to mess with the Clan and certainly not to thieve its property and abduct its staff.

As he turned off the motorway and entered the slip road for Ayton, he observed the Police car, which had been there the last time he travelled this route, at the side of the road. To his surprise, however, this time he was waived down by a Police officer. As the officer approached the driver's side of the car from the rear, Nico slowly wound down his window.

“Good morning, Sir, just a few questions, if that’s alright? Won’t take long.”

“Good morning, officer. Why have I been stopped?”

“It’s part of a random selection of cars today to seek the assistance of ordinary members of the Public in fighting crime. But could you tell me are you the owner of this car and are you insured?”

“Yes! Yes!” Nico exclaimed irritably.

“Thank you sir and where are you are coming from and where are you going to?”

“London and Ayton.” Nico shot back brusquely.

“Thank you sir. And what is the purpose of your visit to Ayton?”

“I have been invited to stay with old friends in Ayton across the weekend.”

“Thank you, sir. Would you mind getting out of the car and handing me your driver’s licence and a copy of your car insurance certificate, sir!”

Nico sighed and took a deep breath. He reached into the glove compartment and pulled out the required documents, which of course many people did not carry in paper form any more. He dismounted, stood at the side of the car and held out the requested documents, as instructed.

"I thought you fellows had all this sort of material on computer, officer. But it just so happens that I have a printed copy of both."

Irritated he handed the documents over to the officer coolly and compliantly, although the officer did not seem to be particularly interested in them and gave them both only a cursory glance before handing them back to Nico.

"Do you come here to Ayton to visit your friends often, sir?"

"No, not usually but at the moment there is an inter-family wedding in the offing and there are things that need to be clarified."

While they were speaking another officer had also dismounted the Police car and was looking into the interior of the car though the windows and now peering in through the open front door and smelling the interior of the car. Out of the blue a thunderbolt probe came from the second Police officer, sniffing in the front of the car.

"Are there any drugs in the car, sir? I mean non-prescription, illegal ones?" The second officer asked politely.

By now Nico was absolutely infuriated at the continuation of the questioning. These clods were clearly fishing. But their net was empty! He tried hard to keep his cool. Experience in London had taught him how to do that especially to what he considered to be predatory Police officers.

No, I don't do drugs, officer."

"There is a faint smell of cannabis in the car, sir. That is why I ask. Would you mind if we had a look in the car and the boot, sir?"

"No, officer I have nothing to hide. But please do it quickly as I have agreed to meet up for a meal."

"Thank you very much, sir."

The second officer began a rapid search of the inside of the car and the boot and having found no trace of what he was looking for, he slammed down the boot door disconsolately and said.

"Thank you sir, for your public-spirited co-operation."

The first officer then said.

"You say you live in London, sir. What sort of work do you do?

"Real estate, officer. Can I go now?"

Yes, you may go now sir. Our apologies for having delayed your arrival with your friends a bit. Hope you're still in time for the meal. Drive carefully."

Fuming with indignation, Nico got back into the car revved up to a loud crescendo and departed at some speed. He completed his journey within a few minutes determined to ask his 'friends' about the incident, its significance and whether it was a common occurrence or a rarity. As he parked his top of the range AMG Line Premium Plus Edition Mercedes at the back of a large Edwardian house, one of only six other similar houses in a secluded cul de sac on the outskirts of Ayton, he was greeted by Tristen Plackici, would-be boss of the Ayton office gang, whom he immediately noticed as directing a weakly forced smile towards him.

Nico's sharp perception began to pick up a message that just maybe the encounter was not going to be quite as satisfying as he had been estimating only a few minutes ago, before the aggravating encounter with the Police on the slip road. Tristen approached the car and opened the door with a hard to maintain forced smile on his face and Nico got out and reciprocated with a similar expression of coolness on his smiling face. Nico could read in Tristen's face that all was not well, but he would find out soon enough what it was. So he concentrated on collecting his things together and handing them to Tristen to be carried into the house.

When he entered the room, where the meeting was scheduled to take place, all the members of the team were assembled to meet him with just one new face and one person missing. Tristen Plackici was obviously going to chair the meeting, though he was looking ever more uncomfortable. Klodjan Shkreli was there, Luan Berisha and Vishnak Asllani also. Roan Kelmendi was not present and apparently in his place was a newcomer, who introduced himself as Moisi Shehu, a thin-faced man probably in his early twenties, but bright-eyed and anxious to make an impression. The reason for the change of personnel was not immediately clear to Nico.

Tristen began by welcoming their guest and explaining the reason for the change of personnel.

"A very warm, welcome, Nico. We are all very pleased to see you again, particularly given your heavy timetable elsewhere. You will have met every one here before, except Moisi Shehu here. Unfortunately Roan, cannot be with us today for two reasons. Firstly he was shot by a woman Police officer in the shopping mall. Once in the arm and once in the leg. Secondly and he is lying now in a hospital bed, guarded by two armed Police officers after himself being arrested on a charge of attempted murder of a Police officer. He is thus out of contact with us except through the lawyer that we have provided him with that is Mary Freeman, a senior partner from the local firm of Pitts, Short and Freeman. As you probably recall, Nico, she has represented us on several occasions already and has always been very successful for our lads. His replacement, Moisi Shehu, has some years of experience with us and is firearms trained. He was formally trained when he joined the Kosovo Liberation Front as a young teenager. Good to have you with us on this very important project, Moisi. Well I've spoken long enough. So I'm going to let you take over now, Nico."

Nico's brain was bubbling with questions and he was a little uncertain, which one would be the best to elicit all the resolutions to the multitude of queries raised so far by what had been said and perhaps more so by what had not been said and his experience on the slip road. So he decided to ask a question about the slip road episode.

"When I was on the slip road to Ayton today, I was stopped by a Police patrol car and two officers, who asked me a whole string of unnecessary questions. Was this just a random check, do you think? Or was it something more ominous."

Tristen brushed aside Nico's query uninterestedly.

"Well it's difficult to tell on the basis on one incident. But there does seem to have been a substantial increase in successful interceptions of our drug transportation deliveries from London and the ports and consequent confiscation of the cargoes. That suggests to us the likelihood of a leak of information to the coppers by some vermin in our midst."

"Have you made any attempt to identify those lice responsible?"

"Not with any success so far, Nico."

Nico realised that he was not going to get any firm response. Once again they were covering up their incompetence and he grew more aggressive and infuriated with them. So he changed tack.

"Tristen, just tell me briefly of the circumstances of Roan Kelmendi's arrest and injury."

"Vishnak Asllani is probably best suited to do that, Nico, as he was on the job with Roan. Vishnak could you respond to Nico's request?"

"Well, Nico. We were doing a job in the large shopping mall. We had been scouting suitable targets in an appropriate context for the whole of the day prior to the shooting incident, when we spied two Police officers, a very young man, probably on probation as a newcomer, and a woman, the latter of whom was a sergeant. We did not fully take into account that she was armed. Perhaps we estimated that being a woman she could not be. Anyway, we pulled our handguns and advanced to engage, when a security guard popped up from nowhere and alerted the two Police officers of our obvious intentions. We were near the reception desk and the women officer promptly darted to the side, at the same time pushing the male in front of her and behind the reception desk, thus totally obliterating their profile. The woman officer, who had dodged behind the stout wooden reception desk, peered round the edge of the desk and 'pop', 'pop' she shot Roan in the arm and the leg just like that. He fell to the floor immobile. A group of shoppers was beginning to assemble as spectators and the mall security guard was on the phone, obviously calling for further assistance. Assessing my position as having become threatened and now becoming more and more untenable, I escaped swiftly and safely. That's all.

"Thank for that very detailed account. Do you think that on reflection you could have done anything differently, Vishnak?" Nico asked probingly.

"No! Given the circumstances and the way the attack unfolded very rapidly and unexpectedly after the first shot. No I do not." Nico rebuffed Nico's implied insinuation that he might have had other alternatives and he persevered.

"So do you think that it is OK to leave colleagues that have been shot to the Police?" Nico persevered doggedly.

“If the particular circumstances demand it. Yes!” Vishnak shot back emphatically.

“Hm?” Was Nico’s single further comment on that question.

Tristen. Would it be possible to hear from the other two?”

“Yes, of course Luan Berisha was leading that one. Luan, would you care to enlighten Nico of your work in the two days since he left us last?”

“Yes, of course boss. Well on the first day we scouted the area around the Police headquarters, checking for properties that might offer a good view of the main entrance. We did not find any of the lower lying buildings that would be suitable, especially in the provision of a rapid escape route. So for the second day we extended our search to higher level buildings, skyscrapers and the like, where rooms were available at a sufficient elevation and with no interruption of the vision onto the front entrance of the station. We found something that appeared to offer that and surveyed the view during the morning and the afternoon. It was in the afternoon that we observed that there was almost no one using the front entrance except the cleaners and people delivering letters, packages and other goods. Someone had tipped off the filth and no officers were using that entrance any more. So late in the afternoon we returned home rather disappointed.”

Nico addressed Tristen and the others gazing icily into their faces.

"So, Tristen. You and your colleagues are telling me that in two full days of highly paid work you achieved nothing. No hits! No nothing! But you lost one man!"

Tristen decided not to accept the debate about the 'high pay' and rejoindered in a placating manner.

"Yes, but we were trying all the time, Nico."

"Trying is an excellent choice of words, Tristen!" Nico exploded laughingly and devastatingly to Tristen's self-confidence.

"Now just listen to this, all of you." Nico exclaimed seething with anger. You're all going to go out the minute we finish here and you will stay out until you've done at least one hit each group at the damnable Ayton Police force. Though I am desperately busy at the moment, I shall be here whatever time you return to hear your account of what you have achieved. Let me just add that you are now on a slender wire of probation. If you do not succeed this time, you will all be on a very rapid one-way ticket to Tirana and this office will be closed. Let me assure you that in Tirana you will carry the blame. I shall say no more. If you find yourself coming back with nothing. Don't bother coming back. Be gone!" Nico shouted at them.

The two pairs departed sullenly and sheepishly and Tristen remained fearfully awaiting further interrogation by Nico.

Andrea was in the middle of an important business deal, the largest she had negotiated since taking over from her mother what seemed like many years ago now. She had left explicit instruction with her secretary that she was not under any circumstances to be interrupted … unless of course it was her mother or the children. The children were at a vulnerable stage in their development and a bit emotionally unstable since the murder of their father only a few short weeks ago The family called it murder but the Police called it culpable homicide as they could not prove 'intention to kill'. But it did not matter anyway, since the hoodlum, who fired the shot, was shot dead by members of the Police Armed Response Squad.

The children, Melissa aged fourteen and Jeremy aged twelve, were both at the local college and at crucial stages in their lives, their personal development and their educational careers. It was all so, so different from when she had been young. Both children had been brought up by their loving family to be independent-minded. Peer group pressures were particularly hard to resist for Melissa to dress, to eat, to behave, to watch unsuitable programmes on wickedly misleading platforms, even the secret apps, on a smart phone and to indulge in alcohol and drugs, all of which she had so far avoided to her cost in terms of social relations at school and outside.

Under the guidance of his loving family, Jeremy had also avoided the vicissitudes thrust towards him by peer group pressure in drugs, alcohol, nitrous oxide, vaping and the internet. He had just ascended the ladder from primary school to secondary education at the local college and was missing his father a lot and finding it hard to work out how his new life fitted into what the Ayton College had to offer him.

Away from her diversion, Andrea returned to a stack of papers, when suddenly the telephone rang. It had been put though by her secretary, Gill, but she was tempted to ignore it. Yet her secretary was ever attentive to her instructions and an excellent performer in every way. She had worked for Andrea's mother and now worked for Andrea. She waited and still it rang. So after a short reflection, she put her papers to one side and she picked up the telephone. When she picked it up she found that it was the Principal of the College, where she was chair of governors. Some major issue of finance or administration or minor infringement of a school regulation perhaps, she suggested to herself.

But what the Principal had to say to her, terrified her into a panic she had never experienced before. There had been an altercation, he said, between her daughter and another group of students. Her daughter, he said, had been stabbed by another student on college premises and had been taken by ambulance to the local A&E department critically ill. The Police had come to the college and were investigating the crime, which on first sight seemed to be about drugs. He expressed his own personal sadness to Andrea and sent his best wishes for Melissa and her complete and speedy recovery.

What should she do when one of her little treasures lay critically ill in a hospital bed? She asked herself. There was only one answer. She must go and join her of course. She whizzed through the office door like greased lightning and as she was departing the office, she called to her secretary, Jill, to ring her mum and ask her to cover with regards to Jeremy and that Melissa had been stabbed at College and was in hospital critically ill.

Perceiving the seriousness of the situation, Gill confirmed that she would do as requested and she expressed to her every good wish and a successful recovery for her daughter. Downstairs Andrea leapt into her car and departed from the college parking area for the hospital, probably thirty minutes journey away, almost comatose. When she arrived, she parked in the hospital's multi-storey car park and walked through the short corridor to the main concourse.

Inside the hospital she approached the main reception desk to ask where her daughter might be located. But there was as usual a queue. Ten excruciating minutes later she was told that her daughter was still in theatre but that Andrea could wait in the waiting area at gate thirty-two and she would be called by the surgeon after completion of the procedure. She dashed down the concourse rapidly and then sat on one of the seats at the reception for Gate thirty-two. She stood up frequently and walked to calm her nerves. Thirty unbearable minutes later she was called by the patient name display panel to go through to one of the offices, number thirty, where she met Mr Abaddi. He was still in his theatre procedural kit and he greeted her in a serious but friendly manner.

"Good afternoon, Mrs Burnley Crowder. I have just finished attending your daughter. She is still critically ill, but no longer suffering from life-threatening injuries. Her bowel had been penetrated and she was bleeding out when she arrived here. But we have managed to stem the bleeding now and she has had a series of blood transfusions. She will need very careful nursing for the next little while but I am hopeful for an eventual full recovery."

"Can I go in and see her, Dr … I mean Mr Abaddi?"

Of course you can, Mrs Burnley Crowder, but she is still under sedation. I would like you to be there with her when she begins to wake up. Perhaps another thirty minutes. If you will go back into the waiting area, I'll ask the senior nurse to come and call you when that point is reached. I am sorry about the wait. I know it is painful, even distressing for you, but we're all trying to do the best for your daughter."

"Thank you Mr Abaddi for your skilful attention to my daughter. I really appreciate it."

"You are welcome, Mrs Burnley Crowder. I have two daughters of my own and I can imagine how heart-breaking it must be for you. Just go now and in another thirty minutes approximately, I promise you, you will be at your daughter's bed-side. In view of her age and her injury, I have requested that she be placed in a single bed ward."

"Thank you for everything you have done for my daughter Mr Abaddi."

"You're very welcome Mrs Burnley Crowder."

With that comment the surgeon left and Andrea returned to the waiting area again, worrying herself sick and with her eyes glued on the patient display panel. Eventually after what seemed like an eternity, the senior nurse came into the waiting area of the gate, called out Andrea's name and summoned Andrea to follow her. They took the lift up to the fifth floor, walked past the ward reception area and to the end of the corridor, where there were two single bed wards opposite each other. They entered the one on the right-hand side and there she was apparently asleep but cushioned comfortably at a slight angle in bed. Melissa, Andrea's daughter! The ward seemed very comfortable, well-furnished and well equipped, with an inbuilt hoist for infirm patients. It also had its own private facilities, as Dr Abaddi had stipulated. Finally Melissa began to stir, open her eyes and after quite a while said. "Hi, Mum!" and then closed her heavy eyes once again. Finally she opened her eyes and said. "Thanks for coming to see me, Mum. Lovely to see you."

Andrea answered with tears streaming from her eyes.

"Hello, Love. Lovely to see you too. But how are you feeling. What happened at the College? Do you know who stabbed you and why, Love?"

"Yes it was one of the Albanian students, called I think Daniel. There was a disagreement because one of his mates had told him that I had taken his drugs from his locker, which was untrue, and I told him so in no uncertain terms. I said I had no interest in drugs and it was probably one of his own mates. He shouted, "Lying bastard" at me and then stabbed me. I felt quite weak and slipped to the floor. I lost consciousness for a while and woke up here in this bed with you at my side."

"I thought the College had taken measures to strictly exclude drugs and knives, even installing one or more special detection alarms."

"Yes! But the system is far from watertight. Some of the kids in gangs avoid the detection alarm by various countermeasures, including reaching their blades and their drugs round the side of the frame to another collaborator. In some cases knives and drugs have also been passed to another member of the gang through the windows in the toilets."

Melissa closed her eyes again and seemed to have fallen asleep once more and Andrea waited an hour or so before she stirred once more. She just briefly thanked her and stood up ready to depart.

"Well, thank you for telling me about the attack, Melissa my Love. I hope I've not over-tired you. Anyway, I can see that I **am** tiring you and the doctor said you needed to rest. So I'll leave you now and I'll be in again tomorrow morning first thing. Night my love. Sleep well!"

"Night Mum." With those two words Melissa's eyes closed again and Andrea left the ward, closing the door quietly.

As she was driving home slowly and safely, Andrea was pondering how she needed to change her life priorities in view of the most recent happening, which had had the effect of making her think that she should get rid of some of her voluntary work and devote a lot more time to the children. She discussed it with her mum when she arrived home and her mother agreed that divesting herself of the role of chair of the College governors was one way she could release a lot more time for the family. She pointed out that this was especially needed now as Martin, their father, was not there anymore and Melissa would need a lot more attention for a very long time before she fully recovered from her traumatic injury. Andrea communicated her decision to the College Principal and gave notice that the next meeting would be the last at which she would officiate as Chair, at the commencement of the meeting.

At the beginning of the next meeting of the College's governing body, it had already spread like wildfire around the members that Andrea was laying down her position as Chair from this meeting onwards and a replacement had already been informally chosen but the appointment would have to be ratified by a meeting of the full Board. It was no surprise that Mr Stanley Beecham-Jones, a retired research chemist at the local university, a long standing member of the Board and local councillor, who often asked about women's rights and people-trafficking had been chosen and his appointment was almost certain to be ratified.

In the intervening period, she was kept busy by her frequent and quite lengthy visits to the hospital to see Melissa, making sure that she had good family time with her son, Jeremy and her mother, and assuring the continued efficiency of her running of her business in town. New clothes and equipment were required for Jeremy and the time-consuming task of purchasing those occupied any free time she might have had, with all the time at the back of her mind, the dreaded day of the meeting when she would step down.

But Andrea did not accept her resignation from the role of Chair with equanimity. The role had brought with it local power and, although she did not seek them, contacts that had been useful in her business affairs. So she dreaded the arrival of the great big hole in her life; the day when most of these things would disappear and she would just be an ordinary member of the Board. She knew it was the right decision for her children but that did not make it any less painful.

When the day did arrive, she took the Chair as usual and at the commencement of the meeting straightway announced that the first item on the agenda would be the selection of a new Chair. As canvassing and negotiations had taken place before the commencement of the meeting, there was only one name proposed and approved unanimously. The successful new Chair was Mr Stanley Beecham-Jones, local councillor, academic and long-time member of the Board. At that point Andrea vacated the Chair and took the former seat of the new Chair.

At that juncture, the College Principal requested the permission of the new Chair to speak. Graciously and appreciatively he spoke of his and the whole Board's sincere thanks for the years Andrea had devoted to the College. She had become universally recognised as a very successful Chair, the second generation of the family to hold the post. He extolled the virtue of her wisdom and hard-working approach and especially the role she had played in the fight against drugs and knives in the College, which was continuing. Finally he said that the Board was gratified not to be losing her completely as she had agreed to remain as a member of the Board sine die.

Many other members also spoke of the excellence of Andrea's service before the Board moved on to the topic of human trafficking and the concern amongst governors about the College's ghost students, conscious that the attack on Melissa had shown once again that the dual problems of blades and drugs were far from solved in the College and in the surrounding town.

Soon the fast-moving criminal scene in the town would accumulate further problematic dimensions for the College making it almost insuperably difficult to solve one issue alone and singly, and emphasising once again the need for multi-agency co-ordinated action.

Chapter Twenty: Rebellion

The four men had been sent out with the specific task of killing Police officers. They left the safe house, aiming for the town centre, feeling disconsolate and insulted at the way the supreme boss from London, Ardajan Nikolaj, Nico they called him, had spoken to them and threatened them with an ignominious one-way return to Albania if they did not comply with what he wanted them to do. The old man was so arrogant and obnoxious.

So why, they asked themselves, would they wish to oblige him, risking their lives or life in prison, if they were caught, or worse. They only had old handguns and any action they took would have to be at close quarters, probably not more than twenty three meters. All the more chance of things going wrong and their being injured or captured like their colleague Roan. And more of the Police seem to be armed than ever now. The men were all feeling profoundly insubordinate.

They needed time and space to tackle what seemed like an intractable problem. Only one solution, that is to go to a suitable café and have a coffee and to talk it over amongst themselves. There they could make up their minds about what course of action to take and whether to solve their little problem by getting rid of Nico. But then, what about the risk in that? The Albanian mafia prided itself that it always paid its debts. So they should really consider other ways of achieving their goal. They decided to go to the Balkan Kitchen Restaurant and have a cup of real Balkan coffee not the swill they had to put up with at their base in the safe house or the usual Ayton cafés.

When they entered the café it was almost empty. It usually was at that time in the morning and they had a good choice of table. They chose one as far away from any other customer as possible and seated themselves around the table. A waiter approached the table straight away. He was clearly of Albanian heritage and they were able to order their drinks in their own language. Swiftly the drinks arrived and Vishnak generously requested that all the drinks be placed on one bill and given to him. Then the debate commenced and Klodjan Shkreli the only one left from the London gunmen in Ayton, spoke first.

"Friends. Just a little bit of a context to what we are being asked to do. For killing someone, a member of another gang, a member of the Public or anyone at all in London, the going rate is around five grand. For killing a Police officer it would be a minimum of double that; ten grand. A lot more if it was a senior Police officer. We have been offered nothing at all by Nico except our usual cut from the business for the latter task. Rather we have been insulted and bullied into doing such a job for nothing. I think that is disrespectful and it seems to me that it offends against the Kanun. What do you others think?"

"Klodjan, I know nothing about current rates in London for a job like we've been asked to undertake. But I agree with you that to be offered nothing is insulting. We need to discuss what action to take here and now today before we act and return to base."

Moisi Shehu spoke next, anxiously as a newcomer to the group but disguising his angst with over-confidence, to make his mark and have his say.

“I agree with what the two of you are saying. But what can we do? That is the challenge we must face.”

Klodjan spoke emphatically.

“In London we have several Albanian groups. But perhaps the most powerful is called Hellbanianz. It’s really a group of youngsters, who have rebelled against the major gang and the way they do business. They have made a great success of it too. We could do something like that ourselves or approach Hellbanianz to join them.”

Vishnak Asllani, a long time Ayton man, spoke next.

“I share your sense of offence. But I am personally not in favour of getting mixed up with that violent and boastful gang of youngsters in London. Their methods do not appeal to me. Rather I think that we should complete our task for today and return to Nico and tell him there will be no more action until he pays us properly for the job he wants done.”

Luan Berisha, also a longstanding Ayton man, added his support to what his long-time colleague was proposing.

“I agree with Vishnak. This issue, in addition to Nico’s behaviour towards us, is basically about money. What Vishnak is proposing has the advantage that this dispute would be just between Nico and us. We’re not getting mixed up with any other body and we cannot thus be called traitors. Simple to solve, when there are only two parties. Let’s go with Vishnak, I say.”

"Fine, but does the action proposed offend against the Besa?" Moisi Shehu demanded with some concern in his voice.

"I don't believe so." Vishnak Asllani stated emphatically. "If we are careful about how we do this, it will not offend against any of the customary moral codes, such as the Kanun, or the new Laws of the state. True we have an obligation to the Firm. But it is not a Besa, and we are not reneging on our word of honour. So here is what I suggest that we do. We choose two Police officers and shoot to wound them in the arms and/or the legs …two shots. Not in the head or body. That way even if we are caught, the penalty would be very much less severe and it would not involve a blood feud situation. We report back to Nico this afternoon and tell him quite correctly that we have done what he asked of us. Now, we shall tell him, is the time for a fair financial reckoning."

There was general acclamation for the proposal and a sense of relief pervaded the group, to the extent that Moisi suggested an additional celebratory coffee. Vishnak advised against it and suggested that they adjourn now, do their jobs as agreed and return home for a formal meeting with Nico at three o'clock that afternoon. It would be important that everyone arrived together for that meeting, he suggested, to illustrate their solidarity. Somewhat reluctantly on the part of Moisi everyone agreed. They all departed to make their hit. Moisi and Klodjan for the rear of the Police station and Luan and Vishnak to the gateway shopping centre as agreed during coffee.

Moisi and Klodjan left their car in the Balkan Kitchen café car park and began the short walk to their target area; the rear of the main Police station. From the start of the short walk to the rear of the Police station, Moisi, the newcomer to the group, adopted a jaunty manner. This was his first experience with a gun and indeed he had had little or no practice with the GLOCK handgun that he had been given by Tristen. But he was confident that he could and would cope at least as well as the 'old man', with whom he was partnered. Klodjan, on the other hand, was an experienced gunman, who had trained in the Kosovo Liberation Army, and had used his gun many times for the syndicate in Albania, in Kosovo, in London and he was now engaged to do so again in Ayton by his London boss. His nerves were ice-cold.

Soon the two men reached the small square at the rear of Ayton's main Police station. They were both surprised at how busy it was and they noted the two armed guards standing outside perusing very carefully anyone, who approached the doorway. Presumably a check was made of entries after they had entered the gate. There was a stream of people, some in Police uniform and some not, moving towards or away from the station entrance and it was rare indeed for anyone to be stopped. Moisi and Klodjan retreated to the edge of the square and sat on a low wall to assess the situation and make their plan.

Klodjan suggested that the best target for them would be one or other of the two guards, as they were static. He also explained that they usually assessed the GLOCK to be accurate at a distance of roughly twenty three meters. So that meant that if they could achieve a clear shot they need not go very close to the guards and that would make their escape much easier.

“Would you like to take the shot and I shall cover you.” Klodjan suggested to Moisi, thinking that the youngster would like the kudos of achieving the hit. “Remember we are not out to kill. So its arms or legs, no heads or bodies. OK?”

“Yes, I’ll do the job.” Moisi volunteered brimming with over-inflated self-confidence.

“OK then choose your target. I suggest the one on the right, who is marginally nearer. Seek your position, fire and depart speedily.” Klodjan advised. “Take your time! Don’t rush it!”

But Moisi knew better and he walked confidently towards the guard, pulled his gun and fired. The bullet hit the Officer directly in the chest and he fell to the ground. But his colleague had seen the confident young man approach jauntily and found something not quite right about him. Just in case, he had taken out his gun and he now fired at Moisi just a split second after Moisi had fired his gun at the other officer. The second Police officer was well trained and experienced and her bullet hit Moisi in the head and came out the back of his skull. Klodjan knew straight away that Moisi was a gonner. He had seen many of those during the Kosovo war. He just turned and walked slowly out of the square and back to the café car park. He entered the café and sadly ordered the additional coffee that Moisi had wanted before his ill-fated departure for the hit.

In the meantime, Luan Berisha and Vishnak Asllani had also left their car in the café car park, walked slowly across town and reached the Gateway Mall. They were now walking slowly down the long concourse assessing the situation and seeking their prey.

"If you make the hit, I will be your back-up." Luan suggested to Vishnak, both of whom were used to working in pairs in situations like that of today.

"Agreed!" was Vishnack's one-word efficient and direct reaction.

Eventually towards the end of their walk down the mall, they had good fortune. At the end of the mall, directly in front of a well-known national departmental store there was a large square of corridor with very few shoppers anywhere near it. Moreover to the left-hand side was an exit from the mall into a large car park, the entrance to which was always crowded. Two Police officers with their backs to the two gunmen had just entered the open space in front of the store walking slowly towards the entrance to the store with no shops to their left, only the wide corridor to the exit.

Vishnak speeded his step somewhat but waited until the two officers walked further toward the store, before pulling his gun, levelling it up and firing at the leg of the officer on the left. The officer fell over, writhing at the pain in his limb. Luan had noticed the other officer begin to turn at the sound of the shot and begin to reach to draw his gun. He reacted instantly by pulling his own gun and shooting the second officer also in the leg. The second officer fell in agony. Luan then rushed up to Vishnak and as they put their guns away, they walked slowly and confidently through the crowded bottleneck at the exit into the busy car park.

"See you back at the café." Vishnak suggested and with a nod of Luan's head, they separated to walk back by different routes to the café for another real cup of coffee. At the café, the three remaining gangsters decided that as it was so early, they would have lunch at the café and drive back together afterwards to meet up with the man from London at the safe house. Over lunch Klodjan explained the fate of his partner, Moisi Shehu, and they renewed their commitment to a serious tête-à-tête with Ardajan Nikolaj that very afternoon. Whatever happened they would show a unified front. But in the interim they asked themselves what the Ayton Police would think with three officers on extended sick leave and two of them with similar non-life-threatening leg injuries? Would they get the wrong message?

When the three men arrived back at the safe house, Nico was by this time packed and ready to depart. He welcomed them back but was surprised to see them back so early and explained that he had commitments in London that were pressing.

"Good to see you back, but where is Moisi? I am afrid I don't have any time to speak with you due to the need to return to London expeditiously now. I shall be gone in another five minutes. Should I take it that you accomplished your task and hit the targets? How many did you kill?"

Vishnak Asllani took the lead and prepared to advance a request for financial justice for him and his colleagues.

"Nico we shall delay you no longer. Moisi will not be coming back and we wish to make a proposal for the payment for the job that we have just done."

"Payment? But you're already being paid your share of the payroll and very generously so too."

"Nico. You know as well as I do that such jobs in London attract a premium payment, sometimes as high as ten grand. Now we're not asking for that, but for something more modest."

"Nico could sense the phalanx of opinion rising against him and decided on an avoidance strategy so as to get away as quickly as possible … and as cheaply as possible!

"Well of course Ayton is not London. But as a matter of interest, I was waiting for your return to see if you had accomplished your allocated task and I had an additional bonus in mind. Payment by results they call it! Eh? I am assuming your task was successfully completed or you would not have returned so early. I should say as I always intended, I am pleased to offer you one grand each pair, half that for each person. Where one of the pair has failed to return only half will be paid the one, who returns. This I shall activate as soon as I get back to the office. We do not have the details of your accomplishment of your gaols. But next time we might have to reconsider the price."

Vishnak was just about to react to the miserable money offer made by Nico, when the Chief of Chiefs stood up and made as if to depart.

“Anyway!” He explained. “I must depart for London this minute or, as with all such contracts, my bosses will be thinking of depleting my bonus or even ‘depleting’ me personally.” He quipped and smiled at the three of them.

His false smile as he uttered these last words was in fact in good measure a humorous threat to warn them not to push their luck, or else! He picked up his valise case and quickly escaped from the room and the house and got into his freshly washed and fuelled Mercedes.

As soon as the Chief Constable was informed of the attacks on her three officers, she sent a message of comfort to those officers, who had been injured, and their families. She also called an early meeting in her office of all senior staff, including DCI Frank Wozny and Detective Chief Inspector Rajan Appasamy, who led the newly established specialised Criminal Investigation Department, and Acting Superintendent Anthony Birch, interim Head of the Armed Police Unit, and both the Assistant Chief Inspectors as well.

Meanwhile news of the attacks had spread like wildfire though the ranks of officers and other staff, many of whom also sent messages of comfort and support to the families of the injured officers. At the explicit request of the Chief Constable, Police welfare officers also arranged to visit the families of the officers injured and offered any assistance whatsoever that might be needed. A collection in support of the three officers was also quickly organised in the large office and quickly resulted in a substantial sum.

When all senior staff had assembled in her office the Chief Constable thanked them for coming at such short notice and said that she hoped it was not too inconvenient for them and their work plans.

"Thank you all for coming together so rapidly and I hope it was convenient for you. The reason for the meeting, as you probably know, is the dastardly and totally unprovoked attack on three of our officers. Initial inquiries seem to indicate that Constable, Jacob Trier on guard duty at the back entrance, was hit in the chest by one bullet. He was wearing his bullet-proof vest and it did not penetrate. But he is nonetheless suffering substantial bruising, although first reports are that he is otherwise unharmed. Police Constable Ronald Price responded to the assailant with one shot to his head and killed him. We are currently investigating who the assailant was, but he appears to have been a very young and inexperienced would-be assassin. Thank goodness! Police Sergeant Sally Pogson was in the mall, when she was hit by a bullet in the leg and she is still in surgery. Her injuries are not life-threatening. Her colleague, Police Sergeant Graham Butter, was also on duty at the big shopping mall and was also hit by a single bullet in the leg and similarly he is still in surgery. I have called you together, because I do not believe that we can allow this provocation by an organised criminal group (OCG) to go unanswered, and I have to ask you for your reactions to the attack and its meaning, given that there were thankfully no fatalities on our side."

DCI Wozny was the first to set out the parameters of his view.

Ma'am, I find the attack itself outrageous and enigmatic. It requires a very severe and swift reaction from us. The fact that none of the injuries has been life-threatening is in my view significant. From this I read that in the two cases of leg injuries someone in the organisation responsible is sending us a message. They could easily have killed the officers. It's only a theory, but perhaps a drug war is brewing between two Albanian cliques as has happened recently on the Continent in Brussels and Antwerp for example. It may be that the message is back off or else next time! In the other case, where the gangster was shot dead by our officer, Constable Price, on guard duty at the back gate, like you, I read youth boastfulness, incompetence and inexperience with guns. As I suggested, Ma'am, my view is that we need to act in response to this outrageous atrocity very quickly and very harshly but also continue to try to work out what the overall meaning of the vicious attacks can be."

Deputy Chief Constable, Rajiv Gundara, was the next to speak and he declared that he agreed with DCI Wozny on the need for a swift and severe reaction and he added a specific suggestion on action.

"I agree with Frank about the imperative of action. We had already begun to plan the raid of a brothel and I think we should pull this forward. We also have intelligence about a large Edwardian house that has been under observation for some time. We believe that this is one of the safe house of the OCG and that sometimes the big fish from London stays there. We believe him to be there at this very moment. Now that would be a coup would it not!"

Assistant Chief Constable Adarsh Khanna also supported the need for an early and fulsome manifestation to the gangsters of the consequences of their outrageous actions. She also added that the brothel bust should have been carried out a long time ago, not least for humanitarian reasons.

"It is the largest brothel in Ayton with somewhere in the region of twenty women imprisoned there, according to our most recent intelligence. I cringe when I think of so many young women, many of them from countries far away and little more than children themselves, subjected to daily abuse and downright inhuman cruelty with no prospect of release and no relief. My understanding is that women in this situation last no longer than six years at maximum before they expire."

Chief Inspector Rajan Appasamy then spoke to the matter agreeing that a speedy and vigorous outcome for the gangsters was essential.

"I do agree with all that has been said about the need for a rapid and severe repost to these criminals. I also agree that the large brothel raid should be advanced to this week. Tomorrow if possible. Action on that establishment is urgent in any case and its closure will deprive the criminal gang of some half a million pounds profit annually and liberate a good number of young women from their cruel bondage. With regards to the suspected safe house in the cul de sac of Edwardian houses on the outskirts of Ayton, my officers have been observing that house for some time. According to our intelligence the Chief of the UK Albanian cartel from London is holed up there currently. We should take that house and him out soonest."

Finally Assistant Chief Constable Maria Clarke spoke supportively for both raids.

"I support action on both raids with the only question being whether that measure of resources could be marshalled and available at such short notice as is being suggested by some colleagues."

The Chief Constable took over the decision.

"Everyone has recognized the need for urgent action by us in reaction to the two attacks. We envisage it as an explicit reply to the attacks on our officers. Given the intelligence we have at this time, I propose that we should tackle them both tomorrow night. Deputy Chief Constable, Rajiv Gundara, will lead the raid on the brothel and Detective Chief Inspector Rajan Appasamy will lead the attack on the safe house, both with the help and participation of the other members of this executive committee here today and of course with an appropriate participation of the authorised firearms officers. DCI Wozny are you happy with that arrangement?"

"Yes Ma'am absolutely."

"Acting Superintendent Anthony Birch, interim Head of the Armed Police Unit, are you happy with that arrangement too? Do you have sufficient resources for the two raids at the same time?"

"Yes Ma'am. We shall be supporting both raids simultaneously. Specifically I personally will be supporting the brothel raid and my Deputy will attend the safe house raid."

"Good!"

The Chief Constable had already stood up assuming that was the end of the consultation, when Assistant Chief Constable Maria Clarke rather boldly added a rider about a unit at the Met, since the Chief Constable had worked at the Met before her appointment in Ayton.

“Ma’am. We have been expanding the number of brothel raids over the last little while and all the follow-up work with the women that implies afterwards is becoming almost overwhelming for us and for the social services department of the local authority. You will probably know the work of the special unit, which the Metropolitan Police have in order to deal with issues arising from raids of brothels, etc. namely The Modern Slavery and Child Exploitation Unit. Would it be possible to think of the establishment of a similar unit here in Ayton? It’s certainly needed and in my view the case for such a unit here is irrefutable.

In the rush to move on, the response that the Chief Constable made, was not quite as graceful as she normally tried to make her usual dealings with staff to be.

“Thank you for that suggestion for the future, Maria. Right, well let’s get to the work of the here and now, colleagues.”

Sick leave and the short time span for the preparations for the two raids was causing enormous problems in the station. Pressing work on preparations of submissions to the CPS, routine patrolling, burgeoning cannabis farming closures, incipient car wash forced labour investigations and domestic and other violence were all suffering. Day-to-day work on things like the investigation of shop-lifting, child and domestic abuse, knife crime, the expansion of the drug mini-empires and other cases of modern slavery were being delayed or even in one of two cases jettisoned.

The progress long expected by the Public on the internal sex scandals within the Force had so far been unforthcoming. There was rumbling in the ranks! But there was definite thunder and lightning from the Public. Nonetheless and just for the moment there seemed to be a need for a thin veneer of false unanimity provided by the reaction to the attacks on the three Police officers.

The preparations for both raids were going ahead in parallel and at some speed, in spite of the shortage of some vehicles and human resources. The whole scene was one of hurried, nay frenetic, preparation and things like the constellation of rooms and the lie of the land around the properties were perhaps not conducted in as detailed a manner as was usually required. Borrowings of some resources, such as specialised vehicles, from local authority departments were necessitated but were willingly provided once those approached had been informed of the purpose.

At eleven thirty exactly the convoys of vehicles began their journey from the back entrance of the main Police station. Some Police officers had arrived in advance at each of the target destinations in separate cars and were engaged in taping areas of exclusion, setting up of traffic diversion signs and covering the back entrances of the properties. All was in place for the commencement of the raids at midnight and the usual warning to be loud-speakered into the properties.

In the case of the brothel raid, as it was expected that there would very well be armed men in the premises, a squad of officers from the Armed Response Unit advanced towards the substantial front door of the large domestic establishment, which was surrounded by a spiked stone wall and locked metal gates. The usual warnings were given on a loudspeaker and when there was no result to the first warnings, a second set was given. Very slowly after the second warning, an aproned middle-aged woman opened the front door and demanded to know what the fuss was and why she was being rushed. She was told that the Police had a warrant to enter and search the property, and she replied that she did not understand what they expected to find as everyone in town knew that this was a brothel and had known for a long time. As the first squads of officers entered the premises they encountered some thirty small partitioned rooms. In most of the rooms they were confronted by scenes that many of them found repulsively sordid in the extreme and distressing.

Twenty women were found in smelly, uncleaned, squalid and frowzy rooms, where even the walls were smeared and dirty with no sanitary installations not even a wash basin in the room. The dishevelled covers and pillows on the beds looked as though they had never seen a washing machine. At the side was a box of condoms, and other materials for their trade on a small soiled bedside table.

Each room had a camera high up of the wall over the bed and oriented to it. In most cases the women were, in the first reaction of the Police, mostly children, who were expected according to the later statements of those, who were willing to testify, to service at least ten clients a day, all day and every day. Many of the girls looked fatigued, emaciated, bedraggled and unkempt, which is not surprising as ledgers found in the house indicated that the business day commenced in the very early hours of the morning and could in some cases ended only on the next day.

The women and girls were treated with great reticence and tenderness by the mainly women officers and each was led slowly and gently to the waiting coach, where they were attended by members of the local authority's social services department. It later transpired that most of the women and girls were Romanian and the house belonged to a Romanian, not Albanian, organised crime group. At least three of the girls had been groomed and trafficked from the local College and were amongst the co-called ghost students being sought by the College itself. On later assessment, some of the girls were judged to be psychologically very damaged and required subsequent special care, counselling and attention in safe houses. Moreover it emerged that this was only one of several brothels that had been established by various OCGs in the town pulling in millions of pounds a week for the gangsters and their criminal organisations.

The other raid had gone smoothly also in the sense that there was no violence. Indeed, some officers felt that it had gone too smoothly and had raised suspicions of some possible advanced leakage of information from the Force to the mobsters. Once again armed men were reliably expected to be present in the building and the advance squad of authorised firearms officers, led by Acting Superintendent Anthony Birch, Acting Head of the Armed Police Response Unit, proceeded in advance. After the usual warning and a good heavy knock on the solid wooden door, two young men, who hardly spoke any English, had swiftly opened the door and greeted the officers in a not unfriendly manner. They were unarmed.

When told that the officers had a warrant to search the property, they had theatrically stood to one side and bowing gesticulated to the officers to please enter and proceed with their search. The premises were large, well and comfortably furnished. They were also cleaned and sweet smelling of cleaning materials. The two young men turned out to be the only two occupants of the house and they claimed that they were resident cleaners, who were paid a pittance in cash weekly but had the rooms in the attic free of charge and free meals thrown in.

An interpreter was needed for an efficient interrogation later but initial questions seemed to indicate that the men were Albanian and had worked at the house in Ayton for several years. On forensic examination, no documents, drug specimens or incidental information was found in the house and surprisingly the premises seemed to have been recently given a good clean. It emerged on later examination that the men had been given a bonus to get the cleaning done quickly.

The two men were taken in for questioning but, because of lack of evidence of wrong-doing, they were turned over to the Immigration Service. The main part of the raid ended at one o'clock in the morning and the traffic and other restriction were fully lifted at that time as well. The house was, however, taped off for possible further investigation.

The evaluation, which followed later that morning was shot through with frustration on all sides. How was it possible that the wrong brothel had been chosen, organised by a Romanian OCG rather than an Albanian one? What had happened to all the occupants of the house, when reliable intelligence had observed several men there earlier that very same day including the Head of the Albanian

Cartel from London, Ardajan Nikolaj? How much in resources and retardation of other projects had the two raids cost? The fact that no members of either OCG were found in either the brothel or the house, would seem to indicate prior knowledge on the part of the criminals. Was there a leak in the house?

These and many other questions were raised with the Chief Constable, some of them in a not very friendly manner. The repercussions of the evening's raids would long work their way through the ranks of the officers of the Ayton Police Force and perhaps particularly the most senior ones and the possible presence of a mole in the Force would cause interpersonal suspicion in the force widespread and long-term.

"A number of members of the Board of Governors have requested in writing an emergency debate about the College's treatment and care of the three young girls, all former students at this College, who were released from months of torment in captivity in an Organised Crimes Group's brothel in our town. I have a list of names in front of me of members, who wish to speak to this matter, but before I, do I would like to invite the Principal of the College, Dr Andrew Ziegler, to make an opening statement. Dr Ziegler!"

The new Chair of the Ayton College, Board of Governors, Mr Stanley Beecham-Jones, local councillor, academic and long-time member of the Board gestured for the Principal to begin delivering his statement.

"Chair and members, it is with some considerable distress that I have to make a statement on the college's treatment of the three young girls, who were freed from a gangland brothel in recent days. I have to admit that the College failed utterly and completely to fulfil its legal obligation of care for these young ladies. Although I was not the Principal of the College at the time some three years ago when this matter began, I have managed to piece together, after discussion with the Police, something of how it began. It would seem clear that the girls were groomed into prostitution by being fed drugs and false kindness even deceitful love. But the key to the commencement was a former member of staff, who had friends in the Romanian mafia in Ayton and was well rewarded for his services in enticing these girls into a brutal, inhuman life of prostitution for the use, nay abuse, of members of the criminal gang."

The Principal briefly halted his report, manifestly distressed by the task he was having to fulfil and continued only in a voice filled with a choking emotion.

"It is not yet clear, as the Police are still investigating this matter, but it would seem that all three young ladies were groomed by the same member of the College staff, whose name I cannot mention at this time, as a number of charges are yet likely to be made against him, not least in connection with his paid attachment to the Romanian OCG. In addition, it is apparent that all three young girls were having difficulties at home, with family break-up in two of the cases and the death of a near relative in another. It would be inexcusable to blame the failure of the care of these three young women on those home travails, but they surely set a context of emotional background, which tells us they actually played a part. Patently, there is a great deal of work still to be done by the College on the whole issue of so-called 'ghost students' to fully recoup its reputation as a caring institution. For the moment I am going to listen very carefully to others and we can seek to then pull all the factors together into a coherent care policy for all our students."

"Thank you Dr Ziegler for that statement, which must have been a very painful task. I'm going to call on our College Liaison Officer, Police Sergeant Mary Rigby, to enlighten us on this tragic affair, as far as she can, given as I mentioned before, the ongoing action on this case."

“Thank you, Chair. There is really little I can say to add to the very courageous statement by Dr Ziegler. If I recall it rightly it was just after Dr Ziegler’s appointment as Principal of this College that the Ayton Police Force and the College agreed the appointment of an Educational Liaison Officer. If only perhaps! I can say that the Police have located the former member of staff involved, he is under arrest and has been charged with child grooming offences and is awaiting the prospect of being faced with further charges. Just to help fellow members understand what that means very roughly grooming is when someone builds a relationship with a child, who is already at risk, so that they can abuse them and manipulate them into doing things they would otherwise probably not do. The abuse is typically sexual and it can include other illegal acts as well. On a happier note the brothel, in which these girls were so cruelly and inhumanely abused over a period of three years, has been shut down and arrests and charges are pending in that connection. The three young women, being of age as they are now, are all residing in safe houses and receiving counselling and other assistance to re-establish their lives. Thank you Chair.”

“Mrs Burney Crowder, as the previous Chair, I should like to ask you to speak next.”

“Thank you Chair. As I believe members will know, my own daughter recently suffered a severe knife attack inside the College. I am happy to inform the Board that she is recovering well. But I mention that as a further three stabbings with a sharp blade have happened in the College since that time and after the introduction too of measures to exclude such blades from the College. Drugs of different strengths are also rife in the college according to reports from some of our students of late. Unspoken we have also had a number of suicides in the College. Predominantly of young girls. Our net of concern and action has to include these young victims of the unpunished tech giants, who are still targeting young people with harmful content. I would suggest a number of actions such as drawing the local Police Force's attention to this unpunished abomination and examining our internet system to make absolutely certain that none of this is getting through to our students. All this as well as an advisory letter to parents. But we need to act to prevent this utter waste of gifted human life, which is entrusted to us here at the College. Thus, we have here a nexus of problems interlinking and interacting, drugs, sexual misconduct, 'ghost students, student suicides and knife crime. Our policy needs to embrace them all in one document."

Mrs Marjory Robinson, Governor and member of the local authority Social Services Department, was the next member on the Chair's list of speakers to be called.

"Chair. I am pleased to be able to endorse what the previous Chair, Mrs Burnley Crowder, has just said. I think that she is right in her comments about student suicides and perhaps we have all as members of this Board been to a certain degree remiss on this matter. But now thanks to our former Chair, we have a chance to change that. If I may I should also like to add that no child protection policy will be successful without the co-operation of other parties, such as for example parents, Police and social services. Given the case that we are speaking about today, it is clear that there was inadequate liaison amongst the three major parties when these young women were groomed. One further point is that we may not be listening sufficiently to the whispers of our own students, which would normally report a member of staff misbehaving, but not necessarily a student. We already have the power to investigate such undertones of sexual misconduct towards students. Of course anyone guilty of such misconduct in public office can have their contract terminated and must be reported to the Police for further investigation of claims that turn out to be bogus sometimes. I would say, of course, in the case of these three students under discussion that the claims were not bogus!"

Mr Bowers, would you like to speak to this matter next?"

Mr Andy Bowers, was a longstanding member of the Governing Body and a very successful local business man, who owned a large furniture shop in the main square,

"Yes thank you Chair. In all the years that I have been on this Board, we have never had to face a crisis like that, which is afflicting us today. Drug taking is rising in the society beyond our walls here in the College as are addiction and deaths therefrom. Newly arriving drugs, many of which like fentanyl have caused thousands of deaths in the United States, are more potent, sometimes up to one hundred times more potent than heroin, and we seem incapable of controlling their arrival or their accompanying criminality seeping into the very fabric of our society. Knife crime is rife and in some cases deaths therefrom have occurred. Gun crime is intensifying and we seem unable to control the criminality which goes with these lawless activities. The accruing criminality from the criminal acts also has a very serious multiplication effect. How are we going to control all those 'infectious diseases' in our College, if we cannot control them in our society outside?"

Former Staff Sergeant Charles Bowen was the next to speak. He was a senior ex-army NCO, retrained as an Information Technology teacher. He was very popular amongst the staff, a recently appointed staff-elected governor and liked to think of himself as a man of decision.

"Chair, we have discussed the issues of drugs and knives endlessly. This, to my recollection, is the second extraordinary meeting within a time scale of a few days about the subject of weapons and drugs penetrating into the College and consequent disputes and stabbings among different groups of students. We have recently had several disputes where knives were used and we have had consequent hospitalizations and one death. There are complex matters interlacing with other equally complex concerns. Some of those questions are partially soluble by us, others are not. For example we can control what our students can access on the internet on the College system, but we cannot control the access that they are given or not at home. We can advise though. We can make the ambience in the College meaningful and enjoyable as a learning environment but we cannot control family break-up in the wider society, although together with social services we may be able to peripherally assist. I say, as I said last time, that each member of staff has a responsibility to examine with a critical eye and find out what the teaching of his or her subject can contribute to the exclusion of drugs and knives in the school and fights in College. But in addition the College itself can install stricter measures and clear sanctions against anyone who infringes the policy. For example, some few students are inserting sharps, blades and knives through the toilet windows to their mates inside. Some students are able to evade the sensors on the main entrance to the College because there are no other sensors at the other entrances. There should be a major publicity campaign with flyers and through the internet to make youngsters aware of the life-threatening dangers of carrying knives or doing drugs. So where do these comments leave us. One! The College Academic Board, as is its right and role is tasked with presenting as a matter of great urgency a comprehensive plan of action to include all the items covered in today's debate. Two! Departments are asked to seriously examine their curricula along the lines I mentioned. Three! Each individual member of staff must examine the curriculum he or she teachers. Four! We should pull our socks up on the efficient and effective use of sensors and other means, by which we seek to exclude drugs and knives from the College. Five! We should generate flyers for students and parents to explain our policy, to seek their help in enforcing it and to emphasise the sanctions available for use against those who infringe the policy, including reference to the Police as appropriate. Six! We should initiate a much closer relationship with our friends in social services and try to offer a counselling service to those students, who feel they need it. That's all … for the moment! Sorry to have spoken for such a lengthy time, Chair, but I really am convinced that now is a time not to prevaricate but to act, by ourselves and with others co-operatively. "

"Thank you Mr Bowen for that sparkling delivery, which I believe has the outline of a policy document. As you suggest we should place the matter in the court of the Academic Board right away, at which you will no doubt speak again. Yes, Mrs Janice Fynan, Finance Officer, you wish to add something I see."

"Thank you Chair. I speak as an assistant to, rather than as a member, of the Governing Body to offer some advice on the financial side of things. Our finances are very stretched at the moment. With a growing burden from the government of unfunded demands, pressure from the inspectorate and the inflationary costs of equipment such as computers, printers and printing paper, and the professional servicing thereof, we are on the borderline of bankruptcy. I am so sorry to be the bearer of bad news. But it is my unpleasant and frequent duty to do so. As I believe we said last time, there is no slack, which would enable us to undertake some of the measures that Mr Bowen has quite rightly suggested. Sorry Mr Bowen.

"Thank you Mrs Fynan, as always, for drawing us back to the unpleasant reality of our financial situation. I think you and I should meet to try to find a groat or two for this very important dimension of the College's legal responsibility to offer care and protection to our students."

There were smiles at the use of the word for the silver coin, a groat, long since discarded. In conclusion, the Chair then drew the meeting to a close, thanking everyone for their attendance at a very long and arduous but richly rewarding meeting. He then indicated to the finance officer and Mr Bowen that he would like a word with them immediately after the conclusion of the meeting.

It all began almost accidentally. The supply of some major drugs was drying up and consequently prices were rising sharply making the drugs more expensive and valuable. Indeed well worthwhile to obtain them free through theft. In Afghanistan the Taliban was suppressing the use of agricultural land and resources for the production of heroin. In Europe imports of fentanyl were being constrained by a far-off summit agreement between the Presidents of China and The United Sates to curb the flow of the drug to the US. More specifically the 'concordat' concerned the targeting of companies that made the constituent chemical compound and the level of production of those wherewithall substances that were used in the production of the synthetic opioid, fentanyl.

The drug fentanyl was very powerful, fifty times more powerful than heroin. The wherewithall substances, which after export from China and some small amounts as well from India, was processed in Mexico and then exported to the North, were deadly. Tablets, wraps or powder was killing thousands of people in the United States every year. A climbing volume of the drug was being exported to the United Kingdom from the US with similar fatal consequences to those in the US, though not on the same mass scale so far.

The two young county lines runners from two different crime organisations were disputing, which one owned the heroin package for the customer, which was resting on the floor in front of them both. Clearly one was lying. But which one? The youngsters were on a delivery trip for their respective drug cartels based in Ayton, the Romanian and the Albanian ones. Somehow their bags had become mixed up and a tugging and pulling of the relevant bag had begun. The argument about the ownership of the valuable product in the bag flared up and gradually became so heated that one of them took out a knife, thinking to scare the other county liner off what he regarded as his goods.

He misjudged the other county lines runner, however, who straightway pulled a gun, pointed it at the other young man's face and with a bullet to the head at close range shot his competitor stone dead. The shot youngster fell to ground and the other young hoodlum wiped the other young man's blood from his face and picked up the bag for delivery to his customer. One of the young men was from the Romanian mob, under the aggressive leadership of Andrei Popescu, closely allied to the Iraqi Kurd mob and the dead man had been from the Manchester mob, with its ambitious and sensitive dual leadership of Chief Gary Buxton and his financial assistant and underboss Giles Campbell, which was closely allied to the Liverpool mob and in which the Albanian clan had interests and investments and links to the Italian NDrangheta. All except the Iraqi Kurdish gang had long-term bases in Ayton.

When word got around that county lines runners were being murdered by others from competitor clans, the scene was set for the start of major confrontations. The new head of the Manchester hoodlums, Gary Buxton, gave the order as a matter of honour that one of the senior Romanians was to be taken out, preferably the top man, and that the number of his county lines runners was to be reduced by two. Unfortunately when the Romanian assassins encountered the Head of the Manchester organised crime group, he was together with visiting mobsters from the Liverpool organised crime group.

The entry of the assassins caused a commotion in the room with the interchange of waves of gunfire and in the mix-up it was two members of the Liverpool gang and one of the assassins who were killed not the originally intended members of the Manchester group. This error led to the involvement of the Liverpool group in the blood feud. From that point confrontations rapidly escalated further. The dominoes were falling fast and in the succeeding months, the other cartels in Ayton became more or less actively involved. Knives had been superseded by guns for most hoodlums and they now became the everyday weapons for most mobsters, reducing the need for placatory words.

Assassinations mounted and took place often in Public places not only with consequent danger to the Public, with consequent Public injuries and in some cases deaths. OCG houses of opponent OCG's were raided and sometimes set alight as the mood of revenge spread and one organised criminal group vented its anger against one or more other organised criminal groups.

As the death toll mounted, property became a favourite means of expressing their anger against the other. Brothels and indoor drug farms were considered fair game and their enslaved occupants were just turned out onto the street without any support or assistance. Sometimes the women were taken over into the establishment of the opposing group.

Premises were raided and pillaged or completely destroyed and worst of all in some of the confrontations innocent civilians were threatened, attacked, injured and some fatally wounded. In some cases assassinations took place on the doorstep or in the home of the opponent as in the case of the head of the Romanian mafia in Ayton, Andrei Popescu, who was shot in the head several times, on his doorstep and in front of his family.

Sometimes the executions took place in a car. That was the case with a six-month pregnant thirty-eight year old woman and mother of three when she was driving with her husband to the restaurant that they jointly owned. The assailant discharged a nine millimetre handgun into their car, aiming for the husband. Usually in such cases there were no witnesses or at least no one, who was willing to state what and who they had seen and even less give a statement and sign it. The man and his wife were killed on the spot.

Throughout Ayton there was a clamour for action by the Police and the Police, Fire and Crime Commissioner strongly expressed his own dissatisfaction and that of the Public at the apparent inertia of the Police. But the Ayton Police Force was already engaged in major investigations into people trafficking, domestic violence, illicit drugs and particularly newer and more potent ones, prostitution, sexual activity with a minor, shop-lifting, common assault, internal investigations into officer sexual misbehaviour, and much else besides. So the Force was consequently desperately short of staff, and especially appropriately trained and experienced officers in the different areas of specialisation and expertise.

Demands from the Public for action on the part of the Police faced the Force with many dilemmas. Firstly the mutually destructive attacks of the mafia gangs should reduce the overall total number of hoodlums in Ayton, which could be seen as an advantage, but all murders had to be investigated. Secondly the destruction of brothels and indoor drug farms reduced the provision of such premises in Ayton and saved the Force the expenditure involved in closing those premises themselves. Thirdly the destruction of drugs and mutual confiscation of cash and nitrous oxide vapes temporarily reduced the value of the amount of investment available for a range of other nefarious activities by the criminal gangs. But the wider community considered that the civilian casualties were intolerable and that action was urgently required by the Police.

Fourthly, each of the murders or cases of arson had to be investigated by the Police and the cost in extremely scarce workforce outlay and financial assets was enormous and mounting daily. In other words the Force was already under considerable stress without this apocalypse in addition. And fifthly where do you look for these mobsters and what evidence is there unless they are actually caught in the act of murder, arson or some other crime?

Meanwhile others were concerned about the internecine warfare continuing in Ayton. But for different reasons. Tristen Plackici with his two so-called advisers, Luan Berisha and Vishnak Asllani, was sitting in the well-furnished front room of the Albanian Cartel's safe house in Ayton. He was lamenting the falling sales and oversupply of their drugs and the consequent complaints from London once again about their performance.

"We've had another complaint from Nico in the East End about the drop in our sales and the consequent overstocking of our stores. This, he says makes them more vulnerable to the Ayton Police Force's raids or indeed raids by other groups in the town, both of which seem to have a predilection for our stocks."

Vishnak responded supportively.

"I do not believe that he can understand the situation we currently face in Ayton, with our fellow mafia groups fighting each other like dogs. There were some more gunfights across the weekend with three fatalities and another arson. I understand that the Chief of the Romanian Firm, Andrei Popescu, was also shot dead in the presence of his family at his front door."

"Yes, I do not think this is good for the trade … for our trade and our balance sheet." Luan added. "But what do you think we can do about it? It seems to me that it is beyond our power to influence. What do you think Nico would do in a situation like this?"

Tristen jumped on the comment.

"Good question, Luan. I think he would knock heads together using his superior force."

"Yes and his force would not be only about the number of guns he could muster, but also the very strong position that we hold in the market for the supply of all the main substances currently."

“Vishnak, Luan. Some good thinking there! What do you think about appealing… with all due modesty of course to Nico to come and help us sort it out? He has a reputation for being good at that sort of thing, doesn’t he?”

“Yes, but we should need to brief him very carefully and feed him the relevant information.” Vishnak added.

“And flatter him as well. After all he is acknowledged to be capo di tutti i capi, as the Italians call it, the supreme boss of bosses as we speak of his role.” Luan suggested to the group.

“Right then! Thank you both very much and that is exactly what we shall do today, er this morning!” Tristen Plackici stated emphatically and gratefully to his colleagues.

Tristen must have engaged a large volume of flattery in his telephone conversation with Nico that day. Nico arrived in Ayton early on the very next morning, emphasising how he had favoured them by reacting so quickly to their request for assistance in spite of his crippling workload. After further discussions and advice, the message was sent out to all criminal gangs in Ayton with a kindly invitation to attend a tea get-together the following afternoon.

As they arrived the next afternoon at the safe house, they were greeted in the hall by two burly gunmen holding AK 47s and with GLOCKS tucked into the back of their belts. All arrivals were invited to place any weapons on the table at the side and to help themselves to the drinks and other refreshments on the table inside the ‘conference room’. As they arrived and entered the room they were confronted by a combined lounge and dining room filled with metal chairs arranged in serried ranks with Nico sitting behind a large weighty table at the front and flanked by two AK47-toting gunmen at the two ends of the table. As the room filled the babble of conversation in the room grew louder and louder.

Nico hit the table with a large wooden gavel and the noise subsided and died away. He spoke with confidence from a well-planned script. He did not read it but looked straight at his audience sharing his scan across the rows and the aisle as he spoke.

"Friends! Fellow businessmen! I am so pleased that you were able to free yourselves from the weighty responsibilities that men such as we all share. After all our job is to make money not attend meetings."

There was a murmur of cool laughter and many smiles at his last comment.

"I have invited you all here today so that we can do even better what we already do. That is make money for our Firms. The last few weeks have made that, our fundamental responsibility, much, much harder, I'm sorry to say! I want to share with you today how we are going to return to our prime responsibility and make more money. Let me emphasise that I speak to you today as what our Italian friends in the business call the capo di tutti i capi, the supreme boss of bosses."

He rested on his laurels for a moment and then hit his audience with the hard truth about the facts on their main and in some cases exclusive supplier of drugs, namely the Albanian mafia in the UK.

"My Firm is in the very happy position of supplying all of some drugs and most of others to you, all at a price so low that you can still make a good profit selling at forty pounds a gram. We also import and control all of the new, more potent drugs that come into Ayton and again sell them on to you at a fair price with an eye to your legitimate benefit. So the present situation of conflict, nay warfare, amongst us is irrational and counterproductive. It does not increase our gains, it reduces our profits. I say again such conflicts do not improve our business and their yields. So here is how we are going to deal with any misunderstandings or conflicts in the future in a market- and profit-friendly way. I am very willing to come down here in the future to help you resolve any disputes in a market-responsive way and peacefully! We are the largest and most powerful syndicate in the country and our leadership has been accepted for this purpose at national level. So the system is tried and tested. It works! There have been no wars in other parts of the country. The system works! Any questions?"

The representative of the Liverpool-based clan, Joe Magee, asked about the assurance of an independent resolution of problems.

"How do we know that you will not just make a judgement in favour of those, who have paid you the most?"

"Good question! Well I have never had to face such an accusation in the past. I do not take any money from anyone except my Firm. It would be the end of me if I did. Just to reassure you, however, would you, Joe, like to nominate someone from the Liverpool Firm to join me to make sure that I am fair in my judgements? Yourself perhaps?"

"OK! That sounds reasonable to me." Was Joe's sharp and rapid retort.

"Thank you, Joe as the leader of the only Firm here, who does not receive its supplies of spice from the Albanian clan, welcome and thank you again. I'll be in touch."

Sensing majority acceptance, and conscious that the meeting could sway in another direction, Nico ended the meeting in a masterfully short way.

"Just a reminder that anyone, who breaches our agreement today by resorting to violence, will face the wroth of all of us. Thank you all most warmly for coming."

"Wow! No wonder the Albanian syndicate chose him as the Supremo!" Tristen said to his two colleagues and they grinned back at him and nodded in agreement.

Chapter Twenty-Four: Suspicion

There had been rumbling in the ranks of the Ayton Police Force for some time now about illicit contacts of some civilian staff and Police officers with one or other of the roughly fifteen organised crime groups, OCGs, currently active in illicit business in Ayton. One officer had already been arrested, charged and convicted of misconduct in a public office for providing restricted Police information against payment to an OCG. But this was considered to be just the tip of the iceberg.

The Police Force was also being regularly and consistently assailed in the Press and mass media for allegedly being institutional racist and sexist. Further bad publicity was accruing about the sexist misbehaviour of some staff and misogynist attitudes and homophobia were alleged to be rampant amongst the officers in the local and national Press. This was a difficult time for an institution strapped for financial resources and requiring the support of the Public to fulfil its statutory duties.

DCI Frank Wozny had responsibility for directing the investigations about internal matters in the Ayton Police Force and keeping the Chief Constable regularly informed of progress. It was Monday morning and time for a feedback session.

"Welcome back, Frank, hope you had a good weekend with the family. Yes, Ma'am we all visited a National Trust property and had some lunch there. Always very interesting and something for all members of the family, young and old."

"I did not know that you had any old members in your family, Frank. Everyone seems so young to me on the odd occasions I have met them. Anyway. It may be that we shall age a little after today's review of progress."

He smiled faintly at her and she reciprocated. Coffee, Frank?"

"No thanks, Ma'am. Just had one in the canteen."

The Chief Constable continued with her examination of the DCI about recent developments.

"So, where are we on the main investigations, firstly into the leakage to the Albanian OCG of confidential information about upcoming raids and plans? Secondly do we have any further information on the filtering of confidential information about staff and their social and financial circumstances held here on our files in the station to other OCG groups in exchange for payments or other favours?"

"On the first matter we have a suspect, Ma'am. Two of our trusty civilian staff, as you know, the one a retired Police officer and the other a woman, who was previously a partner at Jules and Block in the town and later an Ombudsman, are carrying out inquiries under the supervision of Detective Inspector Julie Banksworth. We have also been successful, I'm proud to say, in breaking an encrypted telephone service message revealing collusion and bribery by corrupt lawyers and other Public servants, including a senior serving Police officer here in the Service. The investigators are currently combing through telephone and financial records to obtain final and convincing proof that we can put to the Regional Prosecution Service. We are also hopeful of having evidence from business and street CCTV. But that is still to be confirmed, although the examination of the material has begun. So with regards to your query the present situation is that investigations are still being pursued and we should soon be able to caution and question the suspect."

"Good news so far. Well done! Let's just pause your presentation for a moment, and give me chance to ask a few more questions. Firstly what is the name of the senior officer in the Force, who has been alleged to be colluding with one of the mafia OCGs, and do we know how much he has been paid yet?"

DCI Frank Wozny felt a certain unease about the principle involved in giving the details requested by the Chief Constable. He could foresee the dangers of a potential contamination of evidence and a possible compromise of the Chief Constable's independence for the future procedures that would surely have to take place. He pondered for a short while and then quickly decided what to do.

"Ma'am we are still at the very beginning of piecing together a very complex series of intelligence sources and I don't wish to compromise your own independence in this matter. Forgive me if I do not answer your question about the name of our main suspect, whom we have not even cautioned so far. So, and it is our own interest that it remains so, the person may not even know that they are being investigated. As soon as the person is cautioned, you will know.

“Alright for the moment I’ll go with your judgement on that one. So far! But just update me on where we are with the investigation into the serious attack and wounding of three of our officers.

“Well, Ma’am we are still in the early stages of investigating those. The man, who was shot dead by one of our officers in self-defence has not yet been identified and other witnesses are in short supply, once they know the questions we pose are about the mafia gangs.”

“Does that apply to both attacks: the one in the mall at the Gateway Centre and the one at the rear entrance of the Police station?”

“Less so in the mall, Ma’am. We have already taken a statement from the security guard at the mall and one or two of the shoppers, who were there and volunteered to speak about what they saw. The evidence we are looking for is not yet complete if we are to see any culprits charged with attempted murder. Forensics have completed their work at the scenes there and we should have results of DNA tests, etc. in the very near future.”

“So basically we have insufficient leads at the moment about who sponsored, initiated or executed these attacks?”

“Not so far Ma’am. But we are still working on it. Off the record we suspect the top man in the local Albanian mob.”

“Let me continue with the very serious and damaging allegations concerning institutional racism in the Force, which is a very topical subject due to events elsewhere but also country-wide. The Press are making loud noises about it. Where are we on that one?"

"I am afraid with all the pressure on staff at the moment we have made very little progress. We are desperately short of staff with the background, qualifications and expertise to tackle many of these problems. But in this case the problem is the elusive nature of the evidence. How do you find out about that sort of thing, unless there are specific examples with complaints? At the moment we have no such intelligence."

"What about the allegations of misogynist and homophobic internet communications and, in some cases, of inappropriate touching and insensitive spoken sexual references in the presence of a number of women officers on several separate occasions?"

"We have some six or seven women officers, who have volunteered to testify and we are still taking recorded statements from those officers. On the other hand a number of our former Police officers, who have recently retired, have been given suspended prison sentences and unpaid work for sending sexist, racist and homophobic messages on WhatsApp. I understand that the organiser of the group has also been fined. We are, however, still at the very beginning of the investigation amongst currently serving officers, or rather I should say a series of complaints against serving officers by fellow women officers. But we are not there yet. We are seeking further written statements from other women officers willing to provide us with corroborative evidence. Some few civilian women colleagues have also volunteered to testify on this issue as well."

"What news of the allegations that some of our Police officers, or was it civilian staff, have been combing our files for personal and confidential information about their fellow officers and leaking it to one or more OCGs? Do you know for what reason they are collecting such information?"

"Yes! It seems to me clear that this information enables the OCGs to identify those members of the Force, who are weak and/or vulnerable because of money problems, infidelity that they wish to cover up, drunkenness or expensive drug addiction, etc., and would, therefore be susceptible to bribery or coercion in order to groom them for service to a mob group. Such information can bring a pretty good price on the open market. Sometimes as much as five to ten thousand pounds a dip, depending on the level of th officer being aimed at."

Finally, although it is never finally. Is it? We know that a small group of officers is illicitly combing internal Police records to identify fellow officers, who are having financial or other personal difficulties, such as you have just mentioned, to provide the names of those officers as potentially open to bribery and to furnish information about the workforce of the Force, officers and civilian staff, in exchange for money. In some cases it could also be information of some misconduct, on the basis of which pressure could be exerted on the recalcitrant officer or officers to divulge information to one group or the growing number of OCGs now active in Ayton.

“That is likewise a very damaging area for the reputation of the Force

There are other cases in the offing, so to speak, but the ones I have quoted are the ones that are nearest to fruition. You will find full details and the other incipient cases that we are currently investigating in my weekly report to you, which is now with your secretary.”

“Yes, I began to read it just before this meeting but there were so many priorities to deal with straight away demanding my attention that I did not complete it before your arrival this morning. I hope to do that sometime today.”

“No problem Ma’am. By the way we have discovered the dead body of a young man in one of the sheds at the side of the canal. We have set up a murder inquiry and forensics are there at the moment. This death is one of some twenty homicides in our patch so far this year, which peeked in the recent gang wars. With regard to this body, however, and at first glance, however, given the initial deterioration taking place in the body, the medics estimate the man has been dead for a week to ten days. Obviously a ‘hang-over’ execution from the recent gang wars. The mode of execution was four bullets to the head. He never knew what hit him. We believe he was killed elsewhere and body was dumped in the shed to conceal it for a while.”

“The gang war seems to have quietened down since the visit from London last Monday of the London supremo Ardajan Nikolaj, and the big mafia meeting of the super-syndicate of mafias at The Grange, although the number of deaths from the war is still quite high. Usually such a meeting does quieten the scene for a period and then passions take over again and the killing recommences. One of these days we are going to catch that man, Ardajan Nikolaj, red-handed. I have been promising myself for a long time."

"Yes that would be a good day for us. But this man is clever and well supported by his staff, even those who work in the brothels and indoor farms and certainly his shepherds who organise the county lines business and recruit the youngsters required to staff it. They all know that top-class legal assistance will be provided to them if they are ever arrested."

"By the way, Frank, the number of deaths from what we currently believe to have been synthetic opioid overdoses is also still climbing … more strongly now. That stuff is still getting into Ayton in ever greater quantities and our efforts to restrain the flow are not succeeding, it seems to me. What's your plan of action, Frank?"

"We need more intelligence, interceptions and convictions to take down some of the top people. The OCGs are becoming ever more sophisticated in transporting their poison. The softer drugs are normally transported in containers to Antwerp and less to Rotterdam, with some smaller amounts to LeHavre and Hamburg, then almost at once transferred to factories in The Netherlands for processing, before being transported once again to ports in the UK. Probably somewhere in the region of one hundred and fifty billion Euros plus in value is transported through this route annually. Twenty-five percent of this is intercepted by Europol and the local Police Forces and confiscated, much of it on arrival in Antwerp but some also en route to the other countries. But this is considered a normal on-cost for business by the gangs and they have the expertise and above all the money to find safer means of transportation, especially of the newer and more potent ones, for example by airlift in private planes, by submarine and so on. All of these are markers of the opulence of the gangs. But in the last resort the market is driven by the foolish demand of some members of our community, both young and old for ever stronger drugs. There is a lot of disillusionment out there in our community with many people seeking an escape from what they see as the arduous reality of their lives. Alienation is particularly rife amongst our young people and often youngsters from broken families join a criminal gang with or without incentives to boost their sense of status. From there sadly it's a one-way trip to drugs, addiction and in some cases an early death."

In order to lighten up their meeting, the Chief Constable tossed a happier query to her colleague.

"As you probably recall, this is the time of year when the precept for the Police service is set by the local authority. Although that represents only about one third of the total resources allocated to each force, it is an important element and I hear on the grape vine that due to inflation the increase this year will be large. What would you like to do, if a miracle happened and you were accorded additional funding for your work?"

"In any increase of staff we need to look for up-to-date modern cyber-skills. These really are the days of cybercrime, cryptocurrency and wire-tapping and we need people with the necessary skills in areas like decryption to support our work, regardless of age."

"Well, we could go on all day. But I am afraid that will have to be it for today. I have another meeting this morning with the Police, Fire and Crime Commissioner, Mark Elderson. He probably wants to register his own voice against some of the issues we have discussed here this morning. I have a large mountain of incoming communications to deal with as well. It's getting worse at an accelerating pace too. The bureaucracy required by central, regional and local governments is growing and growing and consuming time and resources from our real job of fighting crime. We are, as you know, having to cut back in areas, where we probably should not. We are, for example, no longer responding to mental health cases. The creeping corruption in society and in our own ranks is a source of great shame to me personally and to all the majority of honest Police officers. But with what additional resources can we fight it? Moreover, in addition to the huge costs necessary to pursue such items, for as long as they prevail in the mass media and Press, they carry with them a declining respect for the Police amongst the general Public and indeed for the whole system of Law and order, including the judiciary. Anyway, thank you as always very much for the report and for bringing me up to date and my sincere thanks also to your team of officers and civilians, who do so much unrecognised and invaluable work, not least in the incident room. I am sure we shall meet again soon. Bye and have a nice day."

"Please give my regards to your wife."

Chapter Twenty-Five: The Interview

"Good morning. Excuse me Ma'am. I just thought you might like to know that we shall be interviewing the suspect in the leakage case, Police Sergeant Anthony Birch, concerning the disclosure of covert information to the Ayton mafia gangs and several conspiracy charges with others this morning at ten o'clock. May I say that, if you wish and have the time in what I know is an overburdened schedule, you could watch, detached from the action, in the observation room."

"Yes, of course, Frank. I shall be there. Thank you very much for reminding me." The Chief Constable responded positivcly.

At ten o'clock prompt four people sat down in the interview room. DCI Frank Wozny spoke first to the tape recorder.

"Interview with Police Sergeant Tony Birch, presently acting head of the Ayton Armed Police Response Unit and his solicitor, a private lawyer, Mary Freeman, from the local firm of solicitors in the town centre, (frequently used by the OCGs in town), Pitts, Short and Freeman. Present also are .DCI Frank Wozny and Assistant Chief Constable, Adarsh Khanna. Sergeant Birch is here voluntarily to assist Police with their inquiries into the leakage of classified Police information to an Organised Crime Group. This is not a formal interview and he is here helping the Police with their enquiries. So just a warning to you that you, Sergeant Birch, are not obliged to answer the Police's questions, and that you are entitled to exercise your right to remain silent, if you so wish. Do you understand?"

"Yes!" Was the rather sullen and curt reaction

DCI Wozny paused for a second to check that all present were satisfied with the introductory statement. No one having objected, he proceeded to begin the interrogation of the sergeant.

"Sergeant Birch. Do you have any previously undeclared relationships with the Albanian mafia crime group, the Mafia Shqiptare cartel, here in Ayton or elsewhere?

"No!"

"Have you ever spoken to in the presence of or by telephone or visited any members of the Albanian mafia or any other organised Crime Group (OCG) in Ayton or outside?"

"No!"

"I'd like you to take a look at this person. Do you recognise or know this man? You may know him as Nico."

DCI Wozny passed across the table two copies of a photograph of a man, who was in fact Ardajan Nikolaj, the supremo of the Albanian mafia super cartel in the United Kingdom.

"No comment." Sergeant Birch responded having looked across to visually consult his solicitor, who had nodded back her assent.

"I want you to take a look at this photograph of these two men. Do you recognise them?"

DCI Wozny passed across the table a copy of a photograph of Sergeant Birch with the same member of the Albanian OCG. In fact the other man with Sergeant Birch who was actually with the same Ardajan Nikolaj, the supremo of the Albanian mafia super cartel in the United Kingdom, known in the trade as "Nico".

"No comment!"

"You recognise one of the men in the photograph do you?"

"No comment!"

"I'd like you to look at this next photograph of two men. Do you recognise either of them?"

DCI Wozny passed across the table a copy of a photograph of two men. One was Sergeant Birch and the other was the former Ayton head of the Albanian OCG in Ayton, and head of the Cartel's regional business, Sebastiano Gjoni, who had been assassinated by one of the other OCGs in the recent mob wars.

"No comment!"

"Sergeant Birch. I'd like you to take a look at this photograph of two men. Do you recognise either of them?" A copy of a photograph of two men was passed across the table by Assistant Chief Constable Khanna. It showed

Sergeant Birch with the new acting head of the Albanian mafia, the Mafia Shqiptare cartel, in Ayton, Tristen Plackici.

"No comment!"

"I'm going to pass an extract from your own mobile phone, showing several listings of the same phone number outgoing and incoming, underlined for your assistance. Who were you calling or receiving calls from so frequently?"

"No comment!"

"Finally I want you to look at this photograph of you entering an Albanian mafia so-called safe house, which was later raided by the Police, including you yourself as part of the team searching for a Police officer, who had been taken hostage. On the evening when the raid took place the property was, however, found to be empty and very recently deserted. Can you confirm that this is a photograph of you?"

"No comment"

"Sergeant Birch. I have here a copy of your Bank account over the past two years."

DCI Wozny passed a copy of the accounts over the table with the amounts to which he would wish to allude all highlighted. He continued with a request for information.

"With increased frequency and in growing amounts from five to ten thousand pounds on each occasion there have been deposits to your personal account from the same source. Could you kindly account for where this money came from?"

"No comment!"

"Sergeant Birch, I have here another photograph of you with three members of the local council, one of them a council officer. Do you know these men and in what connection were you meeting with them."

"No comment."

"Sergeant Birch. I have to tell you that you are now being formally charged with Misconduct in Public Office and you will be remanded in custody with the possibility of further charges of conspiracy. For the information of your solicitor, you will be interviewed again tomorrow under caution at ten o'clock here again. If, however, earlier access to you is required by your solicitor that will, of course, be automatically granted on request."

DCI Wozny then read Sergeant Birch the usual warning.

"You do not have to say anything. But, it may harm your defence if you do not mention when questioned something which you later rely on in court. Anything you do say may be given in Court in evidence."

Sergeant Birch was led away by a Police constable, who came in from outside the room, and taken to his cell accompanied by his solicitor.

Straight away after the end of the interview, the Chief Constable approached DCI Frank Wozny and Assistant Chief Constable Adarsh Khanna to request a short consultation and the three of them went to her office and sat round the coffee table. An offer of coffee was politely declined by the two visiting officers.

"You did very well, Frank, in exposing the lying Sergeant Birch. Are you intending to ask some of the same questions again tomorrow? And as a prelude to what?"

DCI Wozny spoke in response to the question in his usual well-informed manner.

"Yes, Ma'am and some others as well. The unit has discussed the inquiry plan and the specific questions. Our agreed plan is to issue the official warning first thing tomorrow, ask the same questions under caution, so that they can be recorded and used in evidence against him and then move on to the other aspects of his crimes, that is to say that the further evidence that I and my colleagues have collected. It will show that Birch did not act alone in any of this business with the mafia in Ayton. Our further evidence appears to show that he had the active co-operation of his solicitor, two city councillors and an official of the local council, all of whom, except the first mentioned were on the payroll of the Albanian cartel and received huge sums of cash from the main Albanian OCG into their accounts. To be precise, he is also guilty of conspiracy to commit several offences, alone and with others, and unless he agrees to co-operate he will go away for a very long time. The big advantage for us is that this morning has begun the process of stemming the constant seepage of information from us to the mafia and the consequent waste of a large chunk of the resources from our sparse funding."

He glanced across to the Chief Constable and smiled sweetly at her.

"With that gain to our budget, I am hoping for further allocations of urgently needed resource to the prosecution unit, which does such a fantastic job with very constrained resources in preparing and checking the documentation for submission to the regional Prosecution Service. I want to acknowledge the thorough and dedicated work of my colleagues in every tiny step forward."

"Well that's a bit cheeky, Frank. But I shall take it in the spirit it has been spoken in. One of rejoicing at a prosecution on the line, but also a more intensive use of our resources."

The next morning when the interview group convened. Sergeant Birch asked to make a statement.

"Consequent on consultation with my solicitor, I have decided to co-operate fully with the Police inquiry."

The statement was a shock, but a welcome one and one, which would save the Force a lot of money and human resources.

DCI Wozny looked at Sergeant Adarsh Khanna with a broad smile on his face.

Several months later, in the final proceedings in the regional Crown Court, a vast conspiracy of crime involving several arms of government and the mafia Shqiptare in drugs and people trafficking was uncovered and all the accused, including former Police Sergeant Anthony Birch, were sent to prison for a long, long period of time.

Surrounding the jubilation at the cracking of this racket, there was an acknowledgement in the unit that this was really only just a beginning and the next phase would be longer and harder than this one. But for the moment, however, there was a much needed mood of general celebration, which permeated the work of the Force.

A couple of months afterwards, but not quickly enough for him, DCI Wozny received a formal note from the Force finance officer. It was after the referral of the cases of the four men to the regional Prosecution Service, and the notice of the committal to the Crown Court. It stated that after detailed scrutiny by Finance some small amount of money had been found in some dusty corner of the Force's budget. There would be enough, it stated, for him to make two further civilian appointments from the beginning of the following month to strengthen the work of the Incident Unit. It was hoped that this move would accelerate the transfer of cases for prosecution to the CPS, thus yielding further economies!

He smiled to himself and then got on with his work of catching and locking up criminals. He received no communication from the Chief Constable about the finance officer's surprise note.

Chapter Twenty-Six: The Assassin

As Nico drove back to Ayton once more accompanied by an experienced marksman from the London office of the Firm, he cursed the staff in Ayton over and over again. He was obsessed by their incompetence and particularly in the execution of his desired objective of killing the senior Police officers in the Ayton Force, who were shredding his work of building up Ayton as the Firm's most profitable place in the UK. As he drove his top of the line AMG Line Premium Plus Edition Mercedes at some speed on the motorway, he was conscious that there was more than the future of the Firm's Ayton office on the line. His reputation was also at risk as was his prestigious and well-paying job in the UK.

For a moment his attention switched to his companion in the front of the car. Thoma Copja, the best sharpshooter in the London fiefdom and the most independent and expensive one. Still looking young and smartly dressed with what looked like an old-school tie and a well-trimmed moustache. Thoma was not a formal member of the Albanian mafia organised crime group. He worked independently and was paid for each job. He had a full record of success. He had served with distinction as a sniper in the Kosovo Liberation Army and uniquely had ended up with the rank of full colonel at the end of the war. Thoma's record was perfect by any standards.

He never failed. If he had any doubts whatsoever about a job after his advance appraisal, for which he made a nominal charge, he promptly turned the offer down. He never accepted an assignment, about which he had the slightest doubt of its feasibility. In such rare cases, he would normally suggest that the syndicate use one of its own snipers, of which there were several of varying competence and quality. For his part he wanted to maintain his reputation by only choosing the best and safest of the offers of jobs. He took his own time, made his own decisions and normally made his own arrangements for any job he accepted too. There was suspicion in the London branch of the syndicate that he also did jobs for other OCGs as well, though this was never broached in his negotiations with Nico about future jobs.

Nico reverted to his obsession. He complained silently that he was having to spend too much time in Ayton and on its interminable problems. It would be better to abandon the whole business set-up in Ayton and start elsewhere. And in addition the journey had become increasingly tiresome. Above all, the last time he made this journey, he had been stopped by two troublesome local members of the filth and detained for at least half an hour with an array of, to his way of thinking, irrelevant questions. Of course they had found nothing because he made damned sure he did not have anything.

On the other hand, he thought, Ayton could with the right staff yet again be made once more a lavish and rewarding place for the syndicate to do business and make healthy profits. That was especially the case with the arrival of the lucrative new synthetic opioid drugs, over which his syndicate held almost total dominance nationally and in the region. That was the main complaint of the other gangs at the recent meeting that he had arranged for the major OCGs. They wanted a share. It didn't get them anywhere though, he thought, convincing himself that was the end of that particular concern.

"Nico turned off the motorway onto the slip road for Ayton. Unsurprisingly one of the two Police officers, who he considered had pestered him before, waved him down and approached the front of the car. Nico wound down the front window and prepared himself for what he fully expected to be a repetition of the previous pantomime.

"Good morning, sir. Good to see you're on another of your family visits to Ayton. Not long since we met you on your last visit. Another wedding this time sir? See you have another family member with you this time."

His colleague approached Nico's car from the other side. The officers' body cam recorded pictures of both occupants of the car. At once the pictures were uploaded to thc Police station in Ayton.

"Anyway, mustn't keep you." The first Police officer offered. "Have a nice visit to Ayton, sir. See you again next time. Take care!"

He waved to Nico for the car to proceed and Nico cursed him silently and sped away.

"Did you come this way the last time you came to Ayton, Nico?" Thoma asked.

"Well, yes I did." Nico said very hesitantly, because he instantly realised now what Thoma was getting at.

"Were you stopped by the same pair of coppers last time?"

"Yes." Nico ventured, feeling all the time more uncomfortable.

Thoma changed tack.

"When we enter Ayton, could you kindly drop me at the Grand in the town centre? Don't wait! Just pull away when I have taken my things from the boot. The doorman will help me."

"But we've made arrangement for you to stay at the safe house and one of my colleagues has been designated to respond to your every need."

"Well thank you very much. But that won't be necessary." Thoma replied insistently. "By the way, how many others of your colleagues know that I am coming and what job I am going to undertake?"

"Well the men talk among themselves. So I cannot give a precise answer that question." Nico replied shakily and added, trying to make a very weak justification for what he now recognised that Thoma regarded as gross mistakes. "But they are all very Trustworthy. All from Albania or Kosovo."

Anyway, I'll detour for The Grand, as you have requested. We're actually nearly there now. How do we keep in touch?"

"We don't!" Thoma replied insistently. He added very powerfully. "When I have completed the job, I shall contact you directly on a burner phone to give the go-ahead for the payment. In that call I shall include details of any additional expenses and repeat our agreed fee for the job. Then you will not see me again, at least not until our next job together."

Nico managed to stop directly in front of the main entrance to the hotel and Thoma dismounted from the car and was instantly recognised and approached by the uniformed doorman, who helped him carry his large case and back-pack up the steps into the hotel. Nico reached across the cab to say farewell, but Thoma was already entering the open door of the hotel trailed by the rather over-burdened doorman. Nico pulled away in a mood of depression and personal anger at the revelation of his own mistakes. Was he getting too old?

The photographs of Nico and Thoma were received instantaneously at the main Police station by the civilian employee responsible, Jasminder Kaur, a retired Ombudsperson in the incident room. Recognising their significance without delay Jasminder referred the photographs to DCI Wozny in the incident room, who asked another civilian employee, Mary Porteous, to do a thorough check as top priority on the records of the two men. She should look particularly at any details about the smartly dressed younger-looking man with the bright school tie and a well-trimmed moustache. She should feel free to contact our friends at the Met, if she needed to do so.

When Mary, also a retired lawyer from the incident room had obtained the relevant information, including material that was shared by the Met, she provided a copy of the material to DCI Wozny at once and he contacted the Chief Constable and asked for an urgent meeting of the top security team, but excluding of course the disgraced and dismissed Acting Head of the Police Armed Response Unit.

The meeting took place over lunch and sandwiches and tea or coffee were provided for those attending. The Chief Constable chaired the meeting and others present were, the deputy Chief Constable, Rajiv Gundara, Detective Chief Inspector Rajan Appasamy, and the two Assistant Chief Constables Adarsh Khanna and Maria Clarke.

DCI Wozny began the briefing at the invitation of the Chief Constable.

"We have today received several photographs of two men from our officers at the Ayton slip-road. One of the men, the older man, is well-known to us as the Head of the Albanian mafias in the UK, Ardajan Nikolaj, commonly referred to as Nico. He is a frequent visitor to the Ayton region. The other much younger man has been identified by our colleagues at the Met in London as Thoma Copja. He has no Police record but is reliably recorded as a very skilled assassin, working independently, who is not a member of any OCG, but who works the OCG market for assignments from whichever group wants someone discretely killed without fuss or trace of the perpetrator. The Met Police have been on his trail for some time in connection with a number of unsolved assassinations, but in spite of having been invited to a voluntary meeting to assist Police with their inquiries some time ago, they have never found anything to nail him with. My theory is that, locally engaged assassins have proved incompetent and that is probably the explanation for the injuries of our three fellow officers the other week. My theory is that he has been brought in as a last resort to fulfil the pledge to assassinate senior members of this Force. The challenge for us is to decide what further action we can take to ensure that he does not succeed?"

"Do we know, where in Ayton he is staying?" Assistant Chief Constable Khanna asked.

Regrettably not! At least not yet!" Was the brusque and disappointing return.

In the meantime Thoma had advanced to the reception desk and persuaded the young receptionist that he needed a room at the back of the hotel on the top floor, which he had occupied the last time he had visited because he needed his undisturbed rest during the night and the front rooms could be a little noisy at times. The receptionist was sympathetic and Thoma booked and paid in advance for three nights' accommodation, not inclusive of meals. The receptionist summoned one of the pageboys to take Mr Smythe to look at the three available rooms at the back of the hotel and choose the one which was most convenient to him. The receptionist also called a porter so that he could carry Mr Smythe's luggage with him.

The three entered the lift and travelled to the top floor. There he was shown the available rooms, of which one was in the centre and had a lovely view out of the window onto the beautiful mature, perhaps ancient, hedge and row of mature trees with only an unmade private road between the hotel and the hedge. That was the one he chose. When the porter had been generously rewarded and the page boy had received a small token of appreciation, Thoma closed the door and made sure that it was locked.

He then went back to the window and regarded the progress of Autumn on the deciduous trees and the hedge. Satisfied, he began to unpack and ordered a room lunch and large pot of tea, which was delivered very swiftly. He returned to the window and using his now unpacked binoculars spied at least two 'pathways' through the swiftly thinning vegetation, which offered a clear view of the back entrance of the Police station some twenty meters beyond the other side of the hedge and the row of now largely bare trees.

There he noted as well the new fence around the entrance to keep back any would-be intruders. Although it had appeared since he was last there doing his reconnaissance just after he had been given his current assignment, he did not know that it had been very recently erected due to the attempted murder of a Police officer on guard at the very entrance that he was now surveying. But he nodded satisfaction to himself because the new fence would keep back any potential crowding around that entrance and it would also render it necessary for those exiting the building to walk a few yards over clear ground to get into their cars. That gave him additional clear space as well.

Having made his rough calculations about the feasibility of the shot he planned, he sat down and casually ate his lunch, deferring more precise and accurate calculations until later. Not too late however, to miss the exodus from the building at the end of the work day. He wanted to be away again by the early evening for another commission the day after tomorrow. He was also conscious that the longer he had to stay the greater was the danger. He unpacked his equipment and stationed himself in front of the now open window inconspicuously and waited.

In the intervening period, the meeting of senior staff had finished and the group had dispersed to get on with their ordinary jobs or with the search for the elusive Thoma … with no success yet! It was as though he had disappeared from the face of the earth. At the end of the afternoon, the Deputy Chief Constable, Rajiv Gundara, entered the office of the Chief Constable to ask for a lift as his car was in for servicing. She agreed very willingly feeling at the very least that she could reciprocate for his similar favour towards her some weeks ago. They both wanted to avoid having to hire a taxi feeling it could be a potential danger after the new warning signs of a possible attack against senior officers.

Long after most employees had departed at the end of the working day, she rang the car pool and asked for her car to be brought round to the rear of the building, where it would be parked outside the fenced area. They exited the lift together and, with just a tickle of other officers leaving the building, they walked towards the entrance where through the glass doors they could see her car was now parked with the chauffeur inside waiting for them and both back doors wide open on the other side of the new fence. The Chief Constable was carrying a wodge of papers in her arms to be attended to at home that night and did not look up.

They had walked slowly only a couple of meters when there was a crack and the Chief constable stumbled with a hole in the forehead and fell to the ground and her papers scattered like leaves falling from a deciduous tree in Autumn.

Thoma collected his things together including his collapsible long arm weapon, telescopic sight or scope and pistol, packed them and locked the suitcase. He rang the car hire firm, where he had previously ordered a vehicle for a few days under an assumed name. The car firm assured him the car would be in front of the hotel within minutes. He then telephoned reception and said that he had unfortunately just received a call announcing the death of his dear wife and would have to leave this minute. He did not require a rebate and they could add his lunch as a further debit to his card. Could the porter please come and collect his luggage.

By the time the porter came and moved his luggage downstairs, the car, a modest Ford Puma was parked in front of the hotel with a full tank of petrol. Thoma sent a short message to Nico. "Job completed. Payment as usual plus extras as stated." He supervised the loading of his luggage, rewarding the porter handsomely and departed. Within the hour, he was far away from the chaos which had erupted in the meantime at the Ayton Police station.

Chapter Twenty-Seven: Crisis

Like a London smog of the nineteen fifties, a pall of deep sadness descended over everyone in the Ayton Police Force. Mixed in with the revulsion at what was seen in the Police Station as the vile assassination of the Chief Constable and the compassion for her nearest and dearest, there was also a sense of being left leaderless and for the very first time there seemed to be confusion about who was in charge of what in the Ayton Police Force. In fact her death had left the organisation with an overarching feeling of the loss of leadership throughout at a crucial moment in the fight against the criminal gangs. Pending decisions became neglected and even everyday duties were done with a heavy heart and no great enthusiasm.

Numbers on sick leave climbed rapidly and as a consequence the time taken for critical decisions lengthened even more. Submission of material to the Regional Prosecution Service and as evidence for the Courts was delayed, which also brought with it inevitable consequences. The energy and dynamism seemed to have gone out of the whole Ayton Police Force.

One of those unintended consequences of the delays was an increase in the amount of drugs stored in secure warehouses. The warehouses were already filled to overflowing partly because of the postponement of the dates of trials in the Courts This in turn delayed further the transportation of drugs to the only two pollution-free incinerators available for burning drugs in the whole of the Ayton conurbation. The deferment of the treatment in incinerators also meant that decisions had to be taken in a rather ad hoc fashion to store incoming material from new raids in sometimes makeshift, less secure warehouses.

That move, however, in turn rocketed the cases of the successful theft of impounded substances by the various OCGs from the new warehouses and emboldened the thieves. In some cases during the thefts the warehouse guards were threatened with guns, and physical violence was exercised against them. In one case, all the guards were tied up and threatened with a knife to their throat. One of them suffered post-traumatic stress syndrome after his experience at one of the new warehouses.

The deputy Chief Constable, Rajiv Gundara, tried to step into the breach and revive the morale of the Force. But attempting do his own very onerous job at the same time as caretaking the responsibilities of the assassinated Chief Constable proved not only traumatic, but impossible. In fact in health terms the attempt had proved almost fatal for a man of his age. With the Ayton Police Force in almost total disarray, it was perhaps not surprising that in such circumstances the local mobs would seek to take advantage of the situation.

In the days following the assassination of the Chief Constable of Ayton Police there were several instances of Police cars being torched in the streets. In some cases Police officers were spat on, insulted and assaulted when going about their normal duties. Fortunately none were seriously injured. New sale points for drugs were set up by different OCGs audaciously in several parks, outside retail outlets, recreation centres, educational institutions and other Public places. The fence around Ayton College was deliberately breached in several places, facilitating the import of drugs into the institution to be more freely available to the students.

Several Public figures requested Police protection after threats and missiles being thrown at their houses and/or offices. There were vicious fights between county lines runners from different mafia groups, some of which resulted in injuries and in a few cases some of the drug purveyors required hospitalisation and one died from his injuries. Knife and gun fights between members of opposing mafia groups took place in open daylight sometimes in Public places and resulted in some civilian collateral damage, in one or two cases causing serious injury, hospitalisation and in one case death.

Mindful of the serious criminal situation developing on the streets and the serious loss of morale and performance in the Ayton Police Force itself, the Deputy Chief Constable, Rajiv Gundara, called a meeting of all senior staff to sort out the responsibilities of the senior staff, make them crystal clear and subsequently to inform all officers about who their line manager was. If and when necessary clarification of their duties would be offered to officers and civilian staff once more, and the lines of managerial communication between and among them would be clearly and diagrammatically illustrated.

Attending the meeting in addition to the Deputy Chief Constable were DCI Wozny, Detective Chief Inspector Rajan Appasamy, Head of the Specialised Criminal Investigation Department, and the two Assistant Chief Constables, Adarsh Khanna and Maria Clarke. By special agreement, because there was no current head of the Police Armed Response Unit, the most senior member of that

Unit, Inspector Charlie Brangwyn, a man of long service and the utmost proven probity in his work with the Force, was invited to temporarily fill the gap. In order to attempt to demonstrate the objectivity of the group and its decisions, the local Police, Fire and Crime Commissioner, Mark Elderson, was invited to attend in addition as an observer. By the unanimous agreement of the group, Deputy Chief Inspector Gundara was invited to act as Chair for the meeting. He began by thanking them all for their support of himself at this difficult time for the Force and to apologise for any 'snarl-up' at this stressful time for officers.

"Thank you all for managing to attend this meeting this morning at such short notice in spite of the crisis in our Force at the moment. Thank you as well for your support for me personally in the impossible task that I have tried to do to the best of my ability for the last little while. The aim of this meeting is to sort out definitively the load of responsibilities and lines of communication in the Force. I am happy to continue to take on the functions and responsibilities of our sadly departed, Chief Constable, but unfortunately I cannot do that and continue with my existing duties as Deputy. I should say that I have no ambition personally to be appointed in due course as Chief Constable. I am too old for that. So as soon as the next Chief Constable has been appointed, I shall hand over and probably apply for premature retirement. Basically we are looking for someone to take over the role of Deputy Chief Constable. Any offers. Frank, you wish to speak."

"Well, yes, Rajiv. But not to take on the job. I suspect that there are roles in the Force, that cannot be transferred to anyone else and mine is one of them."

"Yes, I agree." Rajiv confirmed.

The next one to speak to colleagues was Rajan Appasamy, Head of the specialised Criminal Investigation Department.

"Sadly, I find myself in the same situation as Frank. I just do not see any possibility of relinquishing my responsibilities. Firstly we have only just started the Unit and we have lots of cases pending, which need to be pursued with all due speed. Secondly if I moved there would be no one in the small team, who at this moment in time would be capable of taking over. Sorry! But quite frankly it is best for the Force if I stay where I am."

Adarsh Khanna was the next to speak.

"Well. It looks as though Maria and I are the only ones left. I am easy about taking on all the roles of both Assistant Chief Constables or to move up to take the temporary job of Deputy Chief Constable. Maria, what do you think?"

"I am in the same position as you, Adarsh. I would be happy to do either role as you have outlined."

Adarsh replied positively.

"In that case I suggest that you take on the temporary position of Deputy Chief Constable. I am sure that you would do the job well and you're young enough to take on the task. It would be a good preparation for your future promotions and I have always thought that one day you would be moving onwards and upwards. In any case I am feeling a little long in the tooth these days."

"That is so kind of you and thank you also for your comments about me. I agree to your proposal. I believe that apart from what to do about the interim leadership of the Police Armed Response Unit, that also concludes a major part of our business today."

Rajiv agreed and swiftly passed the issue of the leadership of the Unit to its longest serving member, Charlie Brangwyn.

"So what do we do about the interim leadership of the Armed Response Unit, which is critically indispensable to our overall plan to close down as many and as much of the real estate and workforce of the OCGs as possible? Charlie, what do you think, having so many years of service in the Unit?"

"Well if you're asking me if I could take on the interim leadership of the Ayton Police Armed Response Unit, the answer is yes, of course! But like some of our colleagues here today, I am a little long in the tooth and I am looking forward to retiring and getting on with my fishing in the next year. I am happy to give you time to engage a permanent replacement for me and at that time I shall be happy to step down and fish!"

Thank you Charlie that is so typically kind of you. Thank you very much." Rajiv expressed his appreciation and continued.

“As a consequence of the decisions made here today, I, and hopefully you too, Maria, will draw up a new flow chart of the management structure of the Force and distribute it to all officers. We shall add an open invitation that if any officer or member of staff is unsure about their line management or responsibilities, they should consult with Maria, soonest. Is that OK, Maria?”

“Yes, of course, Rajiv. You’re the top boss now!”

Maria smiled at Rajiv and he reacted generously with a broad and welcoming grin and then proceeded to introduce the last major decision concerning the next raid.

“Well that is all great news and now we have a chance to hit back at those folk, who are trying to overthrow the rule of Law in Ayton and replace it with the worst kind of anarchy. Now for the next raid! Will it be a so-called safe house, an indoor drug farm or a brothel?”

Charlie leapt up to be the first to speak and expressed himself clearly and rationally.

“My firm view is based on the value of human life. All human lives. It’s also based on the fact that I have a wonderful wife and three lovely daughters, to all of whom I owe so much. So my immediate reaction to your request for us to state where we estimate that we can have most impact is by closing down one of the Albanian mafia’s largest brothels. Coincidentally that raid will deprive the criminal gang of about one million pounds income per year. But the main objective is to free those young women from their cruel and inhuman slavery for good and to put those wicked men, who are placing them in bondage, behind bars."

"Here! Here!" The resounding cry of agreement from all members of the group filled the room.

"Right then! To the responsibility for planning the raid and deciding when. Frank are you willing to ply your usual role of overall officer in charge?"

Yes of course and I can also take the responsibility of calling the meeting and clearing the plans with all departments concerned."

"Charlie, I am afraid that means that, given the size of the establishment and the likely number of armed men there when we raid it, we shall need the authorised Firearms officers to spearhead the raid, fully equipped and with ballistic shields of course."

"Don't be afraid, boss, I am happy to co-ordinate with Frank and I assure you that you will have a keen and well qualified team, well equipped to deal firmly with any would-be malefactors, and as effective a team as you have ever had."

"Thank you Charlie and also to all of you. It is my privilege to work with such a fine group of officers. I am sure that with the co-operative will that you have shown today, we can overcome the problems that afflict the Force at the moment and fight the criminals at the same time. Oh and by the way I almost forgot two pieces of good news for us, bad news for the criminal gangs. Firstly, Thoma Copja has been arrested in London and is helping Police with their inquiries into the murder of the Chief Constable of Ayton. Secondly, our interception team on the motorway have placed a member of the Albanian criminal gang here in Ayton under arrest. He was stopped on the slip road driving a small van by our officers with three kilos of cocaine and a full house of Class A drugs, including cocaine, ecstasy, heroin, LSD, magic mushrooms and crystal meth, as well as some samples of fentanyl all hidden in the boot of his car. Quite a bonanza of drugs taken off the market. He was obviously transporting them for the gang here in Ayton. Just one more proof that these criminals will not succeed! Thanks to our interception team and thanks again to you and good luck!"

There were cries of approval from all members of the group at the first good news since the murder of their Chief Constable.

With that the members of the group dashed away to their old or in some cases new jobs to get on with the work of trying to keep Ayton safe for all its citizens. But would it be safe for members of the Ayton Police Force?

Chapter Twenty-Eight: Compassion

It was the end of a busy day for all three of them. The children had taken part in extra-curricular activities, such as chess and gymnastic club and Andrea had had a meeting at the College about a new scheme to get some of the ghost students back into school and pair them up with a friend and perhaps also a family. Since she had dropped her responsibilities as Chair of the College Governing Body, she had managed to devote much more attention to the children and also to commencing some new ideas, for which she just did not have free time before.

On the other hand, she had not neglected her responsibilities to the College. The outline plan, termed 'College Return', discussed in fragmentary form at the last Board meeting had been proposed to the Governing Board and the Academic Board by Andrea. It had been favourably received on the whole in both bodies, but with some fundamental reservations from some members and with a note of resignation that it was needed by some others.

The three members of the family were lounging in the front room of the small semi-detached house where they had lived all their lives, relaxing and drinking a cup of tea and a piece of Grandma Isabel's very popular chocolate cake. They were all as usual chattering away in a fairly light-hearted manner. The children, Melissa aged fourteen and Jeremy aged twelve, were speaking about what they had done during the day and after the end of the formal day's timetable. Jeremy said he was looking forward to another birthday soon and just could not wait to see his presents. Melissa spoke about her successes at the Gym Club.

The afternoon get-together was a regular occurrence and it was a chance for some humour about the College and its staff as also some serious points about the curriculum. It was also an opportunity for them to exercise their skills of arguing rationally and coolly and for them to share with the others any unusual happenings. It gave them an opportunity as well to raise any problems or concerns where they might seek to ease their own mind by sharing those issues with each other.

Melissa was speaking about her small clique of friends at College and she mentioned Aisha, with whom she had had a particularly close relationship ever since they both joined the College together some years ago. In a rather worried way, Aisha had shared with her that very day during the midday break that during a rather long and boring talk at the mosque on Friday, the Imam had spoken in a derogatory way about Jews and prayed to Allah for the death of all of them and their children.

"Well, I said to Aisha." "I don't know a great deal about these things, but I'll ask my mum this evening and come back to you tomorrow, if that's alright. But I said to her that at first hearing, it does not seem to me a very friendly thing to say. Anyway, she agreed but asked me not to tell anyone else and here I am asking you about the matter she raised in confidence with me."

Andrea tried to respond to her daughter's question in a helpful way.

“I am not an expert on Islamic matters or the English Law, but I do know that we now have quite a large number of neighbours, who are Moslem, both in the country as a whole and here at home in Ayton, indeed in this street too. Without in any way being dismissive or derogatory about what your friend, Aisha, has told you, it is clearly a report of what one person heard and how she heard and interpreted it. So I ‘m going to start my response with a big ‘if’. If the report were corroborated or the gentleman voluntarily confirmed that he had said it, I believe that it would be a very serious breach of the Law, to threaten or advocate the murder of any group of people, no matter who that might be. Imagine also what your friend Aisha would feel if someone said the same about her community or someone said it about our community. Also it seems to me that it does not make for a very friendly society where we could all be happy, but different, celebrating our differences as they say in Canada in French and English there. That’s my off the cuff reaction. Let’s try to celebrate our differences, is what I say. Does that answer your question, Melissa, my Love?”

Jeremy interrupted before Melissa could answer the question.

.”That’s interesting what Melissa just asked because I believe that my friend Muhamad made roughly the same point in conversation with a group of friends in the College recreational area. I like his company and he’s an absolute wizard at maths, and like Melissa I thought to myself I’ll ask Mum about that. By the way we also have a small group of students of Jewish faith in the College, boys and girls, and I felt very sorry for them if they heard what was reported to have been said. I decided there and then that I would go out of my way and make a point of speaking to them the next time I meet one or more of them at school."

Andrea complimented her son and then shared something with them about their own family.

"Well done! That's what I would have done. As you have gathered. I believe that we should be helpful and speak in a civil way about and to others. We are all different and we can learn a lot from people, who are different from us. So let's do what the Canadians advocate and try to do, namely celebrate our differences. That reminds me also that I have been remiss in not speaking about our family and particularly our immediate past ancestors."

"Yes, please do, Mum. Apart from Grandma, Isabel, we know nothing about our ancestors. Who were they Mum?" Jeremy asked intrigued.

"Well for a start, your grandfather, whom you never met was Jewish, born of a Jewish mother and father. His mother died in childbirth and it was his father for a short time and later his bully of an uncle, who raised him. He was born and lived in a small settlement on the outskirts of a small town called Prerov in The Czech Republic, Czechia as it is now called officially. I have never been there, but from the descriptions of my mother, your grandmother, your grandfather, Andrei, described it as having a well-preserved and historic city centre and being situated on the a river called the Bečva. In the past, he said, it had been a major crossroads in the heart of Moravia in the Czech Republic.

She paused for a second to let them catch up and then continued.

"Anyway there was a lot of prejudice against people of Jewish heritage there and during the war, somewhere in the region of fifty percent of the population of Jews in the country had been killed. That prejudice still existed when Andrei was born. When he attended school, for example, the other students made fun of him because he was a Jew. So to cut a very long story short, he decided to leave the Prerov area and went to Prague, the capital of the country. There one day he met a family group of people from Ayton, including your grandma. He was so attracted by what they said about their home town. He was especially struck by the way in which Grandma, a very young woman at the time, said so eloquently about their town in England. It was just after Czechia had joined the European Union, and so he had free access to the countries of the Union. He travelled first to London and then to Ayton. He renewed his acquaintance with your Grandma and they fell in love and had a child called Andrea."

"That's me!" Andrea called out in surprise and Andrea pressed on.

"Your late father and I had two children called Melissa and Jeremy and that is you two."

"Well what a wonderful story you have to tell, Mum. Why didn't you tell us this story before?" Melissa queried.

Well it never really occurred to me. It just never seemed relevant to our lives here in Ayton until now."

"Well!" Said Jeremy. "It certainly seems relevant now!"

"Yes. I think you are both right and perhaps I should write an account of your Grandfather's home and life one day after I retire." She suggested humorously.

"Yes please!" The two children expleted their approval together and Jeremy added. "And why not now, Mum? Please!"

"Well. Let me think about it. I'd like to share with you an idea that I have just presented informally to the College Board of Governors at its meeting today. You know that we have students called 'ghost students' at the College, that means students who attend College and then usually suddenly disappear either permanently or for a short period of time. Many of them are enticed by the mafia gangs in Ayton with drugs or sometimes with other incentives such as fashion clothes, food or foot-ware."

She broke what she had to say and smiled broadly at them both, as if to say, don't despair. I have almost finished and she tried to shorten what remained for her to say.

"Some of them return. Then it often happens that before long they are being lured back again. Some of those who leave again are taken as slave workers to work in appalling, inhuman conditions in indoor drug farms. Alternatively they are used as county lines runners to deliver drugs to areas and customers outside the county lines of the administrative unit, in this case Ayton. Many of these students come from broken families or even no families at all. Some are on drugs to start with, others are not. I think that if we could find some way of giving some at least of these students support by friendship with other students and for those with no family to support them, time with the family of a College friend, that might enable at the very least some of these students to return to the straight and narrow. It might also give the strength and support to resist the further enticements of the criminal gangs and forge a half-way decent life for themselves in the future. What do you think?"

Both Melissa and Jeremy had been educated by both their parents how to present an argument dispassionately and to present a case as coolly and rationally as they could. Their relaxation sessions and the discussions that followed showed the wisdom of this dimension of the children's upbringing.

Melissa answered first. "I think this is a good idea. But I also think it is a rough diamond. It could work or it could fail miserably drawing the participating family and their child or children into the same cycle of drug dominated bondage as the so-called ghost student."

Jeremy added his agreement.

"I agree with Melissa. The plan is very rough at the edges at the moment. It contains dangers for the student and his/her family as well. What you need is to refine the plan and try to pilot in in one or two families before trying it on a more widespread basis."

Andrea acknowledged the value of the idea of a pilot run-through and tried to make it relevant to their lives, asking the question how would they feel, if they were involved in such a plan?

"Let me ask you a follow-up question then. Jeremy you mention a pilot scheme first. Would the two of you be willing to be members of the first pilot scheme?"

"What would that mean for us Mum? In detail I mean for the family and for us?" Melissa asked in a fairly disbelieving tone.

Jeremy added a query about the gender of any prospective guest student.

"Yes, and what would you do about the gender issue? Presumably you would match male with male and female with female?"

"These are good questions, some of which I had not thought about." Andrea responded positively to the concerns raised by her children. "For example if we participated in the first pilot, would we prefer a male or a female? And depending on gender, where would we sleep them?" Andrea solicited some ideas.

"Mum that is an absolutely fundamental question. We only have three small bedrooms and one bathroom and shower cum toilet. There could be an awful queue in the mornings. So there can only be one reply to the question of sleeping. For example if we tried to match gender and location that might work. Or we could put a camp bed in the dining room downstairs or … erect a tent in the garden!" Melissa tried to respond in a light-hearted fashion.

"Yes but putting the visitor in the dining room on an uncomfortable camp bed might cause the very feeling of being excluded, that we want to avoid. If we put the guest student in the dining room, away from all of us and away from the facilities, I think it would just flop." Jeremy suggested rather sharply and Melissa concurred and added a further problematic dimension very delicately.

"Yes and let's remember that both of us, Jeremy and I, are at a very delicate and sometimes problematic time of life, getting used to our bodies changing and new things appearing and happening. I am not sure that I would want even a girl of my own age to be present in my bedroom. It could be highly embarrassing and totally excludes any idea of mixed-sex bedrooms."

"Yes, I take your point having gone through that phase myself many years ago." Andrea responded positively.

"But how about if I moved in with Melissa, or rather put it the other way round because I have a bigger bedroom than Melissa, moved in with me. In that case for example our guest could have their own bedroom near us and on the same floor, whatever the gender."

"Well that is a good idea, Mum. But frankly without wanting to hurt your feelings, I have to say that I am not sure that I would want to be in the same bedroom as you. No offence, Mum!"

Jeremy then opened up the possibility of a completely different arrangement.

“Mum. I wonder how Grandma might feel about a guest student staying with her. Even if the student perhaps had all their meals with us? I just do not know.”

“What a good idea. I had never thought of that. But of course we have not spoken to Grandma about it and she might object fundamentally to a stranger being in the house when she was alone. I just don’ know. But it does add another dimension to our discussion and open up other alternative arrangements such as one of you living with Grandma and the guest student living with the other two of us in this house.”

That idea did not seem to find favour with either of them and both of them made glum faces.

“Anyway, we had better leave it there for the moment. I know that both of you have several subjects of homework this evening and I don’t want to interfere with that. I’ll undertake to have a word with Grandma about the idea and let you know what comes of it, if anything. Thanks again for the ideas and dinner will be as usual at seven o’clock this evening.”

“Fish fingers again tonight?” Andrea joked.

Following her promise to raise the idea of a ghost student being lodged with Grandma, when Isabel dropped of the children from school the next day, Andrea shared the idea with her and discovered something totally different from what she was expecting and that she did not know about and which worried her. Grandma’s reply was perturbing.

I would have loved to participate in your imaginative plan. Unfortunately when I went to the hospital a few weeks ago about some troublesome symptoms, I was diagnosed with mantle cell lymphoma, an incurable blood cancer. Consequently I have to go into hospital regularly to have chemotherapy and receive through a drip a mixture of six drugs including one called rituximab. It is a bit lengthy for me at the moment and I must say that I always feel very tired after the experience, although it is not in itself unpleasant. We are given free tea or coffee and a super choice of biscuits!"

"Mum. I'm so sorry. You should have told me earlier and I could have helped."

"Well I didn't want you to worry then and I don't want to worry you now. But it means that sadly I shall not be able to help with your next brilliant idea, Andrea, my Love. And remember. Mantle cell lymphoma is incurable but not terminal, if treated properly, and I am very fortunate that I have a good team supporting me and a good choice of biscuits." She jested.

And that was how the issue of Andrea's imaginative proposal was left, at the same time as another very serious challenge arose for Jeremy.

After the meeting of the senior management group and the distribution of new details describing the lines of management and communication in the organisation, a newly awakened positive atmosphere seemed to descend fairly swiftly on the workings of the Ayton Police Force. There was a certain amount of confident excitement among the officers designated to participate in the raid of the largest Albanian brothels in Ayton and this gave impetus to the preparations and infected other staff.

The newly agreed Acting Chief Constable of Ayton, Rajiv Gundara had taken to his new role with his usual tenacity, acumen and versatility. He had speedily assembled the team, which would bankrupt the mafia gang, or at least that was the intention. In the main role to lead the entry to the brothel was Charlie Brangwyn, acting Head of the Ayton Police Armed Response Unit, and long-term, trustworthy Police Officer in the Ayton Force.

He, in turn, picked the men from the Unit, who would conduct the first entry to the premises. He checked their equipment and firearms and each man repeated the checks with a partnered colleague. Each man would carry a holstered a self-loading pistol, a Glock 17, in a holster on their person. Long-barrelled firearms', such as the H&K MP5SF and H&K G36C carbines, would be secured in each of the accompanying vehicles and each man was tested in advance in their competent use of these weapons as well. Over several meetings Charlie outlined the tactics that they would employ and at what points they would be deployed. Insofar as it was known, each man was also made aware of the internal disposition of the accommodation in each of the two buildings and the different function of each of the premises, as well as the outside environment and likely escape points for the gangsters.

In preparation for the raid, Charlie had already done a brief recce of the sites to be raided that night, and he was able to brief his team about them. This he did in a pre-raid meeting with all officers the evening before the raid. Both buildings were located some two miles outside the centre of the town on a major dual carriageway and bus route. He informed them. There was a small shopping centre nearby. But it was not a major out-of-town centre for shoppers. Some of the existing stores were now unoccupied and boarded up.

The premises to be raided comprised two buildings on opposite sides of a minor road with both having sides onto a dual carriageway. The buildings had previously housed two cinemas, the Elite and the Coliseum but after alteration, they now served the one as a mafia brothel and the other as a mafia indoor drug farm.

The physical difference between the two sites, he informed his colleagues, was that the former Elite ‘picture house’ had its main entrance straight onto the pavement at the side of the main dual carriageway and was consequently used as a very busy brothel and a great money spinner for the mafia gangsters. The Coliseum, on the other hand, had its main entrance onto the minor roadway about the side of the former cinema faced some twenty meters away from the top of the minor road, where it joined the dual carriageway. It also had a small side door, which looked on to the main dual carriageway at a distance of some ten to fifteen meters away. He alerted the officers that it was likely that most resistance would come from the men in the indoor drug farm, which was a major local provider of cocaine for the local criminal gangs. It was, therefore, also a major money spinner for the Albanian mafia in Ayton.

Just in case some of the officers had not encountered it before, Charlie also briefed the officers from the Ayton Armed Police Response Unit that cannabis plants let off a strongly heady smell when flowering and this smell had likely filtered out to the extent that the whole building would be impregnated with the smell of the plant. The initial reconnoitres had encountered the smell from outside the building. So if not already before they entered, this is the very pungent smell that their nostrils would encounter as they entered the building.

There was an irregular shaped piece of unused wasteland of about ten to fifteen meters in width and at least twenty in length between the side of the Coliseum and the dual carriageway. This land would perhaps be ideal for parking some of the Police vehicles, but the side door could also perhaps be an additional entry point, if needed. Unfortunately, as the deliberately spread street rumour had been that the buildings were being redesigned to act as two competing supermarkets, there was precious little actual knowledge of the inside shape or dimensions of either of the premises and the plans submitted to the local authority were likely to be inaccurate if not downright misleading.

That deficit of knowledge about the inside of both buildings and the duality of the overall sites presented some major logistic problems for the raid. Not least was the question of which one to tackle first or whether to raid them both simultaneously. This latter decision presented, in turn, the further issue of the number of appropriately trained authorised firearms personnel available at that time in the Ayton Armed Response Unit and again how many of the right kinds of vehicles were available. These were some of the problems which were aired but not solved at the pre-raid meeting organised by Charlie the previous evening in the presence of all the senior officers of the Force.

So as the armada of vehicles set off from the main Police Station in the town centre for the raid that night just after eleven thirty for a twelve o'clock commencement, not only had some 'foreseen' problems not been solved but some 'unforeseen' ones remained unperceived and therefore unsolved too.

After a brief discussion, it had been a prior decision on humanitarian grounds, that given the usage of the Elite building as a brothel, the two premises would be raided sequentially, and the Elite would be 'busted' first. So with all the personnel present, including local authority social and welfare services to receive the women liberated from the building and the vehicles parked up on the strip of spare land opposite, the usual warnings were announced at the side of the main road. Unsurprisingly both of the two customary warnings were met with total silence. So, as agreed previously, Charlie Brangwyn and his first unit of three authorised firearms officers, all dressed in bullet-proof vests and bearing ballistic shields before them decided to break down the doors with a ram.

But which ones first? And how? They had brought only one ram with them envisaging a normal house-style entry through one door. Instead there was a row of six transparent, coloured half glass doors, to begin with. What had not been envisaged, however, was a further row of the same number of glass doors, exact replicas, about a meter and a half further into the building. Charlie laid aside his shield and started the hard and fatiguing job of breaking down the middle of the first row of doors, which took a long time. He then handed over the job of tackling the second group of doors to one of the other members of his small three officer squad. Eventually after far too long, the way was clear for the first unit to enter, followed swiftly because of the lack of resistance by the second and third squads.

As the next two more squads entered the premises, what they discovered was an amazing piece of internal architecture, which must have been costly to produce and a living hell for the women who worked there. There was first of all a reception desk and comfortable-looking area fitted with commodious armchairs, coffee tables and a well-stocked bar. There were banks of computers and monitors behind the reception desk, which at the time of the raid were unattended. Clearly the banks of monitors were intended to observe the occupants of the tiny 'hen hutch-like' rooms for the women and their clients. Some few of the tiny rooms were oriented to the immediate exterior of the building but most had no natural light.

As the officers penetrated further into the building behind the reception and monitoring areas they found four corridors stretching back at least fifty meters and lined on both sides by what had every appearance of being pens, of which there were some twenty on each side of each corridor. Most pens, if not empty were occupied by a miserable-looking sex worker, disoriented, emaciated and frightened, usually lying or sitting cross-legged on a stained bed covered by filthy bed clothes. In each case, as they were discovered, the sex workers were solicitously escorted by women Police officers into the arms of the waiting social and welfare services staff outside and gently led to one of the coaches, which would take them to safe houses, for a shower and clean up, clean clothes and a nourishing meal. As not all the rooms were occupied, at the final tally some fifty two women were rescued from sex slavery. At a rough calculation the income from all those sex slaves, assuming approximately ten clients a day, seven days a week would be in the region of going on two million pounds.

Each pen contained a bed, a bedside table and a small wardrobe. There were no toilet facilities or wash basins in any of the rooms, but there was one set of facilities right at the end of each corridor. Each room one had a camera over the top of the bed. There were now four units of armed Police officers on the ground floor and two of those squads progressed upstairs, where in what had been originally the sloping balcony of the cinema, further renovations were in progress and a level floor had been constructed. Although it cannot be certain, it looked as though the intention was to use the upstairs as the main office and thus be able to increase the number of units downstairs.

The interesting thing about the raid was that no men or madams were discovered suggesting that the mafia gang had received advance warning of the intended raid; a great and discouraging disappointment to the men and women, who had carried out the raid. It was only after a thorough search at the rear end of the premises that a back exit from the premises was found behind heavy, cinema-style curtains, which could have led escapees to move to the other building. By the end of the search of the first building, some of the officers, feeling fatigued but also because of the emotional impact of seeing the women in the brothel, were advancing a case to leave the second half of the raid to another evening. This suggestion was overruled by the Acting Chief Constable for resource reasons, even though he could see that some of the men were now quite tired and to a certain degree 'in a state'.

So the search of the second building went ahead and it proved to be a very different and more dangerous task than the first. The usual procedure was adopted at the beginning of the raid of the second building with announcements and warnings that there were armed Police outside with a warrant to search the premises. There was silence. In the second building there was only one large main door and it had a vertically oriented letter box towards the top of the door. Charlie rested his shield to use the ram, and the other two members of the first squad had arrived at the door. At that juncture, the letter box was opened and a large bore rifle was poked through the letter box. Charlie having slightly lowered his ballistic shield to use the ram, received the full force of the shot directly in the face and fell to the ground. The other two members of the first squad retired quickly dragging Charlie's body with them and he was carried on a stretcher to the waiting ambulance.

The Acting Chief Constable, seeking to rally his officers, at once took charge and gathered his officers very briefly together. An explosive charge would be place against the front door and another against the side door, he informed them. There would be two armed squads at the side door ready to enter at the same time as the three squads at the front would also be entering the building. Seeing the need to continue supporting his officers' morale after the severe injury to Charlie, he the Acting Deputy Chief Constable, would, he said, lead the first squad to enter the front entrance. At the sound of his whistle, both doors would be blown simultaneously and both would be blown down inwards. Straight away after that manoeuvre, several stun grenades would be launched into the inside of the building oriented in different directions. These would be followed up instantly by a bevy of smoke grenades aimed just behind the position where the gunmen were assumed to be. Thus all officers would wear their respirators on first entry to the building.

The whistle was blown. The grenades exploded. The Acting Chief Constable donned his mask again. The two doors fell inwards, and the first squad at each door entered and straight away crouched to the side of each door, to allow the next squads at each door to enter. These two squads, each of three men, fired randomly into the interior of the building as they entered. At the front the first three squads led now by the most senior officer of the Force were all now armed with long-barrelled fire arms, such as the H&K MP5SF and H&K G36C carbines, with supplementary clips of bullets. As the three squads advanced from different directions and in different directions, they were engaged by well-armed mafia fighters in pre-prepared defensive positions. The squad that entered by the side door took up positions behind the renegade gunmen, who were now held in a pincer movement. How many it was difficult to tell in the darkness. But there were clearly several of them.

The Acting Chief Constable led the team advancing at the front entrance relaxing his shield to clear some debris to the side. Almost immediately he was hit in the stomach by a burst of machinegun fire apparently from a 1960's Skorpion submachine gun. He dropped his weapon and slowly slumped to the ground.

As a consequence of their gunfire, the two squads of armed officers just inside the two entrances had the identification of the gunmen straight away in their sights and through the smog, each squad opened fire on the positions of the gunmen. Three gunmen were quickly neutralised and a fourth threw his rifle away and hastily raised his hands. He was searched and cuffed and led back to a waiting officer at one of the detention vans. The three gunmen now lying on the floor were checked to make sure they were dead and the squads moved forwards.

As the smoke cleared, the panorama was truly impressive. Row upon row of growing cannabis plants down four columns were being looked after by young men, some of whom were still asleep on the floor, others of whom were awakened by the noise and were now standing up. There was no sign of any supervisors downstairs. Upstairs further gunmen were encountered but they were in surprise and disoriented as a consequence of the stun grenades and the rising smell of the gas grenades. They were swiftly neutralised.

The upper storey of the building had once again been levelled and contained the office, computers, printers and other electronic equipment. There were other tables laden with equipment and supplies for agricultural work, such as work on cuttings and fertilisers and stored in small rooms off to the side, which also contained supplies for the plants below such as fertilizers.

Most of those males found in the premises were working there under constraint in conditions described as modern slavery, no doubt retained in the indoor drug cultivation business by debt bondage or threats of violence to themselves or their family back home. Many of them were no more than children. The keepers, of whom six were found and five were dead and one alive, appeared to be mostly in their twenties or early thirties. The one remaining gunman alive was detained, frisked and cuffed and then formally cautioned before being driven away in the detention van to the Police station.

In the next-day evaluation that took place, there was a very deep ambience of sadness in the room and it pervaded all attempts to have a formal discussion. If only … was a phrase that recurred frequently and some officers could hardly stem their tears. Opinion was split of how successful the raid had been. What were the pros and cons and were the pros worth the cost of the cons. Some officers, especially amongst those from the Police Armed Response Unit, argued that it could not possibly be called a success when they had lost two of their colleagues, a popular man of long service, who was on the brink of retirement and an excellent administrator with a big heart and acumen for good decisions. Both universally liked family men.

All officers present agreed that sincere condolences should be sent to Charlie's and the Actin Chief Constable's family without delay and the family welfare suite should asked to arrange an early visit to both families soonest. The Acting Deputy Chief Constable, Maria Clarke promised that a collection would be organised for them during the following week. There was much to learn from the experience of two raids in one night and the practice of that night was never repeated. One or two officers expressed their concern that the Ayton Armed Police Response Unit was leaderless once again and probably incapable of functioning normally until new appointments could be made. They also raised the possibility of calling in the army in the interim given the ever-increasing violence the Unit had to face in society and particularly in its work.

A final note of optimism lifted spirits a little. Firstly all in all everyone rejoiced for the fifty-two women, who had been saved from a cruel life of sexual slavery and an early death and secondly all officers were absolutely delighted at the massive reduction the raids would cause to the income of the criminal gang concerned.

On hearing about the disastrous loss of the two premises in Ayton and the death of five of their workers, Nico called his crackshot marksman Thoma Copja for further assistance in Ayton. Encouraged by an increased fee for the work, Thoma agreed and both dashed away from the syndicate's base in East London in Nico's car on a lightning visit to the Firm' office in Ayton. Thoma was not a great conversationalist and indeed there was little to say between them. The next mission had already been agreed between them and the terms were similar but the money a little higher than the payment for the previous contract, successfully completed by Thoma only a few short weeks ago.

When they entered the slip road to Ayton from the motorway, it was no surprise to Nico that once again they were pulled over to the side and subjected to what he considered a useless interrogation. After a brief call to HQ, the officer informed Thoma that he was wanted for questioning by the Ayton Police in connection with the murder of the former Chief Constable of Ayton, Patricia Nowak. He was given the option of either coming to the Police station voluntarily or he would be arrested and taken there.

Nico said he would call their solicitor and, of course, Thoma knew from long experience not to answer any questions without a friendly solicitor being present and after an initial consultation with her had taken place. He answered the invitation by saying briefly and courteously that he would accompany the officers voluntarily but was unwilling to answer any questions until his solicitor arrived. When he arrived he was detained for review in a cell for twenty-four hours, but was of course always available for consultations with his solicitor.

So belted up and comfortable in the back of the Police car, Thoma departed with the officers to an unknown future and Nico continued his journey to the old Victorian safe house in a cul de sac in a rather run-down part of the town, a property that passed as a kind of headquarters for the Ayton Firm. He was received by the previous triumvirate, Tristen Plackici, acting as the senior member of the Ayton branch of the OCG and two of his close protectors and gunmen, Luan Berisha and Vishnak Asllani. Klodjan Shkreli, the surviving marksman from the London office who was left to help in Ayton by Nico on a previous visit, was also present

"Welcome Nico! Nice to see you again so soon after your last visit. Are you able to share with us the purpose of your surprise visit? Is it a social call or a seriously official one?"

Tristen asked rather teasingly. Nico ignored the pleasantries and the barb, however and spoke in a slightly acerbic voice.

"I am here to give you and the other Albanian members of the Firm here in Ayton a last and final chance to continue, but as a different organisational entity. A total change of business strategy from the incompetent mess you have made of the current function of the Office here. What I say to you is highly confidential and cannot be repeated to anyone else on pain of death. Do you understand and accept my offer as a besa on your part?"

Confronted by an offer, about which they knew nothing except that it was highly confidential, Tristen made an effort to stall.

"Well of course, Nico, as friends in the same Firm we always stick to the confidential nature of our discussions. Always have done."

"I'm not talking of the past and 'always' this is a besa. Do you accept the terms or not? Each one of you separately? What is your reply?"

The weak forced smile on Tristen's face faded quickly. His chums were no better. Challenged to say, 'yes or no' on the spot, the two gunmen looked at each other and then at Tristen for guidance. As usual they expected that he would make the decision and they in turn would follow suit.

"There can only be one response to your invitation, Nico my friend, from an Albanian and that is the word, 'Po'."

Tristen at last forced out a responsive nod, not really knowing exactly what he was committing himself to.

The other two men explicitly and individually followed suit and nodded giving their word silently.

"Very well you have accepted the besa and you know the blood consequences if you break your oath. So we can now proceed with our business today."

All three men breathed a sigh of relief. But Nico was not finished with the preliminaries yet!

“Tell me in detail what happened at the two premises the other night. In detail!”

Now none of the men, including Tristen, knew exactly what had happened at the two sites, because the only person on the Albanian side to survive had been locked up in a Police cell since the end of the raid. He was accused of illegal possession, supply and production of controlled drugs, holding a child in slavery, child abduction and human trafficking. So once again Tristen found himself in an embarrassing quandary. But he felt he could not admit his ignorance. So he made up a story.

“Yes, well one of the five men, who were killed in the raid, secretly revealed to the filth where the two sites were and what they were for. So the Police had detailed information of how to enter the premises, which they did in the first case, the brothel, without any resistance at all because all the men had fled the place. In the case of the second raid immediately after the first with superior firepower on the part of the Police, their resistance was overcome and five were killed and one man captured. In a nutshell, that’s basically what happened.”

“Do you think that the one, who was captured was the one who grassed on us?”

“Well, it’s impossible to tell because he is incommunicado. So we cannot speak to him, although our lawyer can. Perhaps she could find out. For the moment it’s impossible to tell. But it is a possibility since he survived when all his fellow workers were killed.”

“So, can we clear that one up, because it has cost us an enormous amount of money and the bosses will want to know who was responsible? Will you or one of your underlings contact the lawyer and try to get some info pronto?”

Nico did not wait for an answer but continued with his own agenda.

“Now down to business. Together with our friends in Italy we accept that we have to fundamentally change our way of doing business. The old model of investing in illicit static resources such as indoor drug farms or brothels is too weak to withstand the onslaughts of the Police, as this episode in Ayton has shown only a few days ago. In any case indoor drug farms are expensive to run and in good measure they are now being overtaken by the movement to synthetic opioids. So we have to be more nimble in our operations and that demands a certain legitimacy in our production and markets but also more savvy with regards to where we invest our increasing income.”

He paused to take breath and then unrelenting in his aggressive enthusiasm he persisted.

“As I mentioned to you last time, we are seeking to invest in more legitimate assets, more corporately and more multinationally. We are cooperating very closely to set up a new business model, more like a normal major commercial corporation, quoted on the stock exchange. In the new drug scene, there is a need for joint ventures on the lines of existing classic commercial companies. In this new style of company in conjunction with our friends based in Sicily but located internationally, we shall require workers, who can co-operate as members of small cells with similar cells from other cartels and from several countries specialising in areas such as money laundering, production, supply or sale of drugs, seeing a particular batch through to conclusion and then disbanding. Thus, for example, we need people now, who know the various markets intimately and can make wise decisions on investments, but also have the ability to still push our new drugs."

"I understand, Nico. But what role do you see for people like us?"

Tristen asked totally confused by the continual bombardment of new ideas that had so abruptly dcsccndcd on him.

"Well that's the biggest problem in this whole business. What to do about Ayton and its current staff and business orientation. So let's think of what the assets and deficits are, which would form the baseline for any decision. So let's have a look. Tell me what your assets are here in Ayton?"

Tristen cringed and found himself dumbfounded by the directness of the question and he had to admit that he had never thought about that!" So he had to make something up pretty quickly.

"Well, as illustrated by the weighty profits we make for the Firm every year without fail, this is a good place to invest. We are at the centre of a large population with an expanding demand for what we sell, and we sell at a very competitive price and one which has remained steady for several years now."

"Humph!" Nico responded. "As I have just shared with you, we are now entering a new world of business. What skills do the existing staff have that would match up to the new demands? If we do not have any, we shall have to close the office and move to some more profitable geographical area with new staff, who are qualified to match the new business demands. What do you think? What should happen to the existing staff in that case, do you think?"

Tristen looked at his colleagues in despair and rather feeling out of steam. Luan Berisha saw the problem and tried to rebuff Nico's conclusion that the Ayton branch might need closing. He tried to extol the very modest attributes of the Ayton workers. He also made an effort to pull the exchange back onto more positive and productive ground.

"Nico. We have no need to consider a closure of this branch. You have here a ready-made team, loyal to the Firm and attentive to all the changes needed in the past. You speak of big business and I think the new direction that you outline is a good development, but will take some time to implement. I know little of big business but it seems to me that commercial firms also face the challenge of continuous change in their objectives and modes of working. But they have well-built staff development programmes and in-built assessment with all members of staff assessed each year and a forward-looking programme of personal development, prescribed for them for the following year. To be precise! In the case of this branch of the Firm's business, we have the staff, who have proven themselves capable of change and of learning new skills. All of them could benefit from digital skills training, including things like using a laptop, smart phone or tablet or even a bodycam, encrypture and decrypture and navigation of the dark web. Just for a start! I believe that is what we need here at Ayton and with your assistance, we have the capacity to undertake that task. I assure you!"

"Luan. Thank you. At last! I take your point and with Vishnak's help I want you to draw up such a programme as you have just alluded to, measured against the new skills required by the new style of business I have outlined. I'll give you a whole week to do that and submit a costed programme to me in London on the sixth day so that I can examine it before I come to Ayton the following day. I shall bring one of my underbosses and financial friends from the London Firm with me to assess your plan. Do you all agree? I am warning you in all sincerity this time. This really is the last chance for Ayton and for all of its current staff!"

There was a unanimity of acclaim for the idea of a staff development programme for the Ayton staff, and Tristen breathed a sigh of relief that he had once again survived a sentence of dispatch back to the gang in Albania.

Nico was on his feet before another word was spoken and as he exited the room he called back.

"One week then. Good luck!"

In the meantime, the sharpshooter Thoma had continued his incarceration in the main Police station. DCI Wozny and his team of colleagues in the incident room had been in touch with colleagues at the Met and had accrued the results of their investigations together with what the Ayton CID Force had collected so far in their own inquiries. He and a colleague had interviewed the manager and receptionist with regards to the dates and times of Thoma's arrival and departure. As a result of those interviews they had obtained sworn and signed affidavits that identified those details precisely and indicated the rather agitated state of mind during Thoma's sudden, rushed and premature departure.

The receptionist also reported the transparent and weak excuse for his early leaving, having paid in advance for three days. She also noted that he had left only a few short minutes after she had heard the sound of a weak crack towards the rear of the Police station. The room Thoma had used was examined by a forensics team and traces were found that indicated a long gun weapon had been fired from a situation near the window upstairs and at the back of the hotel overlooking the rear of the Police station. Perhaps more damningly was a match of the bullet that killed the Chief Constable, according to all the three main characteristics, the caliber of the bullet, the lands and grooves, and the rifling twist with the graining of the barrel on the long gun found in Thoma's luggage and which was used to fire the bullet.

The result was a charge of first degree murder, forwarded to the regional branch of the Prosecution Service, an appearance in the local Magistrate's Court and a referral to a session at the Crown Court. It also meant a further period of detention in prison for Thoma, in spite of some eloquent pleading for a release on bail on the part of

Thoma's lawyer, Mary Freeman. The outlook for Thoma was not propitious.

Chapter Thirty-One: Tragedy

The day started quite normally. Grandma came to pick up Andrea's two children, Melissa and Jeremy, from home and to take them to school. Andrea kissed and hugged them both and checked that they had everything for school and they exited the house to get into Grandma's car. Directly after their departure, Andrea dashed away to a busy, indeed overloaded, series of business commitments for the rest of the day. They were mostly in her office in the town centre but with a very important business lunch with a prospective client included at the local International Hotel.

After hugging their Grandma, Melissa and Jeremy crossed the playground from the gate and entered the College's very large building together, passing through the sensor frame erected to exclude knives and blades from being carried into the College by students.

As soon as they entered, they split up and each went to their base classroom. On entering his classroom, Jeremy found that there was only one other student in the room; a mischievous-looking boy called Daniel, who in addition to his school satchel was carrying a heavy-looking backpack. In his hand he held a small wrap.

As soon as he saw Jeremy he walked over to him and greeted him brazenly.

"You're my first customer today and I have something special for you. You can have this wrap at less than half price. For a fiver in fact. Jeremy recoiled and rejected the offer rather abrasively. He had had it drilled into him by the whole family that drugs were a death potion and he should not touch them even if they were offered free. "Steer well clear!" His father had advised him. So he reacted to Daniel's offer rather sharply.

"Daniel, you should not be doing that in College. How did you get them in? It's strictly forbidden and if you're caught you could be expelled from College or reported to the Police or both. No I'm not interested in killing myself with the kind of rubbish that you are selling. Thank you very much."

"Jeremy, you should be careful how you speak to me. Lots of the other kids would jump at the offer I made to you. So you are one of the very few kids, who do not do spice. Just watch out! I knew you were a loner, as soon as I heard you cosying up to Mrs Brogan the other day".

At that moment some of students entered the classroom, as did the class teacher, Mrs Brogan, and Daniel withdrew to the back of the classroom and lifting the lid, he placed his backpack in what appeared to be his desk. The teacher saw him and said to him.

"Hello Daniel. What are you up to? Here so early in the day. You usually linger in the cloak rooms before you come upstairs to the classroom. What were you talking to Jeremy about?"

"Not much, Mrs Brogan. Just exchanging info about last night's homework."

"What was Daniel saying to you, Jeremy?"

Jeremy found himself facing a dilemma, whether to reveal Daniel's illicit attempt to sell drugs to him and risk later serious consequences from Daniel and his drug mates. Or should he tell a lie in support of Daniel's lie. He tried to avoid either option and to waffle his way out of the predicament instead.

"Please Miss. Forgive me as I did not pay attention to Daniel's going on, as I was wrestling to think of a solution to one of the maths homework calculus questions that defeated me last night. And as you know, Miss, my dad's not there to help me anymore. Sorry Miss."

Mrs Brogan, conscious of the tragic circumstances surrounding Jeremy's father's recent death, which had been in the local and national Press and mass media, seemed half-inclined to accept his explanation. She was not entirely satisfied with his comment but the subject went out of her mind when a small group of students entered the room together and one of them asked Mrs Brogan a question about the day's programme.

"Miss are you taking us for French today? Or is it the French lady again?"

"It's me, Carol."

With that brief exchange further students came in and Jeremy's incident with Daniel passed unremarked … that is until the morning break.

Out on the playground at break-time, Daniel approached Jeremy with two or three of his older mates and they took up what he felt was an intimidating stance around him.

"Hello, Loner boy." Daniel began and turning to one of the older boys, he said. "Joe this is the boy who rejected our kind offer of less than half-price spice this morning. He thinks he' better than us. Arrogant sod he is!"

Fortunately for Jeremy, one of the teachers on playground duty, perhaps suspicious of a group of older boys surrounding a younger boy, came over and demanded.

"What are you lads up to here, Daniel?"

"Nothing, Sir." They all muttered as they dispersed. As he walked away one of the older boys threatened Jeremy.

"Just watch out mate. You've not heard the last of this." and he shouldered Jeremy roughly.

Melissa, always intent on caring for her younger brother left the group of girls she was conversing with. She hurried across to a dithering Jeremy and tried to comfort and reassure him that she would look out for him. He was not to worry.

After the end of the academic lessons in the afternoon, both Jeremy and Melissa had extra-curricular activities, Jeremy to chess club and Melisa to gymnastics club. They agreed to meet up after their clubs and leave school together. Jeremy attended chess club in the library on the second floor and Melissa' gym club session took place in the large gymnasium on the ground floor. Invariably Jeremy finished before Melissa. On this occasion he was about to start descending the broad but quite steep set of two staircases, when he saw Daniel and his mates waiting for him. He knew there was an alternative route via a smaller service staircase which led to the side of the kitchen and past the dining hall and thence to the main door of the gym, where Melissa usually came out. He sprinted to that alternative escape route with Daniel and his mates hotly pursuing him. Down the two flights of stairs and past the side of the dining room he raced and through the door of the dining room he saw Melissa waiting for him on the corridor just outside the gym door. She called out to him and walked to place herself between Jeremy and his pursuers, hands on hips with her backpack held in her hand as a potential weapon.

"Leave my brother alone!" She shouted at them. "Or you'll have me to deal with and I will see that you're all expelled from the College and if possible prosecuted. You are dealing with me now and I will not tolerate a continuation of your illegal threats against my brother. Continue and I shall see that you lose more than you can imagine."

Then she shouted loudly so that the teachers in the gymnasium could hear. "Drugs are not allowed in the school. Nor is bullying!"

At that juncture one of the teachers appeared from the gym and looked at Melissa and the boys. He sized up the situation rapidly and took the boys back into the gym to warn them that their bullying behaviour towards a younger boy would not be tolerated and that dealing with drugs in the College was an expulsion matter.

“This is your last warning!” He roared at them and in a cowardly manner they caved in and disappeared down the long corridor with their tails between their legs.

Apart from sour looks in the corridor, that was the last that Jeremy experienced from Daniel and his mates and with the support of his sister, he soon regained his former confidence and learning capacity.

A few days later at the end of the formal curriculum when no extra-curricular clubs were scheduled, Grandma arrived at the school gates as usual on time. The area around the gate was crowded with parents waiting to pick up the children and some smaller children, who had accompanied their mother or father. All official car parking being already taken, Grandma Isabel left her car some way down the road and walked to the periphery of the crowd of waiting parents, waving to her two grandchildren over the heads of the other parents as she saw them emerging from the school doors.

Suddenly there was a crack, followed by several more. People looked up the road to see what was happening. A man running down the road towards the crowd of parents seemed to be pursued by another man running several meters behind the first man and holding what looked like a gun in his hand. The first man had seen the large crowd of parents standing closely together and, sensing a chance of escape, had headed towards them. He had pushed his way into the crowd and there were several more cracks, at which there was shouting, screaming and yelling by most parents in the crowd and those with children reached down to afford them protection. The man with the gun seemed to be frightened by the adverse noise and turned tail. A few brief minutes later a fast racer car sped past the crowd.

Grandma Isabel fell slowly to the ground clutching her stomach. With extreme horror Melissa observed this happening and hastened to assist her Grandma. She told Jeremy also to go to his grandma and see what help he could give her, She then turned round and rushed back into the College and up to the office, where she requested the secretary to ring up and ask for Police and an ambulance to be sent to the school gates, and also to ring her mother to ask her to come to the College urgently. She then ran back to her grandma at the school gates. By that time her grandma's hand was covered in blood and she was lying prostrate on the ground, slipping in and out of consciousness. One or two other people appeared also to have been injured and were variously sitting with their backs leaning on the College boundary fence or, like Grandma, lying on the ground. The College secretary appeared, totally encumbered with cushions, sheets and one of two blankets.

After what seemed to Melissa and Jeremy an eternity a Police car arrived and two Police officers, one female and one male, got out of the car. They were followed shortly afterwards by two ambulances. With grandma being on the ground at the periphery of the crowd, the medics from the first ambulance assessed her first and returning quickly to the ambulance brought back a stretcher and medical equipment including blood transfusion equipment, a supply of O Negative blood and other equipment. The medics from the second ambulance began assessing the other wounded people, who seemed to be less severely injured.

When the transfusion had been set up, Grandma was placed on the stretcher and carefully transported to the hospital. In her most mature voice, Melissa asked if she could go with her Grandma and, age being difficult to assess, and a relative being potentially useful to be able to give the necessary personal details about the casualty, she received the agreement of the woman medic. Melissa hurriedly took Grandma's mobile from her handbag and gave it to Jeremy, shouting to him above the hubbub of crying and talking to ring his mother and then hastily pursued Grandma, the medics and the stretcher to the waiting ambulance with the back doors open. She reached the ambulance just in time to enter before the doors were closed and she was strapped in by the woman medic, who stayed in the back of the ambulance with Grandma throughout the journey, as, siren sounding, the ambulance sped towards the A&E Department of the main Ayton hospital.

Unloaded and taken straight to a nurse for triage and then rapidly onto a doctor for pre-operative assessment Grandma Isabel was rushed on a stretcher to an operating theatre for emergency surgery, while Melissa was still giving further details to the nurse in the waiting room. Shortly afterwards, when her mother, Andrea arrived, she took over the task of giving Grandma's personal and medical details to one of the nurses in A&E.

After what seemed like hours of stressful waiting the nurse returned to them and said that the surgeon, who had done the operation, would like a word with them. She led them to the privacy of a curtained one-bed ward and invited them to take a seat until the doctor arrived. The surgeon, Mr Michel Carmichael, entered and took a seat facing them. He then spoke softly and sympathetically to the two of them.

"Your mother has been grievously wounded. She has taken a bullet wound in the lower abdomen and is seriously ill. Her injuries are currently life-threatening and she will be under sedation for some considerable time to come. But, you'll be reassured, that we have managed to stem the bleeding and stabilise her. Once she has been taken to one of our one-bed wards, you may go to see her under the supervision of one of our nurses. Do not try to stir her or even speak to her yet. Although her injury is life-threatening, that does not mean that she will definitely die. She will have a first-class team looking after her and she has tolerated the long operation fairly well. She seems to me a tough one, your mother and Grandma does. I am hopeful but I would not say I am optimistic. But then I am a surgeon."

He smiled pleasantly at them both and began to depart excusing himself as he had so many patients to deal with that day.

Andrea and Melissa thanked him very much for care and attention he was giving Grandma Isabel Burnley Crowder and he hastened from them to his next patient.

Chapter Thirty-Two: Finale

Ayton was becoming more diverse; more multicultural, more multi-ethnic and more multicredal by the beginning of the story told in this series of books. In a sense, Ayton had always had minorities, for instance of Huguenots, Jews and Armenians, who settled in the town and plied their trade. They were already well integrated into the economic and social life of the town, while in many cases wishing at the same time to maintain their own cultures and sometimes their own languages side by side with the culture and language of their new home without any discord being caused to either.

From the end of the Second World War there had been new influxes of settlers. First of all small numbers of so-called displaced persons mostly from Europe, especially Poland and the Ukraine, whose own country had suffered from a cruel and disruptive war followed by takeover by alien and sometimes neighbouring powers. Settlers from British colonies such as the West Indies, came next and settled in the town and with admittedly some frictions were absorbed into the workforce of the still booming woollen textile and car industries and other local employment opportunities. After those influxes people were recruited from the Indian subcontinent to take on night-time work in the mills or act as bus conductors. New Polish churches were soon established and Ukrainian Catholics attended local Catholic churches but for separate services.

After the start of the Ukraine-Russia war migrants from that country and new citizens from Hong Kong began to arrive and settle in Ayton. Large numbers of new citizens from a diverse selection of other countries and cultural backgrounds fled persecution and threats and they had also successfully come to find their new homes in Ayton. New retail and recreational outlets being were quickly established, some of which expanded the gastronomic and cultural opportunities in the town. As an example, some streets soon had residents from Thailand, Georgia, Afghanistan, Hong Kong Bangla Desh, France and the remaining original population of the area as neighbours and sometimes as friends.

More recent times, however, had seen successive mass immigration into the United Kingdom, many of whom either came directly to Ayton to settle or were placed here in local migrant hotels. Local churches and other religious centres responded very generously to assist the newcomers, but inevitably pressure on health and welfare and other Public services became intense. The employment opportunities had also narrowed and become more specialised as the woollen textile industry declined and other manufacturing hubs were exported to lower income countries, to be partially replaced by employment opportunities of a more scientific technical and technological kind.

War in the Balkans then added to the seemingly ever-changing composition of the population. Many of the displaced and expelled immigrants came to Ayton legitimately in need of assistance with the establishment of a new life and home for themselves and their families. With these legitimate immigrants, however, criminal cartels used informal means of entering the countries, to perpetuate their criminal activities in larger centres of population such as Ayton in the UK. Drugs and human trafficking spread rapidly, answering an ever-growing market demand from buyers in the local population. The drug habit spread to younger people and often, at schools, Colleges and universities consumption of drugs became rife.

As the potency of drugs accompanied the rise in demand, more people of all ages became consumed by drug-taking to the point where they were addicted. Many, became ill, some seriously, and an escalating number required remedial or rehabilitation service and far too many died. Sometimes potent drugs were hidden as a component in a wrap or tablet, with the consumer unaware and this also resulted in many deaths. Uninhibited, the internet was also propagating the sale of such substances mixed in some times with harmful subject matter content that led to suicides, mostly amongst younger people. Educational and social institutions, rehabilitation, remedial and welfare services and hospitals and other medical and convalescence facilities became overwhelmed with an increased wave of quite focussed demand.

Faced with the rapid increase in drug consumption and collateral criminality as well as restricted resources and financial cutbacks all aspects of Law and Order were challenged by insuperable demands. Criminality was also diversifying, computerising and internationalising and becoming more violent. New harder drugs were being filtered at first and then flooded into the country by internationalised cartels, sometimes comprising many different criminal organisations from several different countries.

It is in the context of these fundamental changes that a fairly ordinary family such as the Burnley Crowder family had, like many other citizens of Ayton new and older, lived and contributed to their society and to the health and welfare of their fellow citizens over four generations. Emily had commenced the practice, most recently Izzy known as Grandma Isabel, and her daughter Andrea had continued the family tradition of contributing to voluntary and charitable life in the ever larger conurbation and that had continued in the face of some serious setbacks. Successive generations had chosen to support the efforts of educational and other cultural institutions to fight the menaces that particularly confronted young people and to seek to improve their life chances.

Emily had passed away approximately ten years ago and her daughter Izzy, now Grandma Isabel had retired some years ago. She had recently been critically injured by an assassin's stray bullet outside the College, where she was waiting to pick up her grandchildren. The assassin was pursuing a runner from an opposing gang in one of the frequent outbreaks of intergang warfare that happened periodically on Ayton's streets. Such intergang conflict often unintentionally affected members of the Public adversely and even on occasion mortally.

After weeks of post-operative care and months of residence in a convalescent home, she never returned to her home just down the avenue from her daughter, Andrea, and her grandchildren. Instead, Andrea found her a place at an old people's care home in Ayton. There she revelled in new-found friends and as a member of a so-called management committee, she fully exploited the opportunities such membership offered to improve life, cuisine and facilities in the home.

She saw the birth of two of her great-grandchildren and the entry into the reception class of the local primary school of the first one. She died quietly in her sleep at the great age of eighty seven years. The memorial remembrance occasion at the City Hall was filled to overflowing and many eloquent tributes were paid to her wide and energetic efforts across her lifetime to assist her fellow citizens of all backgrounds in Ayton.

Andrea, her daughter, and the daughter of her deceased husband from Czechia, Andrei, continued to run the family consultant business in the centre of town, which had been founded by her mother. Isabel had two children, who during the period of this novel lived with their mother at home, while attending the local College. They both did well with their studies, actively resisting peer-group pressure to engage in drug-taking and alcohol, At the end of their studies in Ayton College, they both went up to Imperial College in London, Melissa to study engineering like her mother and two years later Jeremy to study economics and business studies like his father.

Eventually on the retirement of Andrea many years in the future, Melissa would take on the ownership and management of the consultancy firm in Ayton, marry and have three children all daughters. On completion of his studies at Imperial, Jeremy took over the management and ownership of the financial service business in the town centre, which had been founded by his father and looked after on a caretaker basis by his father's assistant manager. When he married, he and his wife, Eva, whose family was of Jamaican background, had two beautiful children, a girl and a boy.

The Ayton College, of which three generations of the family had attended, later become members of the Board of Governors of the College. Two of the family's generations had also provided Chairs of the Governing Body. In their capacity on the Board all three of them pursued the objectives of preventing the incursion of illicit drugs into the College and its grounds. Another aim was to cut down or eliminate the number of suicides of students at the college and a third was to try prevent blades and knives of different kinds from entering the College and to thereby reduce the number of stabbings in the College. Finally all three were very active in finding ways of rehabilitating at least some of the ghost students back into studentship at the College and a second chance at an inspiring and satisfying life.

The issues of drugs production, conveyance, selling and human-trafficking, both linked with the brothel market in the town had not been one of the major priorities of the Police Force in Ayton before the beginning of the wars in the Balkans. As a result of successive conflicts in that region, the drugs business, organised by regional or local godfathers at that time had supported migration of Albanian criminals to the UK and with them the drugs and people trafficking businesses.

In the UK as well as in Ayton drug use and sale had rocketed to the point where the Albanian mafia had a large majority control of the trade in some major drug lines. That structure was changing by the beginning of this final part of the series to much more co-operative and multinational control and involvement of the Albanian and other transnational outfits into joint enterprises or with the structure of large classic commercial companies and investing their dirty money in perfectly legal businesses such as real estate. Although remaining separate for example, the Albanian mafia was very closely linked with the most powerful mafia in Italy, the Ndrangheta.

Along the lines of some of the Italian mafia, with whom the Albanians had very close relations, these moves were deemed to necessitate a capo di tutti i capi, who had an oversight of all branches of the organised criminal group in the UK and links with those of the same organisation on the Continent. In earlier time this position had been occupied by Tristen Rexhepi an even cleverer supremo than his successor. In a joint action of the London and Ayton Police Forces Tristen had been arrested and taken to London under caution for cross examination. He had been cautious and clever in covering his tracks. He hired the cleverest lawyer in the country and the charges were dismissed and he went free.

During the period of time covered by this final book, the main occupier of the office was Ardajan Nikolaj, mysteriously known to his accomplices as 'Nico the Greek'. He was not quite so clever as his predecessor. Over a number of years he had been the supremo of the mafia super cartel in the United Kingdom, which groups together all the Albanian organised crime groups of significant weight, most of the transnational OCGs and a few of the larger regional groups here in the UK.

Nico, like his predecessor, had been extremely conservative and clever in avoiding being convicted for anything, though he was arrested on several occasions. He used his workers to do all the dirty work for him and the Police had never been able to pin anything on him or at least not enough to present to the Regional Prosecution Service, nor for that matter the Prosecution Service in London. Towards the end, however, his dissatisfaction with the performance of his subordinates in some UK regions caused him to become impatient and less cautious. He imagined that with more hands-on experience by him, he could achieve what his underlings could not achieve. He began to make mistakes.

At the same time, units from the Met and the local Ayton Police CIDs working closely together were able to assemble a catalogue of some twenty charges, including human trafficking, multiple offences against children, a range of drug charges and running brothels, with which he was arraigned. He was convicted at the Crown Court in London and was sentenced to some eighteen years in prison, the latter part of which would be served in an Albanian jail.

Nico's coopérants did not long outlast him. All staff at that Ayton branch of the syndicate were cleared out, including the newcomer, Daniel Kristoja, Luan Berisha and Vishnak Asllani. They were all considered to be incompetent by the mafia super-bosses and were invited to return to Tirana forthwith for further service elsewhere.

From Tirana each was sent to a different location at the different extremities of Albania, in small settlements in the remote parts of the country, where their reward was pitifully small. Vishnak was relocated to the Shkoder branch, Daniel to the area around Theth and Luan to the region surrounding Doberdol; this latter for only six months! They were replaced in Ayton by a new boss and underboss and new staff, who were all loyal and experienced adherents of the new classic business approach of the mafia gangs worldwide.

With the major changes in the organisation and also in the modes of working of the local mafias and the murder of two senior officers, new appointments were needed at the top of the Ayton Police Force. In a competitive process, Maria Clarke, Acting Deputy Chief Constable of the Ayton Police was appointed to the permanent position of Chief Constable, one of the youngest in the country. As Deputy Chief Constable, Detective Chief Inspector, Rajan Appasamy Head of the Criminal Investigation Department of Ayton Police was appointed. New recruits to the Ayton Force were appointed to fill the gaps left by the promotions and retirements of other staff, two of the replacements officers recruited were from the Met.

Other Works of Fiction by the Author

New Life in an Old Town: Part One of the Ayton Cycle (Available as an e-book and paperback)

The Hydra (Available as an e-book and paperback)

The Fit Country (Available as an e-book and paperback)

Back-to-Back (Available as an e-book and paperback)

The Final Mission (Available as an e-book and paperback)

Turbulent Times: Growing up in the Edwardian Era (Available as an e-book and paperback)

Deception: Part Two of the Ayton Cycle (Available as an e-book and paperback)

A Boy's Story: A Novella (Available as an e-book and paperback)

The Endless Struggle: Part Three of the Ayton Cycle (Available as an e-book and paperback)

The Silent World (Available as an e-book and in paperback format in late 2023)

Armageddon: Part Four of the Ayton Cycle (In preparation for publication in early 2024)

The House on the Blind Site (In planning for availability as an e-book in mid to late 2024)

Happy Poems and Games for Young Children (Complete but unpublished; awaiting a poetry editor and illustrator)

Printed in Great Britain
by Amazon